YOU CAN CHOOSE YOUR FRIENDS BUT . . .
You can't choose your relatives. Whether you've got some family event coming up that you wish you didn't have to attend . . . or there are relatives coming to stay whom you'd really rather avoid . . . or you actually like your relatives and just never get a chance to see them . . . you'll find visiting with the families in *Rotten Relations* a truly unique experience.

From the problems that come along with being the son of Santa Claus . . . to the twists and turns of an assortment of fairy-tale marriages . . . to a whole new take on the Salem witches . . . to a deposed ruler's version of the Sleeping Beauty fiasco—here are highly original tales that will make you look at your next family reunion in a whole new light.

ROTTEN RELATIONS

edited by
Denise Little

DAW BOOKS, INC.

DONALD A. WOLLHEIM, FOUNDER

375 Hudson Street, New York, NY 10014

ELIZABETH R. WOLLHEIM
SHEILA E. GILBERT
PUBLISHERS

http://www.dawbooks.com

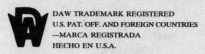

CONTENTS

INTRODUCTION
  by Denise Little   1

HOME FOR THE HOLIDAYS
  by Pauline J. Alma   3

WITH A FACE ONLY A MOTHER COULD LOVE
  by Jenn Reese   25

SWITCHED
  by Nina Kiriki Hoffman   42

THE TRICK OF THE TRICKSTERS TRICKED
  by Josepha Sherman   64

THRICE TOLD
  by Von Jocks   73

DYNASTY
  by Bill McCay   102

SERPENT'S TOOTH
  by Susan P. and Bradley H. Sinor   107

MIRROR, MIRROR
  by Jacey Bedford   120

AFTER THE BALL
  by Pamela Luzier   142

PEGGY PLAIN
  by Devon Monk   163

HEATHCLIFF'S NOTES
  by David Bischoff   175

CUCKOO'S EGG
  by Jody Lynn Nye   199

RAPUNZEL—THE TRUE STORY
  by Robert Sheckley   220

AMONG THE STARS
  by Susan Sizemore   246

KING OF SHREDS AND PATCHES
  by P. N. Elrod   265

INTRODUCTION

by Denise Little

EVERYBODY has one—a relative who makes you blush, a skeleton on the family tree. Most of us have more than one. But a select few among us deal with something much worse than a merely embarrassing relation. Some of us have rotten relations—people who make us run screaming for the hills in the hope of staying alive. Since I'm from Texas, where everything is bigger, and that includes the guns, I've got a couple of those lurking in my background, hiding among the crowd of my wonderful and colorful family members. When those rotten relations show up at a family picnic, they can clear out the place faster than a bad karaoke singer. So I've always been comforted by fantasy and fairy-tale stories with really rotten relations—the ones that put the bad guys on the map. From the Wicked Stepmother to King Arthur's kin, from Hamlet's family to Rapunzel's dad, they made the lives of their families very, very interesting.

So interesting, in fact, that I wondered what it would be like to look at their stories in depth. Wouldn't it be fun to read about a rogues' gallery of rotten relations from the annals of fiction and fairy? Especially if we did it from the point of view of the plotters and schemers . . . I asked a number of writer friends of mine if they'd like to play in that universe. It turned out that I wasn't the only person fascinated by the villains of the piece in the old tales. So here, for your amusement, are gathered a collection of new and original stories of rotten relations—most of them old favorites—who have been brought to life again by some of the genre's most talented authors. Though there are some surprises in the mix, too. I hope you enjoy the voyage. I know I did!

HOME FOR
THE HOLIDAYS

by Pauline J. Alama

Pauline J. Alama is the author of the fantasy novel The
Eye of Night and winner of a second-place Sapphire
Award for the short story "Raven Wings on the Snow,"
published in Marion Zimmer Bradley's Sword & Sorceress
XVIII. Her work has also appeared in Marion Zimmer
Bradley's Fantasy Magazine and A Round Table of
Contemporary Arthurian Poetry. A survivor of a Ph.D
program in English, she works as a grant proposal writer
to support her cats in the style to which they've become
accustomed. "Home for the Holidays" is her first profes-
sionally published humor piece. No reindeer were harmed
in the writing of this story. Her website is at www.geoci-
ties.com/paulinejalama/paulinealama.html

"YOU'D THINK once—just once!—Dad could
be home for Christmas," I said, hunched over
a Northern Comfort and a slice in a dark and smoky
corner of the Frozen End. "Every year it's the same.
Out all night on Christmas Eve, he flies back in the
middle of Christmas Day with a massive sugar hang-

over, and falls into bed without a Merry Christmas to anyone."

"Don't let it bug you, Sharp," Luna said. "Parental attention is, like, so overrated. My parents are always trying to drag me to some lame Traditional Elfin Music Festival or something."

Luna's an elf—one of the *lios alfar*, the light-elves, with a heroin-addict-thin figure and vampire-pale skin that looks eerie with her black clothes and black nail polish. Her hair is dyed black, too, and done in spikes around pointed ears with five or six earrings apiece.

"You think that's lame?" I said. "My dad still wants me to try out the new line of toys every year. Like, *hello*, you may not have looked at me in years, but I'm almost thir*teen*, you know?"

Luna made a gagging motion, then signaled the bartender for another Pix Elation, getting dirty looks from a couple of red-jacketed old-timers down the bar. There's no drinking age in elf bars, but that doesn't mean the old geezers will let you alone there. Luna showed them her tongue stud, slapped down her money, and grabbed her glass from the bartender. "You see?" she said. "If he hung around more, it'd just be more time for that kind of crap."

"Maybe," I said. "But it pisses me off how everyone sees him like this great jolly old dad who loves kids so much. Yeah, right. As long as it's other people's kids. He doesn't see *me* when I'm sleeping. He's not home when I'm awake. He doesn't care if I've been bad. What the hell's it gonna take?"

"You should do like I did. Call him on this Christmas crap. Embrace the Old Religion," Luna said. "Like I keep telling my parents, if they'd quit stooging for the fat man and reclaim what's ours, we could be *gods*. People used to worship us, you know. They *sacrificed* to us."

Yeah, a bowl of milk at the door, like a stray cat, I thought, but I kept my mouth shut. I may be just the fat man's kid, but I'm not a total ignoramus: I know the word for gods was *aesir*, not *alfar*. They were totally minor figures in the old pantheon. The *aesir* used to piss down on them from Asgard—why the hell else'd they all become Lutheran? But I just nodded and acted like I agreed because it's part of the deal. I let her go on about being gods and call her Luna instead of Lucia, the number three name for elf girls, and she calls me Sharp instead of Santa Junior. It's worth it. Besides, she had a point. "Why do your parents work for my dad, anyway?" I said.

She wrinkled her nose. "They say it's such a nice *family* business."

I rolled my eyes. "Same old bullshit. The whole 'family' thing. Like, I hardly get on Dad's schedule. Black Peter sees more of him than I do, and he's practically retired. It's worse since Dad took over the Three Kings' outfit. Months of negotiations in Mexico, conference calls from Spain at all hours, and now he insists on going out personally on Epiphany, too. Rides a burro behind the three camels. Comes home with saddle sores. Takes days with the personal trainer to get over it."

"Whoa," Luna said. "Santa Claus has a *trainer*?"

"You have no *idea* how obsessive he is. 'The difference between jolly fat and sloppy fat can be just a pound or two. No one wants a sloppy Santa.' " I did my best Dad impression. "That trainer sees more of him than I do."

"That must cost a fortune," Luna said. "Where's all the money come from? I mean, he just gives stuff away. Where's the profit in that?"

"Duh! Licensing. Like the Olympics. You don't think all those ads get to use his face for *free*, do you?"

"Wow. And he's, like, everywhere," said Luna.

"Everywhere but home," I said.

Then Luna's beeper went off. "Oh, crap. That's my parents, wanting me to go to some lame St. Lucia's Day festival. They'll kill me if I don't get out of here. See you round, Sharp."

"Later, Luna," I said.

With Luna gone, there was no reason to hang around the bar any longer, getting hostile stares from Dad's loyal retirees. The North Pole is a company town, so everyone knows who I am, and they all have this attitude like I should keep up the family image. So I took the monorail home through the tunnels of the North Pole Compound, waited for the tin soldier housekeeper to let me in, and hung around my room for a while, looking for dirty pictures on the Internet. But that gets boring after a while, you know.

"There is nothing to DO around here?" I yelled at nobody, and kicked one of the toys that carpeted the floor: a build-your-own Strategic Defense Initiative kit that was supposed to be the hot toy for boys a couple years ago but bombed. That felt pretty good, so I kicked another toy, but you know, it's just like playing with them: it's only fun the first time. I was almost at the point of taking out my homework when I decided, what the hell, I'll try to get hold of Mom and Dad.

As I slipped out the front door to the travel tunnels, the tin soldier asked, as it was programmed, "Where are you going, Chip?"

Chip. Gag me. That dorky nickname Mom and Dad gave me, as in "chip off the old block." As if. "Call me Sharp, you stupid hunk of tin."

"Where are you going, Chip?" the thing repeated. Its programming isn't that sophisticated.

"Out," I said, and the stupid thing accepted that as an answer, filed away in case Mom or Dad asked it where I was. I set off down the compound tunnels and took the monorail to Santa's Workshop, the headquarters of North Pole Enterprises. I've had my own magnetic key for ages, so it was easy to get in and take the elevator to Licensing and Marketing: Mom's domain.

Licensing and Marketing is always busy, but in December it's swarming, and the phones ring day and night. Elves and sprites of every size, shape, and pantheon bustled back and forth, some giving a sugary smile to the boss' kid along the way, others not noticing. But Black Peter, standing over the open drawer of a file cabinet, slammed it shut with a clang and called, "How ya doing, Sharp?" He grinned at me, showing a mouthful of teeth that would scare a shark, which I guess is normal for a hobgoblin. He beckoned me over, and when I was close enough to hear, dropped his voice to a stage whisper: "I hear they got some cool war toys in the banned gifts department."

"Aw, Pete, I'm too old for that stuff."

"Too old? Oh, soooooh oooooooohld!" Pete teased. "Some day, kid, you won't be so happy to say that."

"Aw, come on, don't *you* get that way on me—"

"How old d'you think *I* am, Sharp?"

I couldn't exactly remember—seventeen hundred years? eighteen hundred?—so I just said, "Older than Dad."

He laughed so loud that the brownie in the next cubicle, bent over a ledger, gave him a dirty look. "Yeah, that's right, Sharp," Pete said, rubbing his left horn, "I remember your Dad when his big snowy beard was just a little blond peach fuzz, and he was just a small-time street mummer. We used to have quite an act: the Boy Bishop and the Devil, that was our first routine. I taught him a thing or two."

I'd heard the story before. Back when Dad was single, Pete was his partner: Dad handled the gifts, and Pete handled the punishments. Now no one remembers his part of the act. He got transferred to a back office job in Mom's department, enforcing contracts. It didn't seem fair. "So why don't *you* run this place?" I said.

"Who says I don't, behind the scenes?" Pete chuckled. "Maybe there's no better way of punishing some rotten kid than to give them what they want. Maybe it's me that took over the operation, after all. You ever think of that?"

I nodded, figuring that this was like Luna's goddess complex: I'd better just let it slide. "Hey, Pete, you think there's any chance I could see Mom sometime soon?"

"You can see her right now—I got a TV in my office," he said.

"TV?" I echoed like an idiot.

"Yeah, TV. You know, the box with the shiny pictures?" Pete said. "She's live on that homemaking show. Didn't you hear about that?"

"Homemaking? My mom?"

"Sure. Take a look." He led me into his office—a big plush one full of pictures of him and Dad in the old days, when it was a two-man act, and newer pictures of little hobgoblins with braces who must be his grandchildren—and switched on a small TV in the corner.

I slumped in one of those hard wicker chairs he had put in there to keep contract breakers on edge, and watched Mom in a ruffled apron mixing a big bowl of cookie batter and beaming her sweetest candy-cane smile to the back of the studio audience. "This is *so* bogus."

"But the ratings are terrific," said Pete. "She's got a softer touch than Martha Stewart, they say."

"I'm gonna yack," I said. "They're not really gonna eat what she's making, are they?"

"There's a premade batch of cookies waiting in the oven for her to show off at the end of the show," Pete said.

"And people fall for this?"

Pete shrugged. "People believe what they want. Don't knock it—it pays your allowance."

"I'm gonna gag," I said. "So Mom is where? Hollywood?"

Pete nodded. "Got it in one."

"She took the sleigh?"

"Nah, she was traveling light, so she just saddled up Comet. You know your mother loves a good ride. She'll be back around 9:30."

"What a drag. Guess I'll go look for Dad."

"Want me to walk you there?" Pete said.

"I can find the way myself, you know."

"Suit yourself, kid," said Pete, and went back to his files.

I was kind of sorry I'd blown him off when I got to Dad's office and found the door closed and no one to talk to. Oh, he was there, all right—I could see the light under his door—but there might as well have been a "Do Not Disturb" sign. Dad's secretary was gone—she never stays past 5:30—so I buzzed the intercom on her desk and waited for Dad to respond.

"Millie? You still there?" he said.

"No, Dad, it's me."

"Chip, I'm sorry, but I'm in the middle of a conference call. Come back at 7:15 and I'll be free." He said it in that friendly, jolly-old-elf tone, but he hung up before I could say anything in return.

I could have rung again, but he would have ignored it, so I sat back in Millie's chair and put my feet up on her glass-topped desk.

Inga from Finance popped her head out of the office and smiled nervously at my feet. "Oh, hi, Chip. I didn't know you were here."

"It's not Chip anymore. It's Sharp," I said.

"Oh. I see. Well. Waiting for your dad?"

I shrugged. "Guess so."

"There's some great video games down in the showroom that might help you pass the time," she said.

"Why is everyone still trying to push toys on me?" I said, but I went down and tried one out anyway, and frittered away the time until 7:00. Then I went back up to the executive floor to see if I could catch Dad a little early.

Fat chance. His door was still closed. I sat down at Millie's desk and turned on her computer. It didn't exactly take a genius hacker to get in. Millie's passwords are always the names of her kids or dogs. This time it was "Sherwood"—her second son's name—that opened up all North Pole Enterprises' files for me.

I went into the Licensing folders to see what Mom was doing playing Happy Homemaker for a gullible public, but the memos were boring, all about Q-ratings and Nielsens and crap. *Holiday Living with Mrs. Claus.* What a crock of flying reindeer guano.

At 7:15 I buzzed the intercom again. "I'm sorry, but it's running a little late, son," Dad said.

"Whatever," I said, and this time *I* hung up on *him*. I opened up Client Records. The database password was the system password backward, as usual. Good old Millie.

I opened the first record: Aaron, Adrienne. Wish list: Veterinarian Barbie. I deleted "Veterinarian," made it "Bestiality Barbie," then closed the record.

At the other end of the alphabet, I found Zywicki, Wesley. Wish list: Harry Potter books. I shook my head, highlighted "Harry Potter," and changed it to "dirty."

Dad's door was still shut, so I opened another record, and another, and another, getting my creative juices flowing: "Lots and lots of really violent war toys," I put in one wish list. Peacenik Dad would really hate that. But it got better: "A dildo." "An Uzi: a real one." "A brain. I lost mine somewhere." "Tits." "Anything to build up my collection of guns and explosives, because I really, really hate my parents, my neighbors, my school, and YOU!!!!" I was just typing the final exclamation point on that particular masterpiece when I heard a stagy "Ahem!" behind me.

I didn't even bother to close the record. "Hi, Dad."

He wasn't in his red suit, because it was Casual Day, but he looked even dorkier in a red-and-green plaid flannel shirt and suspenders with little clusters of holly printed on them. His cheeks were like roses, his nose like a cherry—he must have taken a shot from that bottle of Northern Comfort in the bottom left drawer of his desk. His face wore that gently troubled look that makes me want to jump up and down and scream. He took me by the elbow, gently but firmly, and steered me into his office. "Now, Chip—" he began.

"I'm not called that anymore. It's Sharp. Can't you get that through your head?"

He ignored that. "I appreciate that you're exercising your creativity on these wish lists, and I know how important self-expression is at your age, but you need to find a more appropriate outlet for your creativity. There are all kinds of outlets for creativity around here. There are paint and draw programs on this computer. There are paper and markers in the conference room. There are paints and Legos in the staff lounge—"

"Again with the toys! I'm too old for that stuff—"

"If you want me to validate your sense of maturity, you should show you're mature enough to consider the impact your actions have on others—"

"Well, none of this would have happened if you'd been there at 7:15 like you promised," I retorted. After all, the best defense is a good offense.

He got that little wrinkle between the brows that tells me I won a point. "I can see this upsets you, but I wish you would accept that I have responsibilities that I just can't put aside. For a lot of children—and many adults, too—I'm responsible for Christmas."

"Well, maybe I don't want to go along with that Christmas crap any more," I said. "I've been thinking a lot about—um—about the Old Religion, you know. Like, the Old Gods, you know, don't they deserve respect, too?" *That'll get a rise out of him,* I thought.

But Dad just smiled and nodded. "I'm glad you've been thinking about these issues, studying diverse mythologies. After all, mythology is our business. But if that's what's been troubling you, I don't think you need to worry. Many of our valued customers these days are pagans who have their own equally valid version of the Santa story. We don't fear that kind of diversity. We embrace it. When you're older—when you're running this business, and I'm just the old retired Santa—"

"I am NOT going into the family business!" I yelled.

"We'll see," said Dad, with a smug smile that made me want to smack him. "I didn't think, either, when I was your age, that I would be holding together a holiday entertainment empire—"

"Why do we always end up talking about your business?" I cut in. "Why don't we ever just do stuff like other guys do with their dads—you know, go to a hockey game, or even just watch TV together?"

"Of course we'll do things together—when the holiday's over. You know this is my busy season," said Dad.

"So, like, if we got Canadiens tickets for December 28—"

Dad winced. "I mean after the Twelve Days."

"Jeez, Dad, you used to be *done* after Christmas Day. Now by the time you're done with the Twelve Days, you're ordering the Easter Bunny's candy. By the time that's done, you're looking at new toys for next year. Give me a break."

"I can't take off after Christmas Day. Epiphany's a lot of work," he said.

"So why is that your job? If those Three Kings are

supposed to be wise men, why can't you let them handle it?"

"I owe it to all my customers to ensure the highest quality holiday experience. How would it look for the business if I left my Hispanic customers to a subsidiary without giving them the same personal touch I give my English-speaking public?"

"You always act like you have some noble reason for everything, but it's just a cover-up. It's all about you being in charge. You have to take over everything. Like—like—the elves. They used to be gods," I sputtered. "And Black Peter—he's been in the business longer than you. He used to be your partner; now he's just a back-office hack."

Dad shook his head. "Pete's a very gifted performer. I'm the first to admit that. He created an unforgettable character, Black Peter the punisher—so unforgettable that when the act changed with the times, we couldn't change the image of his character. But we couldn't keep him the way he was either; punishment just doesn't fit the modern spirit of Christmas. And besides, he wasn't a good role model for African-Americans."

That one threw me. "He's not African or American. He's a hobgoblin."

Dad shrugged. "Be that as it may, we had to show sensitivity to the way he might be perceived in certain communities. He had to transfer to behind-the-scenes work. And as contract enforcer, he's found another role that uses his talents well. Believe me, if he'd wanted to stay in the spotlight, he'd be in Hollywood right now, making science fiction movies. He's come to like being behind the scenes. It means he can spend Christmas with his grandchildren."

"Yeah, *some* people *care* about that," I said, and the sarcasm was strong enough to get through even his hide.

"Chi— *Sharp*," said Dad, "it's not that I don't want to spend Christmas with you. It's just the nature of my job. You *know* that. I *have* to work on Christmas. But you could come with me. You used to like going along in the sleigh—"

"That's kid stuff," I said.

"Sure it was—the way we did it when you were little, checking out what everyone got," Dad said. "This would be different. More like an apprenticeship—"

"No way! I am NOT going to grow up to be you!"

Dad opened his mouth to reply, but the phone rang, and he picked it up instead. "Oh. Uh-oh. Oh, *no.* I'd better come over there." He put down the receiver. "There's elf trouble in Packaging—the same old rivalry, the *lios alfar* and the *svart alfar* can't work together without someone starting a fight, and once one of them gets going, all the old wars start again, light-elves against dark-elves and all that nonsense. I've got to run. We'll pick up this discussion later." With that he disappeared like a six-pack in a room full of *svart alfar*, leaving me alone.

I could have gone back to vandalizing the Christmas lists, but that really hadn't had enough impact: he'd forgotten it already. What I needed was something that would hit him in his public image. Then he'd have to notice.

If only I could get to that studio where Mom was filming, get out on camera with her, and go all Jerry Springer telling everyone how bogus she is. I could dare them to actually eat what she mixed up. But the show would be over before I got there, even if I could take the fastest reindeer, the one she had with her.

Still, a plan started forming to embarrass Dad—not on TV, but you can't have everything. I headed for the stables, grinning in anticipation.

It was past feeding time and way past the time for the wranglers to take them out to exercise, so the reindeer were alone when I came in. They've known me forever. I can remember feeding them carrots when I was three, helping Dad harness them when I was seven. They nuzzled my hands and I petted them, like I've always done. The stable still felt more like home than any other place I knew: warm and crowded and comforting.

It was also smelly. Flying reindeer guano is pretty good fertilizer, and they've found a market for it as a novelty Christmas gift for gardeners, so the stable hands don't let any of it go to waste. The manure pile in the corner was starting to look like a small mountain. I shoveled some of it into a bucket, then threw back the tarps and uncovered the sleigh. The bucket fit nicely into the compartment where Dad usually keeps a giant jug of coffee for his midnight rides.

Harnessing the reindeer was easy. I'd helped Dad

do it a hundred times, and they seemed downright eager to get to work. Cupid looked a little awkward without Comet by his side, but it couldn't be helped, and I was sure the seven of them were more than strong enough to pull the sleigh.

I hadn't been flying with Dad for years, but it couldn't be hard. The dark-elf engineers had added a computer guidance system, so the thing must practically fly itself. I set in a flight plan to hit a couple of houses near Buffalo, New York, and then crash the Sabres/Canadiens game—might as well kill two birds with one stone.

When everything was ready, I opened the gear closet and rummaged around till I found Dad's red suit. THE red suit, you know. It was kind of big on me, but with the black belt at the tightest notch it stayed on. I leaped into the sleigh, grabbed the reins, and activated the automatic stable door opener.

The reindeer charged forward without even a "Now Dasher, now Dancer" to get them going. Before I could even get my bearings, the lights of North Pole Enterprises dwindled to tiny stars below me. It was such a thrill to see it so far behind, knowing I was free to go wherever I wanted, that I couldn't help shouting out loud: "Woo-hooo!"

The reindeer responded with an aerial flip. I am not exaggerating. I wish I was. Next thing I knew I was upside down, the Northern Comfort and pizza sloshing around disturbingly in my stomach. If I hadn't had the seat belt on, I'd have been a little red-coated splotch somewhere in the Yukon.

At least, that's where I think we were. The guidance computer kept saying, "You are now off course by fifteen degrees west." I yanked the reins left to correct it. The reindeer turned left—and kept turning left until we were headed back the way we'd come from.

"No, no, you stupid animals," I yelled, pulling the reins the other way. They wheeled around again, then steadied as I let the reins go slack. I took a deep breath.

"You are now off course by sixteen degrees west," intoned the guidance computer.

I gave it a savage punch. My fist hurt. "Please establish flight plan, beginning with current coordinates," said the computer.

"Son of a bitch!" I yelled. The reindeer jerked forward and flew like bats out of hell. I couldn't do anything but hang on, trying to curse quietly so I wouldn't excite them anymore. Leafless woodlands and snowy fields sped beneath us and then, finally, the lights of towns.

I waited till the lights clustered so thick that I knew I had a city under me. I pulled the reins. "Down, Dasher. Down, Dancer. Down, all of you." They swooped low over a crowd in a square. It was perfect: a tree-lighting festival with a brass band and a whole herd of bundled-up people stamping their feet against the cold and swaying with the music of Christmas carols.

I didn't make my move till they started pointing and yelling. Though the wind carried their words away, I knew what they were saying: "Look! Santa Claus!" Bending over the side of the sleigh, I upended the bucket of reindeer guano. "Merry Christmas, you losers!"

The shit broke up in the air into glittering silver powder that drifted down over the people's heads. It looked like pixie dust. From the way the crowd was giggling and cheering, I'd say it *was* pixie dust.

"Waste recycling field activated," said the computer.

"Recycling," I muttered bitterly, still leaning over the side to watch. Well, that explained how Dad could drink so much coffee and get around the world without a bathroom break.

"Obstacle ahead," said the guidance computer. "Obstacle ahead. Obstacle ahead."

I straightened up and saw the cathedral in front of us, but not before the reindeer did. They shot straight upward—it must be a reflex—and started charging straight up the wall with the runners of the sled scraping the stone.

To the top of the porch, to the top of the wall—well, not quite to the top. There was a gargoyle jutting out dead ahead of us.

"Oh, shit!"

Dasher swerved left to avoid it, Dancer swerved right, and the rest of them went wildly in all directions. The harnesses tangled around the gargoyle; the sled, with me in it, dangled down, turning and rocking in the wind, like an amusement park ride from hell.

I wondered whether I should try to jump down from there. I looked down at the ground swaying and spinning below me. *Bad idea*, I thought as the

Northern Comfort and pizza came back out the way they went in.

"Waste recycling field activated," said the guidance computer. The crowd beneath me, pixilated on pixie dust, was applauding. Apparently they thought it was all a wonderful unannounced part of the show.

"Hello, down there," I shouted, without knowing what language these people spoke. "I'm stuck. Can someone help me?" But the brass band played on, and I don't think anyone heard me.

The harness creaked, stretched to the limits. *This is it*, I thought. *I'm going to fall down and die, crushed in a pile with Dasher and Dancer and Prancer and Vixen and Cupid and Donner and Blitzen. I wonder if Dad will even notice I'm gone. I guess the wranglers will tell him in the morning that the reindeer are missing. He'll miss them more than me.*

I looked out mournfully at the reindeer struggling on their end of the harness, each one flying out a bit and then sagging back. *They're going to die, too, and it's all my fault.* "Sorry, guys," I said. "I didn't mean to hurt you."

The crowd wasn't even looking at me anymore, distracted with something else, cheering and pointing. But I didn't care any more. I shut my eyes and waited to die.

"Chip! Get out the tow rope!"

I opened my eyes again. There, hovering beside me, was Dad on the burro he uses to follow the Three Kings. "Chip—or Sharp, or whatever—get the tow rope. Hurry! It's in the front compartment—no, not the coffee compartment, the one next to it. Got it? Fix one end of it tight to that ring. You know how to tie a good strong knot?"

"Yeah." My fingers were stiff with cold and fear, but I managed. I tossed him the other end and he fastened it to the burro's harness.

"Steady, Pepito," he said, giving the burro a pat. "You stay steady, too," he told me. "No quick moves."

I nodded dumbly. The only quick move I had in mind was that my stomach might turn inside out again at any moment.

Dad brought Pepito close to the gargoyle to examine the tangled harness straps. "All right, Blitzen, you first," he said. "Come on, girl. Up and over. There's a good girl. Donner! Donner, old boy, come up this way. Good boy!" With that, one by one, he coaxed the reindeer through a series of maneuvers to undo the tangle of harness straps till they could pull the sleigh past the gargoyle, all on the same side, to the roof. It sloped wildly, but it was better than dangling in midair, so Dad stopped there to put on the spare harness and let Pepito into the sleigh with us.

As he took up the reins, he shouted down to the crowd below us, "Merry Christmas to all, and to all a good night!" The crowd went wild, and we took off.

As the snowy fields passed beneath us, I fidgeted. Finally, I couldn't stand it. "Okay, when do you start?"

"What?"

"When do you start yelling at me? Oh, wait, yelling doesn't fit the modern image of Christmas. How about that long speech I have coming about how I need to consider the impact of my actions on others?"

Dad stared straight ahead of him. Then he sighed. "I don't know what to say."

"Great. This is just like us. We just won't say anything to each other all the way to the North Pole. Or after that. Aren't you even going to tell me how I screwed up? How I could have killed the reindeer and myself and half the people at that tree-lighting ceremony?"

Dad looked at me, and this time I couldn't read his expression. "I could. But that would seem a little redundant now, wouldn't it?"

"Well, say something!"

It took a while. He sighed again. "Been a long time since we've been for a ride together, you and me."

I stared at him to see if he was being sarcastic.

"Too long, I guess. The time gets by me," he said. "Christmas, Epiphany, Easter—it's always something." He patted Pepito fondly. "This little guy, he's not used to this kind of exercise, catching up with reindeer. Maybe he needs to take it easy till next year. The Three Kings managed by themselves for years, you know. They'll be okay."

"Yeah," I said, still looking for the catch.

"It's pretty nice out here, isn't it?" he said, gesturing at the starscape above us.

"I guess," I said. It was a pretty awesome night, with a perfect crescent moon.

"How about this: You do the rounds with me Christmas Eve, and I'll take you to a hockey game on Epiphany?"

"Sounds okay," I said, turning away so he couldn't see how wide I was grinning.

WITH A FACE ONLY A MOTHER COULD LOVE

by Jenn Reese

*Jenn Reese's work has appeared in anthologies such as
Prom Night and Sword & Sorceress XVII, as well as
on-line at "Strange Horizons." She has degrees in English and Archaeology with an emphasis on Medieval
studies, so she couldn't resist writing a story about Grendel and his good pal, Beowulf. When she's not writing,
Jenn practices martial arts, plays strategy games, and
keeps an on-line journal at www.sff.net/people/jenn. She
currently lives in Los Angeles with her one husband,
two cats, and three computers.*

"MEN ARE PIGS," my mother said as she
scraped the bones off her plate and back
into the soup kettle. "No, they're worse than pigs.
They're . . . *men*." She stirred the soup with the dull
dagger I had given her as a present on her last birthday. "They tell you you're beautiful. They say they
love you. Then you get pregnant, and BAM! They're

25

off to find some braided young bimbo who'll listen to their lies."

It was a familiar lecture. I could recite the whole thing when I tried, which wasn't often. I picked the fish carcass off my plate and crunched down on its brittle skull. Mmm, tasty.

"Are you listening to me, Grendel? Because I don't think you are." She tapped the stirring dagger on the side of the kettle and laid it gently on the dirt by the fire pit.

I cringed. Mom was really upset. The scales on her cheeks had flushed dark green, and her eyes glowed ever so slightly with hellfire.

Plus, she never said my name unless she was really serious.

"Yeah, I'm listening, Mom."

"Oh, is that so? Then why did I find a sword in your cave this morning when I was dusting?"

Busted!

"Uh . . . I . . . There was this really big spider, see . . ."

"Don't you dare lie to me," Mom said, her eyes fully ablaze now. She took a step closer and wagged a claw at me. "I see there's more of your father in you than I thought. How long before you run off to fight your little wars with your buddies instead of helping out around the lair?"

Sooner than you think, Mom. But I'm not as stupid as I look, so I said, "I'd never do that, Mom. I love you."

I had to wait till full dark before swimming up to the surface. Growing up in a cave complex under a lake will play havoc with your eyes. Besides, Mom's ears were too sharp until the second flask of mead had her snoring on her mat by the fire. I hated lying to her, sneaking out every night. But there are some things a man just has to do, and I was a man.

Or at least half of one.

I sat by the edge of the lake and played with the krakens for a while. Fang and Freckles, I named them. Freckles, in particular, loved to be scratched on the snout. Then I ripped out a small tree and played fetch with Fang, though he insisted on doing three somersaults in the water before he took the tree in his toothy maw and brought it back to me.

Finally, it was time to go see Dad.

Mom didn't want me to go. She'd told me endless stories about his selfishness, about how he loved his sword and his fame more than he loved her.

But why would she have loved him in the first place, if he wasn't pretty cool? I mean, every kid dreamed of being a prince, and I actually was one! My dad was a king. That made me a prince, almost by definition.

Maybe Mom was the one with the problem. Maybe she was just trying to cloud my judgment so I wouldn't want to go live with my dad and leave her alone in the lake. She was the selfish one, and it just wasn't fair.

I trudged through the swamp, ducking under strangling branches and jumping over drowning pits. Some wolves ran along with me for a while, but I wasn't inclined to play. I needed friends who could actually talk. Friends—*men*—who I could practice fighting with, who could introduce me to girls. I'd spent way too many nights fishing with my mother and watching the lichen grow on my ceiling.

King Hrothgar—*Dad*—had been busy building a huge wooden hall, big enough for me and even Mom to come and live in, if things worked out. At night, if I got there early enough, I could sit in the woods nearby and listen to them, my dad and his men, drinking and laughing.

When I got there tonight, a minstrel was singing. I settled into my regular spot, a nice-sized crevasse in the gnarled roots of an old tree, and closed my eyes to listen. The man had a beautiful voice, so clear and strong. I could sing, too, but not as well. My mom said I sounded like a kraken in heat. But maybe I just sang too much like a man for her. Maybe my father would be proud, and let me sing in the hall for him and his men.

The minstrel sang about God and the world and how everything He had created was special in its own way: the sun and the moon, the beauty of each leaf of each branch of each tree, the multitude of creatures great and small that walked, flew, swam, and slithered over the earth. I listened, and it was as if the minstrel was singing the song just for me. Different meant special, he told me with his music. Special meant good.

Tonight.

Tonight, I would finally have the courage to enter that great hall called Heorot and take my rightful place at my father's side. Tonight was the night I'd been waiting for my entire life.

Of course, I couldn't just burst in there in the middle of the merriment and expect my father to welcome me with open arms. I hadn't been invited, for one thing, and I didn't want everybody to fuss over me, for another. I mean, did my father even know that I existed? What if Mom never told him about me?

No. Better to wait until most of the people were asleep. Then I could just sneak in, wake up my father, and have a decent chat with him. That way, if he started to cry with joy at my return, none of his subjects would have to know. Until I let it slip later on, that is. What long-lost prince doesn't deserve a few good tears?

Slowly, the lights were extinguished inside Heorot. I ate a few rabbits while I waited, though I wasn't really hungry. Nervous habit, I guess. I finished off the warren, then made myself stop. No one wants a pudgy prince, even of the "long-lost" variety.

It was time.

I brushed the bunny bits off my chest and stood. Mom would understand. She said she hated Hrothgar, my father, but I'm sure that was an exaggeration. Heck, once Dad saw me, maybe he'd even divorce his new wife and go back to Mom. But I was getting ahead of myself. First, the joyful reunion.

I tiptoed on my claws to the head of the hall and

walked up the four sturdy wooden steps to the hall's great golden double doors. My hand shook as I threaded one claw through the iron door handle and pulled it open.

For a moment, I think my heart actually stopped.

The hall seemed even bigger on the inside, and it was filled with the warmth of a smoldering fire and a host of sleeping bodies. Like lifting up a boulder and seeing a million tiny grubs squirming in the once-hidden soil. Only these grubs—these men— weren't moving. They lay in bundled heaps around the floor, their snores echoing in the wooden beams of the high ceilings. I smelled beer and mead and cooked meat, saw dim firelight dance along the gleaming metal of the swords and armor and shields hanging on the walls and strewn in almost every corner and crevasse of the place.

Women, too, lay among the men. I could smell the soap of their hair and see the soft fabrics of their gowns twisted among the dark-dyed wool cloaks and blankets. So many people! How they must relish each other's company and the bright spark of conversation that flies between them.

But which one was my father?

It was difficult to walk with so many bodies on the floor. I almost tripped twice, and barely caught myself by grabbing onto an iron sconce sticking out of the wall. The third time I tripped, however, it was the body beneath me that I grabbed onto.

The man's eyes opened instantly. He lurched beneath my grip, opened his little mouth, and let loose with the loudest scream I've ever heard. I now know what the phrase "bloodcurdling" means, firsthand and personal. Before I could even let the man go, the humans were all moving, all screaming. Those glittery bits of metal came down off the walls in a blink of my eye.

It wasn't the reception I'd been hoping for.

I stumbled backward, accidentally ripping apart the man I had tripped on. His flesh just came off in my claws like he was made of flower petals. Of course, the ensuing gouts of blood only made things worse. Angry screams now filled the hallowed hall of Heorot. I felt sword after sword snap against my legs, my back, my arms. Someone even got in a good jab with a spear right at my groin.

"Wait!" I yelled, but I guess nobody could hear me. They were too busy with their own war cries and panic. I tried again anyway. "I want to see Hrothgar! Hrothgar is my father!" Nope. Nothing. It was like trying to argue with my mother.

Retreat was my only option. I waded through the men, flailing my arms to protect myself. Bits of them came away with every swipe, but it really couldn't be helped. They weren't giving me a lot of choices. Like flies, they swarmed around me, buzzing with their little grub anger and their glinty grub weapons. My left claw got stuck in someone's eye, and when I pulled it out, the man's whole head ripped off his shoulders. I decided to take that bit with me. No sense in wasting the good meat.

I thought they would follow me back into the woods and to the lake, where I was sure I could talk to them more reasonably, maybe introduce them to my mother and get her to tell them about Dad. But strangely, they didn't seem to follow me past the clearing of Heorot.

I dove into the lake, ignoring Fang and Freckles, and swam down to our subterranean home. Mom was still asleep by the fire, her tangle of black hair piled under her head like a pillow of giant spiders. She'd never looked so lovely.

Back in my cave, I flopped onto my sleeping rags and tossed the man head into the corner. Just didn't have the appetite right now. How had things gone so far awry from my plans?

But then it hit me. Dad hadn't been in the hall, after all! Surely, he would have recognized his own son and put a stop to all that mayhem. Surely, his wisdom would have led everyone down the path of reason and friendship!

Yes, that was definitely it. And tomorrow was another night.

My father didn't raise a quitter.

Okay, technically he didn't raise me at all, but the idea was still sound. Never give up. Men didn't back down when the odds seemed to go against them. I'd heard tale after tale of heroism every night I spent listening outside my father's hall. Men valued courage and strength. If I did nothing else, I would prove to them that I possessed both.

Night after night, I went to Heorot.

Sometimes they were awake, but they never gave me a chance to explain myself. Always with the weapons, these men! I came for conversation and camaraderie, and left only with body parts. Father was testing me, I decided. Any son of his had to prove his worth to the whole kingdom. But how many men did I have to kill? I stopped counting after three dozen, mostly because I just couldn't count any higher than that.

Then one night, a few months into this whole "testing" process, the hall was empty. I couldn't believe it! Even the great oak doors hung open, too heavy to swing in the wind. I went inside for a look around. Splintered wood littered the floor like fish bones in our cave. The walls, once shiny with gold and swords, stood blood-splashed and silent in the darkness. Not even the hint of a fire still played in the hall's many fire pits.

I fell to my knees, shattering a small bench that had somehow remained intact until then. Where were the minstrels, the warriors? Where were the bawdy lasses with their long braids and their swirly skirts? Where was my dad?

I cried then. Alone in the darkness of Heorot, I cried like my mother did in the early morning when she thought I was still asleep. I cried, and I didn't care if it made me look weak or stupid, because that's how I felt. Weak. Incredibly stupid.

Alone.

Mother was awake when I got home that night. I could tell by the ring of yellow around her eyes that she'd been crying, too. I crawled out of the water and went to her without a word. She didn't need words. She hugged me to her scaly bosom, and I let her do it. She put her lips against my ear and whispered, "I love you, Grendel."

My whole body relaxed against hers, the aches in my neck and back driven away by the power of her soft voice. When she spoke again, I stilled my heart in order to hear her more clearly.

"And you're grounded for twelve years," she said.

A lot of lichen grew on my ceiling in twelve years. And I ate a lot of fish. But in that time, my mind had spent more hours with Dad than the rest of me spent with my mother in our lair. I went with him on imagined battles, his most treasured and feared warrior-prince. Together we sailed the whale-road, the great expanse of water that started at the shore and never, ever stopped.

Father and son, King and Prince.

Oh, and I learned how to masturbate, too.

On the last night of the twelfth year of my grounding, Mom cooked us a huge kraken for dinner. Fang and Freckles had produced a few too many offspring, so we were just doing our part to help out—for the good of the lake, and all that.

"I hope you've learned your lesson," Mom said. She used her knife to scrape a huge chunk of kraken onto my plate, along with way too much seaweed. "Men are evil."

"Well, I'll admit that they weren't exactly brimming with kindness," I said, "but the idea that everything in the universe is either good or evil is a little simplistic, don't you think?"

One has a lot of time for self-reflection over the course of twelve years.

"I don't really care about the universe," Mom said, "I just care about you. When I told your father I was pregnant, he left me. What makes you think he'd want you back now?"

My immense courage? My intense loyalty? My flawless green skin?

"I dunno, Mom. Maybe he's sorry. Maybe he didn't have any other kids, and he really wants one. Maybe he needs someone to give his kingdom to when he dies."

"Oh, don't give me that crap!" Mom smashed her fist down on her plate of food. Kraken bits spurted out in every direction. "Have you learned nothing in the last twelve years?" A little piece of intestine caught in her bangs jiggled as she talked. I couldn't take my eyes off of it.

She slapped me then, hard enough to make my eyes wobble inside my skull.

"Go," she said quietly. "Get out."

I shook my head, not understanding.

"Leave!" she screamed. "You want to be with your father so badly, then go to him! Find out, once and for all, what men are really like!"

She stood up and turned toward the wall of the cave, her body shaking with silent sobs.

"Mom, please—"

"Go," she said again. And this time, I obeyed.

Heorot brimmed with light and laughter as I approached. Men sang in loud, out-of-tune voices.

Mugs of beer clattered against each other in raucous toasts to dragons and long sea voyages. Women giggled in what I suspect was an alluring manner.

And everywhere I heard a new name mentioned, again and again. The name *Beowulf*.

Twelve years is bound to add a little smarts to a person, even me. I climbed a huge tree next to the hall and clambered onto the roof. I made a lot of noise, scraping the scales of my knees along the wood, but no one seemed to notice. I crawled along, pleased with my ingenuity, until I found a decently-sized hole with which to spy on the world of men.

For the first time, I saw my father.

King Hrothgar sat on a high-backed throne of polished wood and gold. His face was much like what I'd imagined: regal and surrounded in thick well-groomed hair of silvery white. The simple crown around his brow sported glittery stones of every color.

His wife—the strumpet—sat next to him on a smaller, less flamboyant chair. She was pretty, I suppose, but lacked my mother's strength and obvious charisma. Hrothgar would forget about this thin, gangly woman soon enough.

The scene was perfect. All it really lacked was the entrance of a long lost son to give it some oomph.

And then another man entered my field of vision. Judging from the swagger in his step and the haughty rise of his nose, I pegged him as this Beowulf I'd been hearing about.

What followed was worse than my most terrifying of nightmares. Worse even than the time I had caught my mother cooking naked. It was the stuff of hell itself.

Beowulf, it turned out, was a big hero up north. He spent the next hour regaling all of Heorot with greatly exaggerated tales of his bravery and strength. Yeah, like he really swam for five days in his chain mail. It wouldn't have been so bad if they'd all pointed and laughed, like I wanted to do. But no, the entire hall believed, revered him even more. Even Hrothgar, my wise and beloved father, smiled and spoke to Beowulf as a son.

As a son!

Dad even did that man-to-man embracing thing, where they almost hug and then slap each other on the back. Everyone cheered. Women swooned. Men envied. Even Hrothgar's little strumpet flirted with Beowulf when she handed him a goblet.

That should have been me down there. That should have been me!

And all that posturing, all that bragging. "Oooh, I'll kill the monster without wearing any armor! I'll kill the monster without using my sword!" It was insufferable. I shimmied across the roof and back onto my tree.

I'd show this Beowulf the meaning of strength. I'd show him courage! Dad had showered his gifts upon the wrong person, that's for sure. Well, Dad would be retracting those gifts come sunlight tomorrow, and he'd be taking them from Beowulf's dead body.

Or whatever bits of his body I decided to leave behind.

* * *

Okay, so it didn't quite go as I planned.

It was dark! There were a lot of blankets! I ripped up the wrong guy. Beowulf just lay there and watched me do it. Never said a word, never even called the alarm. Some hero. Just lay there and bided his time until I got to him.

I have to admit, the little grub was strong. I went for his throat, but those beady eyes snapped open and he grabbed my arm instead.

Locked together, we smashed our way around the hall. We broke all the newly rebuilt stools and tables, all the half-filled mugs and crumb-covered plates. I growled. Beowulf grunted. The crowd cheered us on and tried to keep out of the way.

On the plus side, I got away.

On the negative side, one of my arms didn't.

I ran as fast as I could back to the lake, holding my shoulder as the blood gushed out between my clawed fingers. My head throbbed in time with my heart. So much pain! I jumped into the lake. The cold water stabbed at my wound till I thought I would pass out. With just one good arm, I couldn't swim down to our lair. Could barely even keep myself under the surface.

Freckles to the rescue. She took my torso in her maw, sank her teeth gently into my flesh, and took me home to Mother.

When Freckles broke the surface of our little lair lake, my mother rushed to my side. She dragged me to the fire, pulling with every muscle, and I could do nothing to help her. Her eyes glowed red, her mouth expelled great puffs of fishiness with each new strain of her muscles.

"Beowulf," I mumbled. "Beowulf."

His name was the only thing I could say. Other words flooded my mind, words like, "I'm sorry," and "You were right." But the only ones that made it to my mouth were his name, over and over again.

"Shhh, Grendel," Mom said. She smoothed the hair out of my eyes and kissed my forehead with dry, scaly lips. "No one does this to my baby," she said. "No one does this and lives."

Then the world fell into a darkness not even my cave-grown eyes could penetrate.

I awoke to Mom's toothy smile as she waved my dismembered arm triumphantly over her head. "I got it, son!"

"Ung?" I said eloquently.

She knelt beside me and helped me sit up against the cave wall. Then she mashed my errant arm back into place on my shoulder. My vision blurred from the sudden renewal of pain.

"Hold it there for a few days. It'll knit back into place, good as new." She licked two of her fingers then used them to clean some bloody residue from my reunited limb. Mom spit cleans just about anything, it turns out.

I stared up at Mom and grinned, hoping she understood how much I really did love her. And when the pain grew too great, I closed my eyes and slept again.

For the first time in years, I was happy.

*   *   *

The next time I awoke, it was to the sound of my mother's last scream.

Beowulf stood over her, gripping my childhood sword in both his hands. She lay at his feet, blood flowing freely from a deep cut in her neck. Beowulf's own blade lay discarded in the dust a few feet away. Useless. Only my sword had been strong enough to pierce my mother's hide. To kill her.

It was all my fault.

"Fiend!" I yelled.

Beowulf turned and looked at me, his eyes hidden in the shadow of his helmet.

My wounded arm hung limply against my torso. I used the good one to brace myself against the wall as I stood. "Murderer," I hissed. "Woman-killer."

"Come get some," said Beowulf.

We met in a mind-splitting clash of steel and claw, scale and flesh. Gone were his petty promises of no weapons or armor. Gone, too, were his pretty clothes and perfect features. What I faced now was a monster. A wild beast. A *man.* And what I was, was so much more.

I was my mother's son.

Beowulf slashed me across the thigh. I backhanded him across the face. We circled. We snarled. We grappled and hissed and traded insults.

Finally, I got a good grip on one of Beowulf's arms and twisted with all my might. The sword—my sword—fell from his shattered hand and thudded to the dirt-strewn floor. Beowulf the Big Hero wailed like a little girl.

"An arm for an arm," I said.

For the first time in many, many years, I didn't think about what my father thought of me. I didn't care if he thought I was brave, or strong, or honest, or handsome. He didn't love me, and he never would.

I wrapped my claws around Beowulf's head and squeezed.

Mother had always known that. Why couldn't I have listened when she was alive?

Beowulf's head popped off of his neck. I brought it to my mouth and bit into his crunchy skull.

Well, Mom was right about something else, too: Men *are* pigs.

But they taste more like chicken.

SWITCHED

by Nina Kiriki Hoffman

Nina Kiriki Hoffman has sold more than two hundred stories and several novels. Her works have been finalists for the Nebula, World Fantasy, Mythopoeic, Sturgeon, and Endeavour awards. The Thread that Binds the Bones won a Horror Writers Association Bram Stoker Award for first novel. Her Fantasy novels include The Silent Strength of Stones, A Red Heart of Memories, Past the Size of Dreaming, and A Fistful of Sky. Her third short story collection, Time Travelers, Ghosts, and Other Visitors, came out in 2003, as did A Stir of Bones, a young adult fantasy novel. Stir made the American Library Association list of books for the teen reader, the New York Public Library list of books for teens, and was a finalist for the Horror Writers Association Stoker Award. In addition to writing, Nina works at a bookstore, does production work for a national magazine, and teaches short story writing through a local community college. She lives in Oregon and has cats.

I WAS TEN when my father married my stepmother, and her daughter, Musette, was nine. My
wicked stepmother, Habila, was cleverer than most
wicked stepmothers; she had read the old tales before
she married my father.

My father, on the other hand, was just like fathers
in the old tales, too stupid to realize she only married
him for money, and that she loved her own daughter
and hated me.

My own mother had been a beauty and a saint, so
lovely everyone adored her at first sight, so kind we
had benches built in the garden for the beggars and
the troubled who came by each day to ask her for
aid and counsel. She was not as openhanded as she
longed to be, for in those days Father still had some
sense, and knew he had to maintain his wealth and
not bankrupt himself if he wanted to sponsor Mother's charities for any length of time. He made her a
daily allowance, and she had to decide carefully how
to spend it to benefit the most people. This served
her well; she did not give equally to the liars and
the genuinely destitute: she learned to tell who told
the truth.

In all her charitable work, she kept me by her side,
and taught me, as she learned, how to deal with others, how to tell a schemer from a pauper, how to be
kind and good and careful.

She had been dead only a year when my father
married my stepmother.

My stepmother was a clever and accomplished

woman. She had her own dark beauty. Her lips were redder than my mother's had been, and this, I think, owed more to her passionate nature than to any art. Unlike my mother's golden hair, my stepmother's hair was bog black, shimmering and iridescent as a raven's feathers in the sun, and her eyes were a blue so deep they looked black in any light but daylight.

My stepsister Musette was as dark as her mother, but in some ways innocent. However, her mother loved her so much and catered so to her every whim that Musette believed everyone should defer to her. In this one area, my stepmother was at first blind to reality: she did not see that Musette offended those she considered her inferiors with her high-handed ways.

Soon after my father met Habila, he brought her home to dinner. I did not know what to think. She was beautiful and acted kind, and my father had been so melancholy since my mother died—as had I—that I was glad my father had found someone who gave him even a moment's comfort.

Habila took pains to charm me. "Oh," she said to my father, "Prudence is a lovely child. How sad you must be, dearest one, with no mother to care for you."

I *was* sad, so I took this for sense. I let her hug me, fool that I was, and took comfort in the warmth of her embrace. Father and I had not touched each other since the day of Mother's funeral. We had retreated into our own cold sadnesses. I had not known until Habila held me how hungry I had become for even the falsest of human comforts.

I had watched my mother learn to tell the deceiver from the honest person, had tried to continue in her traditions, seeing petitioners each day, with my father's blessing. But I was confused and could not always determine who to give alms to. Usually I gave a little to everyone.

Habila petted me and said what a good, kind child I was. She told Musette to be nice to me. Musette found this difficult; she had never had to be nice to anyone, but she tried. She let me touch her dolls, but she would not let me play with them.

My father's courtship of Habila lasted a month. Then they married, and Musette and Habila came to live with us.

"Oh, my Prudence, everyone loves you," Habila said to me the morning after her wedding. We were in the dining room, where Cook had set the breakfast buffet. Habila and I were the only two awake so early. She had come down before me, in time to watch Cook set the buffet. I came before Cook was finished, and Habila heard me thanking Cook for everything, as was my daily habit.

"Do they?" I said. I set toast and scrambled eggs on my plate and brought it to the table, set it at the place beside Habila's. I wondered when she would hug me again. She had embraced me at every meeting before she wed my father. I stood beside my chair, uncertain but hoping.

"How could they help it? You are all that is good and kind." She studied me, but she did not hold out her arms.

I wasn't sure how to respond, so I curtsied.

Musette stumbled into the room in her slippers and robe then, her dark hair disarrayed, her cheeks flushed. "I want chocolate!" she cried after she had studied the buffet and discovered there was no cocoa there. She strode to the bellpull and tugged it hard. Cook came up three minutes later. "What took you so long?" cried Musette. "I want chocolate! Now!"

Cook nodded and fled.

"Oh, dear," said Habila. She touched my shoulder and said, "Sit, child. Eat. Your eggs are getting cold."

I seated myself beside her and ate. Musette filled a plate with pastries and climbed up onto the chair on the other side of her mother. When Cook brought her a cup and a pot of chocolate, she tasted it and threw the cup on the floor. " 'Tis not sweet enough!" she cried. "Make it over, and this time flavor it correctly!"

Cook fled again.

"Oh, dear," said Habila.

She spent the morning baking, despite Cook's protests at the invasion of her space. By lunchtime, my stepmother had made her first spellcakes in my father's house.

At lunch she set a dark cake on my plate, and a white cake on Musette's. "From now on," she said, "you will each eat one of these with every meal. Eat it first, before you eat anything else. It is the only thing I ask of you."

My dark cake was sweet and rich. I thought it wouldn't be a hardship to live off such cake entirely.

Musette didn't like her cake so much. " 'Tis too sickly sweet!" she cried.

"Eat it," said her mother. In that moment she looked different: her eyes held storm, her mouth shaped anger, and she grew until her wild dark hair brushed the ceiling.

Surely my eyes deceived me.

Nevertheless, Musette ate all of her cake, and never protested again.

At supper that night Father noticed our treats. "What is this?" he asked.

"Something to aid our daughters' complexions," said Stepmother.

"May I taste?" Father reached toward my plate.

I wanted to hide my plate in my lap. I didn't want to share my cake with Father! It was mine, mine alone.

"No!" cried Stepmother. "That is just for Prudence. Only girls get any benefit of it."

Father looked forlorn. Stepmother said, "Never mind, Louis. I'll make you your own special cake for breakfast tomorrow."

I ate the rest of my cake quickly, before anyone could take it from me.

Stepmother made Father a yellow cake that looked as delicious as the cakes she made for me and Musette. After he ate it, he became sleepy but contented. That was no good; she had to bake him something else for breakfast and lunch, or he became too stupid to do business, and Stepmother didn't want that; but she was delighted to have him sleepy and happy after supper, so he had yellow cake with every evening meal.

The week after I first started eating my special

cake, I became too impatient to meet with petitioners any longer. I gave the housekeeper the day's alms to disburse, and granted her discretion over who to give them to. I discovered some time later that she had decided she and her husband, the butler, were more in need of alms than any of the beggars who no longer thronged our doors, but by that time I did not care; I was dipping into the alms myself. A woman needed ribbons and jewels, after all.

Two weeks later, I looked at the hair in my brush and noticed that it was darker than I expected. I studied myself in the mirror and saw that my curly blonde hair was turning dark and straight, and my eyes, formerly sky blue, had gone lavender. At lunch that day I studied my stepsister as she ate her white cake and noticed that her midnight hair had streaks of blonde in it now, leaving her odd-looking and piebald. Her dark eyes had flecks of green in them.

In the following month, my stepsister and I changed our coloring: she was fair, her hair a shining crown of wheat-blonde curls, her formerly olive skin lightened to peachy pink, her dark eyes to a sea blue-green; my hair had gone to cave black, my eyes darkening to pansy-purple. Now when we went out shopping with Stepmother, strangers mistook me for her true daughter, and Musette for the adopted one. Musette no longer cried and cursed either. She never sent anything back or complained of Cook's behavior or the laziness of the maids.

More things bothered me than formerly. My tongue's sensitivity to taste increased. Some flavors upset me so I couldn't finish my food. Meats tasted rotten; sweets were cloying, and when the bread was too dry, it felt like I was trying to swallow sawdust. I never got an apple but I found a worm in it.

The color of light changed, too; to me it always seemed stained with smoke, so that I saw no true sunlight any longer, and often there were scents in the air that made me sneeze.

Sometimes I complained.

Father always stared at me as though he couldn't believe the words that came from my lips. Stepmother smiled, and encouraged me to rage until I got my will. Musette, who had complained of the same things when she first moved into our house, grew increasingly quiet. She served herself the meat with the gristle, the burned ends of bread, and left the choicer cuts to me. What I left, after Father and Stepmother had been served, Musette snuck to the dog under the table. If there was more, sometimes she took it outside to give to the poor.

Later, the housekeeper set tasks for Musette: clean out the fireplaces. Draw water from the well. Do the mending. Take the laundry from the line, iron and fold it.

Stepmother watched and did not interfere. She only smiled.

I watched, and thought: Musette deserves it. She's the interloper here. It is my house, after all, and she is just a latecomer. She *should* help.

One of Father's apprentices stopped by the house after a year-long sea voyage. He had not seen me since before my father's wedding, and he called Musette by my name, and asked for an introduction to me. I screamed at him, but it only confused him; he did not believe I had ever been Prudence. He never came to the house again.

I grew to enjoy my own reflection as my hair and eyes darkened. None of my old gowns suited my new colors, so I had to buy others, in ruby and sapphire and emerald. No longer would I dress in pastels. I gave my old clothes to Musette, until I realized how nice she looked in them. Then I made sure to shred them and put them in the donation box for the poor.

By then, Musette had learned how to mend, and sometimes, when her own clothes were worn to pieces, she rescued my old gowns from the box and mended them. I let her do that. I always knew where the mends were, and I took secret joy in the thought of her wearing what was flawed, even if it looked fine to others.

When Musette was sixteen and I was seventeen, an invitation to a ball came from the local prince. It was addressed to all eligible ladies of the household.

"Musette is not eligible," I said. "She has nothing suitable to wear. Besides, look at her hands. They are ugly." Laundry soaps, scrubbing, and scut work had roughened Musette's skin, and her nails were short and ragged.

"Prudence is right," Stepmother said. "Musette will stay home while Prudence goes to the ball." And she helped me dress in my sapphire-blue velvet gown. She bound up my black hair in a braid crown around my head, and sent me off in my father's best carriage to the ball.

The prince danced with every young lady who came to the ball, but I fancied he enjoyed my company the most. He danced twice with me, an honor he had not shared with any of the others. The floor was polished crystal, and the walls were lined with mirrors: when I saw us reflected as a couple, the prince in pale blue and I in dark sapphire, his hair gold as coins and mine dark as night, I thought: *we are the perfect couple.*

At ten, though, the doors opened to admit one more maiden.

The herald announced her as the Unknown Princess. She wore a ballgown of pink overlaid with silver net, and her hair was a cloud of pale gold around her head. Her neck was long and graceful, her face beautiful, her crystal slippers tiny as she stepped with small clicks down the stairs into the ballroom.

All music and speech stopped for her entrance. The prince, who held my right hand in his left, and rested his right hand at my waist, released me so suddenly I would have fallen, save I was prepared for this. He abandoned me and walked toward the new arrival.

I studied her face as she descended the stairs, and thought: I know her. Then: Who is she?

Then: *Mother?*

She was the image of my mother's portrait, taken just after my mother wed my father. The portrait hung in the front parlor over the fireplace. After Mother died, I had visited there every day, though we never used that room unless we had visitors. I had stared at my mother's face, longing for her to come back from the dead, praying that she would advise me as I tried to continue her charitable works. For a time it seemed I heard her voice as I listened to the petitioners, and I had thought my judgments sound.

I had abandoned all such work years earlier.

This was not Mother as I had known her. This was Mother before I was born. This was the person I should be.

This was Musette as she was now.

The perfidy of my stepmother came clear to me in that moment.

As if pulled by strings, the prince advanced to the base of the stairs, and when Musette alighted, he took her hand in his. The music started then, a waltz, of course, and they glided over the floor in a space left bare by everyone else, who still stood, awestruck, staring at the prince and my stepsister. Musette was lovely, every step sure and floating. Her hands were concealed in elbow-length gloves. I had never noticed before what small feet she had.

"Miss Prudence?"

The man at my side wore a dark green velvet jacket and darker green unmentionables, and his figure was too slender and short for admiration. His face was clever rather than handsome, and his dark hair was thin on top. His dancing golden eyes protruded a little. I had known him for five years, as he was a business acquaintance of my father's, and often came to dine with us. He always wore some shade of green. He never left the house without me calling him "that frog" behind his back, which never failed to make my stepmother laugh, and my father protest that Mr. Baton was one of the best businessmen he knew, and I was not to make fun of him. Musette always shook her head, her eyes downcast.

Five minutes ago I would have said something cruel and sent him away, secure in my belief that the prince was mine. Now I said: "Mr. Baton?"

He held out a hand, and I took it. We danced. His steps were shorter than the prince's, of course, but he was energetic and lively, and his sense of rhythm was perfect. Unlike all the other men there, he did not spend the next ten minutes gawking at Musette.

Later in the evening, when I had danced with several other men, Mr. Baton claimed my hand again and led me to the chairs at the side of the room, seated me beside a little table, and went off to find me refreshments.

I looked around the room while Mr. Baton was gone, surveyed all the young men who were here. My stepmother's years of planning had borne fruit tonight. Musette, the classic mistreated princess-in-hiding, would have the prince. I would be cast off. The love and tolerance Stepmother had shown me, encouraging me in her own image instead of in my mother's, would evaporate now, I was sure. It behooved me to make my own plans.

Mr. Baton was not as handsome as other men here who were not the prince. He was not as tall as most of them, and his shoulders were narrow. The lack of hair, would that bother me? He could always wear a wig, as many in society did.

Did I need height or strength or even hair in a husband? Mr. Baton was rich. Though not noble, he had interests in a number of businesses; he had a fleet of ships, three dry goods shops, part share in the lending library, an upcountry textile factory, and a fine house on a square not two blocks from my father's house.

His eyes were lively, and his hands were dry in mine, not moist and clammy like some of the younger men's. His breath was always fresh and sweet, not rank with rotten teeth like some, or ripe with the scent of onions and garlic, like others. I had seen appreciation in his eyes when he looked at me.

He brought me a plate of pastries and a flute of champagne. He seated himself beside me while I nibbled. I did not pout because the creampuff filling was too sweet, or complain that the champagne bubbles made me sneeze. I smiled at him.

"Miss Prudence," he said. "You regard me differently from the way you have in the past. Dare I hope?"

"What do you think of *l'Inconnue*?" I asked.

"Who?" He glanced around. "That creature in pink, the so-called Unknown Princess?" He lifted a quizzing glass and studied her as best he could between the men who thronged around her. "Pretty enough, I suppose, but she does not look as though she has much wit."

"What would you say if you learned she was kind and good-hearted and not at all stupid?"

"Good for her. Perhaps she'll make an adequate queen."

I set my half eaten pastries on the table, placed my champagne glass beside them, and reached for his hand. He let me clasp it; indeed, he looked surprised and pleased at my forwardness.

Almost I heard my mother's voice again, though how that could be I did not know: I had eaten my regular portion of dark cake with my dinner that night. Perhaps enough hours had passed since then for the effect to lessen. I had a choice to make: I could entice this man into offering for me, and live with the security that would come of such a marriage, or I could tell him the truth about myself—if I even knew it—and let him make a more informed decision. My mother's voice advised me to tell the truth. "Mr. Baton? When I don't dye my hair, I fear I look much like the Unknown does."

"Impossible." He let the quizzing glass fall among the other fobs on his watch chain, and studied my face. He reached up and touched my hair just above my ear. Something in his eyes quickened then. "I spoke too soon," he murmured. "I see how it may be so." He cocked his head. "Do you plan to stop dyeing your hair?"

I looked away. "The choice may not be mine," I said. Now that Stepmother had her royal son-in-law, her happy daughter, would she ever make me spell-cake again? Who would I be without its influence? I had forgotten who I was when my real mother died; I only knew who I was now. Once the effect of the cake wore off—

"Would you even consider my suit?" he asked.

"I would, of course. But you don't know whom you ask to marry. I don't know myself."

"I have detected a touch of sorcery around your

father's investments," he muttered. "They are sometimes too successful."

"I've been under a spell as long as you've known me," I murmured, then wondered how I could admit such a thing.

"Is it a spell that enhances understanding? Do you anticipate it wearing off now?"

"Yes," I whispered. "No. I believe my understanding is my own, but everything else about me—"

"Ah," he said. He leaned back. His hand dropped to his thigh.

We sat silent beside each other. I gazed down at my sapphire velvet skirts with their insets of white satin. From the corner of my eye I watched as Mr. Baton surveyed the company, much as I had before. Was he searching for a better candidate for a wife? Most mothers and fathers would welcome him as a son-in-law, I suspected. He was successful and well-received.

By the prince's invitation, every eligible young woman of worth, and several worthless ones, should be here in the ballroom tonight. Perhaps he could not have his pick. But there were many he could choose, I was certain, girls who would be obedient to parents, who in turn would be obedient to economic pressure.

"Miss Prudence," he said at last, "thank you for favoring me with such relevant information, so prejudicial to your person. Given what you know and suspect of your own nature, if you should make a promise now, would your future self consider it binding?"

"Yes," I said. Suppose I lost my acquired selfish self. Surely the saintly self I used to be would never break a promise.

"I have already spoken to your father, though I feared I had no hope of winning you. He has given me permission to court you, but he says the final decision must rest with you."

"You prefer me to Musette?"

He lifted his glass and studied the Unknown again. "Musette," he said. "Ah. Of course. I much prefer you."

"I may be more like her tomorrow."

"And she?"

"I don't know. My stepmother planned this. After tonight—surely they will announce the betrothal tonight—she may have further plans. I don't know if she'll allow Musette to revert to her true self after she weds the prince, but I believe she will no longer care to keep me as I am."

"I believe I could love you either way. Could either of you love me?"

I smiled down at my skirts. "This is surely the oddest conversation I have ever had."

"It's not the oddest one I've had, but it is crucial to my future."

I glanced sideways at him. His golden eyes—so prominent—and yet, his mouth, so clever, with such a lovely, twisted, rueful smile on it. Why had I never appreciated him before? Perhaps it was so easy to see the flaws in him that the true heart lay hidden. I reached for his hand, and said, "I do believe I could love you either way."

"Miss Prudence, will you do me the honor of becoming my wife?"

Could I ever hope for more? Was I not lucky to be offered this much? I was fortunate indeed, no matter which self I became on the morrow. "Mr. Baton, I will."

He smiled. "Miss Prudence, would you care to take the air?"

Oh, dear, I thought. He means to kiss me.

Of course, you silly goose. He surely expects that in his wife.

"Gladly, Mr. Baton." I rose to my feet.

"Please. Call me Remy."

We went out through the tall French doors to the balcony that overlooked the gardens. Light from the myriad candles in the ballroom leaked through the many glassed, uncurtained doors to spill in rectangles of gold across the ground. Other couples stood there, leaned on the stone railing above the gardens, spoke in soft tones.

Remy led me past the others, down the staircase to the graveled garden path that led past yew hedges and beyond the light. Tonight I almost enjoyed the air, as I had not since my stepmother moved into the house. Almost I could taste cool wet spring and fresh grass.

In a small alcove in the yew, Remy pulled me close. I was an inch taller than he was. I thought: *How nice this is. Who would have thought it comfortable to dance with someone the same size? And yet, when I danced with those other men, none kept pace so well with me, or felt so comfortable with his arms around me, not even the prince. There is something to be said for being the same size as your husband.*

He tipped my chin down, and I leaned forward to meet his lips, thinking of his crooked, clever smile.

He tasted of champagne and shyness. *This is sweet,* I thought. *I will be able to put up with this the rest of my life. Indeed, perhaps I will enjoy it.*

The kiss began as one thing and changed into quite another. What started with me leaning just the smallest bit forward, my hands gripping his head, ended with me tilted backward as he loomed above me, my hands having slid down over his shoulders to press against his chest. At first I was frightened, then terrified. He wrapped his arms around me to keep me from falling. "Prudence?" he asked. Even his voice had changed, deepened until I didn't recognize it.

Was this one last trick my stepmother played on me?

"Let me go."

Gently he released me, steadying my shoulders with his big hands so that I didn't collapse.

"Who are you?" I asked in a shaking voice when at last his hands stopped gripping my shoulders. In the starlight he was nothing but a shadow that blocked the sky. How tall was he, and how did he come to be in my arms?

"Your fiancé."

"Mr. Baton?"

"Prudence. You were not the only one under a spell. But I was forbidden to speak of it until you broke it for me. I apologize for wooing you under false pretenses."

"But—"

"I hope you can forgive me. I promise I'll make it up to you the rest of our lives."

"Remy. Who are you?"

"You know me, Prudence. Only the envelope has changed."

"Really?"

"Truly." One of his hands reached for mine, and I let my hand disappear into his, which was now big enough to enfold it completely, but he didn't; he left me room to slide my thumb over his and grip him back. "I anticipate some trouble when I go back to the firm. It may be that I'll have to present myself as my own son or brother. I'm sure I can work it out, though. I have all the knowledge I need; I'll be able to convince them."

We walked back toward the palace, Remy a large presence beside me, his hand warm and dry around mine. At least that hadn't changed; but that made me wonder about all the other things that might have happened. Would I still be able to dance with him? He was taller than anyone else at the ball, I could tell that even in the dark, just from where the sound of his breathing came from.

Only the envelope had changed.

I couldn't promise him I would stay the same inside when the spell on me was broken, and he had accepted me even so. Who was I to complain?

We climbed the stairs to the balcony, where light waited, and I looked up. And up, and up. He was not quite a giant, but almost. His shoulders were broad, his face more handsome than the prince's, his hair thick and dark and no longer disappearing. In fact, he had a respectable amount tied in a tail at the back of his neck now. His neck was a whole subject in itself, thick and mighty as a young tree. He still wore shades of green, but his clothes had grown with him.

He paused in the light and looked at me. "Will I do?" he asked.

"Oh, Remy." I couldn't keep the irritation out of my voice. I had just convinced myself of all the advantages of a short paramour, and now here I was, stuck with a giant one.

He laughed and leaned to press his forehead to my hair. "My love, your dismay does my heart good," he said.

"I expect I'll get used to you," I muttered.

"Excellent."

The clock struck midnight as we went back inside, and Musette pushed away from the prince and ran off into the night, leaving behind a crystal slipper on the stair. Anxiety swept the crowd, and gossip, people wondering who the mysterious princess in pink had been; plainly the prince was smitten. He made his foolish declaration from the stairs, that he would marry the woman whose foot fit the slipper. By then Remy and I had regained our seats, and I had given him the rest of my pastries. He vowed he was hungry, and I wasn't surprised. There was a lot of him to maintain now.

He saw me home not too much later, riding with me in my father's best carriage, but he walked off after he had kissed me good night, much to the outrage of the housekeeper who answered the door. "I'll call on your father tomorrow," he said.

I went to get a cup of water in the kitchen. Musette sat by the hearth, back in her rags again.

"You should have been there," I told her, feeling it was required of me. "I was sure the prince was mine, but then, very late, a vision in pink appeared out of nowhere, and the prince spent all the rest of the evening dancing with her, until she ran off at midnight, leaving behind only a glass slipper. No one knows who she is."

"Oh, Prudence," Musette said. "I know you knew me."

"You do?"

"I saw you staring. I saw you blink when you recognized me. I saw you dance with the frog! How could you, Prudence, after all the times you've teased him?"

"Oh, well," I said. "I'm going to marry him. The prince vows he'll marry the one who fits in your slipper, so your future is assured."

"You'll marry the frog?" she cried. She leaped up and came to me. "You don't have to do that, Prue. I'll marry the prince, and then you can come live with me in the palace. We'll find you a much better husband."

"No, no. I am content."

We went upstairs together, and bade each other good night; for once, we both meant it.

In the middle of the night I woke and stared at the ceiling. My fiancé. Who was he, really? Who had cast a spell on him, and how long ago? Would he ever tell me?

In the morning, I found a piece of chocolate spell-cake on my plate, the same as every morning. I looked at Stepmother.

"What?" she asked.

"Is this any longer necessary?"

"Don't you like it?"

I was salivating as I stared at it. But I was confused, too. Remy and I would wed, whoever I happened to be. He had liked me better than Musette, but he had only known us as each other. If I could stay the way I was now—would he be happier?

Maybe Stepmother would give me the recipe.

I said, "Last night I became engaged, and I'm sure Musette will be, as soon as the prince knocks on our door with her slipper. Need we maintain this masquerade any longer?"

Stepmother smiled. She came around the table and kissed my forehead. Musette wandered in, yawning against the back of her hand, and Stepmother set a plate with white cake in front of her as she sat.

"Children," she said. "Eat."

THE TRICK OF THE TRICKSTERS TRICKED

by Josepha Sherman

Josepha Sherman is a fantasy novelist, freelance editor, and folklorist. In addition, she had written for the educational market on everything from Bill Gates to the workings of the human ear. Her newest titles include: Mythology For Storytellers, and the Star Trek: Vulcan's Soul trilogy. Visit her at www.sff.net/people/Josepha.Sherman.

NOW, YOU MUST know at the start of this that where you have one Trickster, you have trouble. That's what he's about, after all, Mr. "Let's See What Happens When I Do *This*"—trouble.

But of course there isn't just one Trickster in the world. No, that would make the world run too simply, in one straightforward direction! Clearly the One Who Set Things Up has a very strange sense of humor, because there is no such thing as that.

Consider this: In the wide spaces of sand and rock,

there should be more than enough room for everyone.

There is not.

So: First we start with Coyote the Trickster, he who can be man-shape or beast-shape as he wills it. Coyote had staked out his territory a long time ago, in the beginning of the setting-up-of-things, and had selected for himself a fine range of open space and brush, with plenty of places for a coyote to hunt and a Trickster to work his tricks.

Then we must continue with Iktome the Trickster, he who can be man-shape or spider-shape as he wills it. Iktome, too, had staked out his territory a long time ago, in that beginning of the setting-up-of-things, and he, too, had liked the idea of all that open space and brush. Plenty of places for spiders to spin and a Trickster to work his tricks.

Well, it didn't all quite work out the way either had planned. When they were done choosing, they found that their two territories ran up against each other.

"You have to withdraw!" Coyote shouted.

"I was here first!" Iktome snapped back.

"I was the first!"

"I!"

"You're lying!"

"Of course I am, I'm a Trickster! You're lying, too!"

"Well, yes, but . . . give up this land!"

"You give it up!"

Back and forth the words flew, and got them nowhere. Yes, they sounded just like two children, those two, or maybe like two human men. But at last it occurred to them both that they were wasting time, or rather, that nothing was changing. And that is not the right thing for Tricksters, who must forever change. So they went their separate ways.

But of course that wasn't the end of it. Things started happening, all right—to each other.

Iktome was stalking some nice, fat ducks that were sitting on a lake as though just waiting for him. The air was still. The sun was casting his shadow behind him. Those ducks were almost his. Iktome licked his lips, almost smelling them roasting on a spit. He leaped—

Aie! The ducks were gone, the lake was gone, and Iktome was falling into an empty pit!

Coyote!

Frantically, Iktome changed from man to spider, casting out a web to stop his fall. He crawled up out of the pit and became man again.

"I'll get you for this, Coyote!"

The next day, Coyote was going along when a rock said to him, "You lied to me."

The surprise wasn't that a rock was talking to him. Rocks often did, back then in the days when the rules were still fluid. The surprise was that this particular rock was talking to him.

"I have tricked a few boulders in my day," Coyote said. "But I don't remember ever tricking you. So good day to you."

But the rock groaned and rumbled. It pulled itself free of the earth and started rolling after him. Coyote glanced over his shoulder and started walking a little faster.

The rock rolled a little faster.

Coyote walked a little faster.

The rock rolled a great deal faster.

Coyote broke into a trot, then a run. The rock was right behind him now, and if he didn't find a way to stop it, he was going to be a coyote rug!

Iktome! This has to be Iktome's plot!

Try to trick a Trickster? Coyote raced to the edge of a cliff and turned to face the rock. "Oh, dear, a cliff. Whatever shall I do?"

The rock rolled forward. Coyote leaped straight up, the way a coyote leaps up to catch prey. The rock rumbled over the edge of the cliff and crashed into pebbles at the bottom.

"I'll get Iktome for this," Coyote said.

Well, the long and the short of it was that Tricksters just don't make good warriors. Coyote tried to trick Iktome. Iktome tried to trick Coyote. On and on the cycle went.

And at last the two Tricksters grew bored with their game. This endless ring of tricks and countertricks was starting to lose its challenge. They met by mutual agreement, each standing carefully on his side of the territorial dividing line.

"We are wasting perfectly good time," Iktome said.

"And perfectly good tricks, too," Coyote agreed.

"Have you been watching that new race, those humans? They look promising."

"That they do."

"Good people to play tricks upon."

"Looks like it. Plenty of those folks to go around, too."

"More and more of them every day."

But standing and trading polite words and doing nothing else simply isn't in a Trickster's nature.

"Truce," Iktome said.

"Truce," Coyote agreed.

"Tell you what, Coyote. Come to dinner at my house to show there're no hard feelings between us."

"Sounds good to me," Coyote said. "That's very kind of you, in fact."

"Tonight?"

"Tonight."

So off Iktome went to his home, which was a sturdy longhouse with a thick sod roof and even a door. "Wife? Oh, wife!"

She came to the doorway, wiping her face with a hand, a harried look on her face and her long black hair in disarray. Iktome's wife was a fine-looking woman, with high, broad cheekbones and that mass of gleaming hair, but right now she looked very much as if she wanted to slam the door in his face. "What is it, husband? I was just trying to get dinner started, and the fire wouldn't catch, and the food—"

"Exactly. We're having a guest for dinner." Ignoring her sigh of exasperation, Iktome continued, "Coyote."

"Coyote!" she gasped. "Husband, is this wise?"

"Don't question me, wife. Coyote and I have made peace. And he *will* be my guest for dinner!"

"Really?" She ran a hand through her disarrayed

hair, trying to smooth it down. "And just what were you planning to feed your guest?"

"What—"

"Do you know what I was doing just now? I was trying to make us something decent to eat out of three dried roots and a handful of berries! That's all that's left in our larder, husband. Unless you hunt us up something else, that's all our guest is going to be getting, too."

"Humph." But he knew it was the husband's job to bring home the meat. Without another word, Iktome stalked off to find them some. He wasn't going to waste any energy in actually hunting anything. What good is a Trickster if he can't trick? Iktome turned himself into a human and tricked two human hunters out of a fine haunch of buffalo. Back in his true form, he lugged it home to his wife.

"There is our dinner," he told her. "Be sure to roast it as well as you can. I wish Coyote to be impressed."

With that, off he went again on his wanderings.

"Of course he's gone," his wife muttered. "He's never around when there's work to be done. Well, I knew what it would be like when I married a Trickster. Roast the meat. Yes, I'll roast the meat. But will I get so much as a taste of it? Oh no, not with two Tricksters at dinner. Be lucky if there's still a scrap of root for me, and a roof still over my head."

But what else was there to do but stop complaining and start the meat roasting? She added wild onions and sage, thyme and wild garlic. And pretty soon . . .

Mmm . . . how good the roast smelled. So

savory . . . she should taste it, just to be sure that it wasn't burning.

Carefully, she cut off a small piece and tasted it.

Oh yes, wonderful! It was roasting perfectly.

But maybe she should taste another piece, from down here, to make sure it was roasting all the way through. She cut off a piece and tasted it.

Mm, yes, it was roasting perfectly, indeed.

Another taste? Well . . . just a small one . . .

The woman lay back on the pile of buffalo hide robes, almost too full to move, almost purring with delight. One taste had demanded another, and that taste had demanded another, and at last she had tasted her way through the entire roast. Ahh, that had been *good*.

Too good! Nothing left but the bone.

She sat up in horror. What was left for her husband's dinner? And he was bringing a guest!

"Now what am I going to do?" she wailed.

Meanwhile, well, no matter what oaths have been sworn or promises made, a Trickster cannot be anything but what he is. He must be true to his nature. And so, as soon as he saw Iktome wandering away, Coyote went stealing off to Iktome's house, getting there long before dinnertime.

"Hello in there," he called. "A guest is calling you."

This happened just when Iktome's wife was bewailing the meal she'd eaten and was wondering what she was going to do. At least, she thought, this sweet-voiced visitor couldn't be her husband. He wouldn't have sounded so polite.

As soon as she saw who stood there, her heart sank. Just as if she didn't have enough trouble already, here was Coyote himself ready to start more.

"I'm your husband's guest," he said, "Here for dinner. I'm a little early, but Iktome sent me on ahead to meet you. He said that while we're waiting for him, you should offer me hospitality." Coyote grinned, showing very white teeth. "Every kind of hospitality."

She knew perfectly well what he meant. But instead of shouting in outrage or drawing back in fear, the woman merely looked him up and down, considering. Coyote in man-form was very pleasing to see, jet black of hair and gleaming green of eye. His skin was smoothly copper and his form was slim and lithe. Oh, yes, he would be far more lithe than any spider. And there was no Iktome here to interfere. How interesting . . .

"Well, of course I must show you every kind of hospitality," she purred. And her grin matched his.

Ah, but they had a wonderful time then, sometimes there on those buffalo robes, sometimes, heedless, on the bare earth floor. On and on . . . and at last even a Trickster could do no more. Coyote lay panting on his back, eyes closed and body worn and sated. Beside him, he could hear the woman stirring. Now she was getting to her feet. What could she possibly be doing? Lazily, he opened his eyes a slit to see—then opened them all the way in wild alarm.

The woman was now kneeling beside him, a very

large, very sharp butchering knife in her hand. She was smiling, and Coyote really didn't like the look of that smile.

"Uh . . . what are you doing?" Coyote asked.

"Why, I am just following an old family custom!" she said cheerfully. "Just lie back and relax. We've had our fun. And now, as our family custom states, I'm going to cut off you balls!"

"No, you are not!" Coyote yelped.

He nearly bowled her over in his frantic scramble to get to his feet. Then he raced from that house as fast as coyote legs could gallop. He shot by Iktome, who was returning home, nearly bowling him over as well.

"What—why—Coyote! Where are you—"

"Get him!" his wife yelled, brandishing the knife. "He stole our roast! Stop him!"

"Why, that flea-bitten useless *thief*!" Iktome roared, and chased after Coyote.

What about Iktome's wife? Well, she just stood in the doorway of the house, smiling and twirling a strand of long black hair in one hand, and watching the two Tricksters disappear into the distance.

What a good day this had turned out to be. She'd just had a good meal and a good . . . playtime. And now she'd tricked not one but two Tricksters as well.

THRICE TOLD

by Von Jocks

*Von Jocks is very distantly related to Nathaniel Haw-
thorne, acclaimed nineteenth-century author of both* The
Scarlet Letter *and* Twice Told Tales, *a story collection that includes the famous "Young Goodman
Brown." However, Von is also a fan of good witches
and woman's fiction (a genre Hawthorne jealously dismissed as written by "a damned mob of scribbling
women")—so nepotism hasn't helped him! Von teaches
literature and creative writing at Tarrant County College in Texas (where she does often force unwilling stu-
dents to read Hawthorne), and writes romance novels
as Evelyn Vaughn.*

"NAY." OLD GOODWIFE BROWN laughed,
but with an edge to her voice. "Nay, sir. My
husband is no witch."

The judge, seated at her planked table before its
high fireplace, hastened to reassure her. "These are
not the dark days of yore, Goody Brown. There shall
be no hangings on Gallow's Hill, no matter what foul

73

truths you tell me. 'Tis a new century, and those times are past."

And fair riddance to them, thought Goodwife Brown. The judge himself had sat on the tribunal that had condemned over nineteen people to hang in the summer of 1692, to say nothing of those who'd died in prison. Unlike some jurors and judges, he had ne'er shown remorse. 'Twas a blessing that those days had passed.

Besides, the bread had tasted awful that year. Moldy.

The judge said, " 'Tis for my own understanding that I still seek information about which families in Salem Village might yet be of . . . well . . ."

"Of occult persuasion?" suggested the good wife tartly.

"There shall be no harsh consequences for the truth beyond those dispensed by God, Goody Brown. I shall divulge what you tell me nowhere but in my journals, and those are mine alone."

"I already speak the truth," the woman insisted. "My husband is not a witch, though I might have wished him so."

The judge's bushy eyebrows climbed his forehead. "What madness do you speak?"

Goody Brown looked toward the cradle by the fire, where soundly slept the latest of her many grandchildren, and smiled. She knew that even with her hair silvered and her hands worn by age, her smile held more than a dram of beauty. "Let me relate to you a tale. . . ."

1.

I was quite certain of Thomas when we married
(*quoth Faith Brown, for Faith was indeed her Christian
name*). Mind you, we married young, I not sixteen
years old and him little past twenty. His father had
died the year previous, of smallpox, and Thomas inherited business, land, house—all of it. 'Twas a
proper time for him to marry. As the Bible instructs,
'tis better to marry than to burn.

And, oh, we felt a fine fire, from our first sighting
of each other! On a business visit to Andover, from
whence my own family hails, Thomas first met me,
and I him. He was tall and slim, gracefully wrought,
handsome in black clothing. I . . .

Well you may not think it to look at me now, but
I was quite the beauty. Already I had rejected many
offers of marriage, from suitors young and old, for
I meant to settle for none but the best of men. From
the moment mine eyes and Thomas' met, I knew
with the certainty of youth that we must be
together.

Perhaps I was too forward, too free. Thomas
Brown was a godly man, for all his youth. But he
seemed pleased by my affection, and soon we
married.

The cock crowed before dawn, on the day of our
wedding, but I refused to think ill of it. Doubt, after
all, can be its own sin! I was young. I thought that
the meeting of our lips, of our bodies each night in
our marriage bed, was love. I thought his gift of pink

ribbons for my matron's cap was love. And I foolishly thought that, because I loved him and believed him strong, 'twould be so. Sometimes wishing could make it thus . . . but sometimes it cannot.

For three long, wonderful months, with no proof to the contrary, I believed I had chosen well.

Then the dreams began.

Perhaps I should not speak of this, Judge, but that I've led a full life. I shall test your promise of secrecy and tell you that my dreams, from childhood, oft proved prophetic. Thus I was sorely disturbed when I dreamed of my dear-heart, Thomas, on a dark journey into the forest.

I dreamed of him not loving me any more.

I dreamed of witches.

2.

Ah, Judge. I see your interest in that quick enough. Remember that I was three months new to Salem Village, and that this was some years before the trials. Yet even I had heard rumors, through my husband, of the witches.

"They meet in the woods outside of town," Thomas would whisper, holding me late at night. "Some say they fly here from places as far as Boston—or farther! They are evil, of course . . ."

"But why are they evil?" I asked, and he but laughed.

" 'Tis nothing my precious Faith need have any knowledge of," he would reassure me. Though I wanted to question his praise of ignorance, he was my husband, so I believed him.

Once the dreams began, my battle against doubt grew more difficult.

Thomas scoffed at my superstition. "My sweet Faith," he would chide me. "Trust that nothing dark can touch us, lest we allow it in."

How could I argue with such as that?

Until late October, that is! Yes, *that* night—the night that pagans and papists celebrate as All Hallow's Eve. The leaves had already turned, and many had fallen. The air grew chill—and my Thomas told me, of a sudden, that he must take a journey.

" 'Tis but for one night," he said, and proved his assurance by taking no pack. "I shall be back in the morning."

'Twas merely afternoon, and already the air shivered with power. Even then, I did try to trust him.

For perhaps the first time, I failed.

"Dearest heart," I pleaded. "Prithee, wait until sunrise and stay with me tonight, in your own bed."

I will admit, Judge, that the dreams of losing his love distressed me even more than did those of witches. But I sensed them all intricately linked, and thus I feared them.

"On this of all nights must I go," he assured me, for the first time swayed not even by the temptation of our marriage bed. " 'Tis the fulfillment of a promise I made, one I must keep before the dawn. Surely you do not doubt me so soon?"

Doubt him? Nay—I was yet too young and in love to allow myself the sin of doubting my dearest husband. But I did not fail to note how easily he dismissed my pleas. What could be more important to him than I? Should *he* have asked *me* to stay, would I not have done so in a moment?

That he did not . . . it left a sour taste, mixed with the fear in my mouth.

"Say thy prayers and go to bed at dusk," he instructed me, as if I were but a child, to be comforted by ignorance, "and no harm will come to thee."

A wife should be able to trust her husband, in such a promise. Despite him leaving on a mysterious errand, on so dark a night. Despite this being a town which he himself had admitted was haunted by witches. Despite her own woeful dreams.

But left alone in our empty little house, in a strange new town, I found it increasingly difficult to deny my own good sense for the mere memory of his. Besides, I heard the neighbor's brindled cat mew, a strange howl which unsettled me.

In making my bread, I spilled the salt. As I cleaned it up, I heard the cat mew again.

Then I dropped a knife—and it stuck in the floor, point down. Do not deny, Judge, that you recognize the illness of these omens as surely as did I! For perhaps the first time in my life, I found myself glad that our Puritan faith does not approve of the vanity of mirrors, for if I had owned one, it surely would have broken. But perhaps as bad, the cat mewed yet again.

And stopped. Thrice it had mewed, and no more. 'Twas then that I could no longer deny the certainty in my heart. Pulling on my good wool cape, I went out the door—into a near-deserted town. I knew the good folks of Salem Village far less than did my husband, of course, who had been raised there. But in three months of marriage, I had met several whom I thought I could trust. I walked down an almost silent, twilight track to the house of old Goody Cloyse, who had taught Thomas his catechism in his youth.

The house, like the town, stood strangely empty.

Drawing my cape tighter around my shoulders, as if mere wool could ward off the chill in my soul, I hurried to the meeting hall and the home of the minister.

His home was equally deserted.

Running now, I made for the cabin of Deacon Gookin. I almost wept with relief to find his solemn wife there, so shaken was I by the near-empty town. But her husband, she sternly told me, had gone out.

"He will be back on the morrow," said Goody Gookin, from her doorway. "If you have need of him then."

Like my own husband! "Do you know whence he has gone?" I asked, increasingly desperate. "Do you know if . . . if 'tis a good errand? If 'tis safe?"

Goodwife Gookin said, "Do not ask questions you do not wish answered, Goody Brown."

And she shut the door between us.

By then, I no longer wanted my questions answered. I *needed* them answered! Thus I left the Deacon's house and, with autumn's early darkness heavy upon me, I ran to the outskirts of town and the one place where I believed I might find help—were its resident not gone with the others!

I went to the small, overgrown cottage of that town pariah, Esther Prine.

Aye, Judge. *Her*. The woman you'd have hanged first of all back in '92, had she not possessed the good sense, or perhaps the foreknowledge, to leave town to a better life well before you and yours began your deadly witch hunt.

3.

I'd ne'er walked the path to Esther Prine's home before. As you well know, she was no longer received since the birth of her natural son, long before *my* arrival in the village. 'Twas an overgrown trail that led there, deep with fallen leaves, tangled with thorny vines. Worse—I knew my Thomas would not approve.

I forced my feet to continue, even so.

As I rounded the last copse of trees, into the moon-lit view of the tiny cottage, its front door opened. Out stepped Esther herself in her best dress, beautiful and proud for all her sin and shame, and bid me welcome.

"I thought you might come, Faith Brown," quoth she with shameless familiarity. "If you had more courage than your husband."

I slowed my step, unwilling to be so insulted by even a rumored witch, much less an accepted trollop. "How is it you speak so freely of my good man Brown, when you have no such man of your own?"

"You are indeed an innocent, to think that!" She smiled as she spoke and, as when the sun bursts through a rainy day, the chill left our conversation. "But this night's visit is not about me, I trow. If you are here to do what I suspect, your time is short. Come in."

Wary, I nonetheless followed her into her herb- and bread-scented home. Her little boy, the mark of her shame, sat before her hearth, playing with sticks and stones. The air of the single room held surprising comfort.

"What could you mean?" I asked. " 'If I am here to do what you suspect.' Even I know not what I could possibly do in the face of this mystery—or if I should do aught at all!"

"Yes, you do." She drew a bowl down from a high shelf, a black and shiny dish, and set it on her table. Then she poured in water from a bucket. "You know in your heart where your husband goest, Faith Brown. If you did not, you would not be able to see . . . *this*."

I looked down into the water she had poured— and gasped.

Reflected in the surface of the bowl I saw my own dear heart—my husband. Walking in the woods.

With the devil.

Do you doubt me, Judge? Even now? Ah, you think I should not know the devil's form so easily, but you forget—all of us in Salem Village have had close doings with him, of late! In truth, he vaguely resembled my husband, or how my husband might look several scores since.

And he carried an ornate walking stick, carved like a snake.

"Then there *are* witches in Salem," whispered I to Dame Prine, looking up from the magical proof of it.

"There are many witches," agreed the beautiful Esther. "Good and bad. That one—he is of the bad. Most of the people who follow him do not wholly perceive the difference; they believe one magic to be either as dark or as harmless as the rest. This man, this *creature's* powers, they come from an old Indian magic even I should not wish to trifle with, and my own family's magic goes back to the time of Druids. Were I you, Goody Brown, I would go home, lock my door, and pray the night passes uneventfully. Your husband's soul is his own, to keep or lose as he will."

I looked back down into the bowl, never once doubting that the image I saw floating across the water truly was my Thomas—my Thomas, making perhaps the greatest mistake of his young life. "But how can it be that he should do such a thing? He comes from a godly family . . ."

"Odd," said Esther, "that you should say that." And she waved her hand over the bowl. At that, I heard Thomas' voice, as if from a deep well, stating that he meant to return from whence he came, that he had scruples.

"My father never went into the woods on such an

errand, nor his father before him," quoth he. "We have been a race of honest men and good Christians . . ."

But the devil interrupted him. "I helped your grandfather, the constable, when he lashed a Quaker woman through the streets of Salem. 'Twas I who brought your father a torch from my own hearth, to set fire to an Indian village . . ."

With a grimace, Esther waved her hand again over the bowl and silenced his distant voice. "Your husband continues to protest," she told me, perhaps as a kindness. "But his willpower is not such that he can keep to it."

"But he is a good man," I protested. "He is a strong man. He would never . . ."

My gaze drifted back to the bowl of water, to what could be proof of Thomas' weakness—or could simply be a lie by a demoness.

"If it helps to know it," said Esther, "you seem to be his best reason for returning."

But I could see, in the water, that his stop proved temporary. He began to walk with the devil, yet again.

"Is it true?" asked I. 'What the old man said to my husband?"

"That he was friends with the elder Browns? I could not say for certain. The devil can lie, Faith, which is why doubt can be so insidious. We can only trust what our hearts say is true, and hope God lets our hearts hear clearly. Sometimes, it is only what we wish to hear."

I could not think of a reason I would wish to believe that my husband was on his way to a demonic mass, and thus I believed her. As to why my husband would wish to believe that he was following some family tradition in his journey . . .

It hardly bore thinking.

"I meant," I said more solemnly, "is it true that Thomas' father burned an Indian village, and that his grandfather publicly lashed a Quaker woman?"

Esther's eyes seemed kind. "Aye," said she. "That part is true."

Perhaps I had married too soon, at that.

But married I had. So I straightened my shoulders and said, "I must save him."

"Nobody can save another person's soul," said Esther. "In the attempt, in the pride and distraction of trying to oversee *them*, we can too easily lose our *own* salvation."

I held her gaze. "He is my husband."

Whatever else he was—or was not—I believed that must be honored.

Esther nodded and went to the stone fireplace. She drew a loving hand over the top of her little boy's head—such a beautiful child, to have come from such supposed sin, although it seemed to me he favored the minister suspiciously. Then she retrieved a short-handled hearth broom.

"There is a way."

4.

Perhaps you will not believe me, Judge, when I tell you that I flew to the witches' meeting.

"There are some who would insist you must use darker magics than mine, to do this," said Esther. "That you must anoint yourself with the pressings from smallage, cinquefoil and wolfsbane, along with fine wheat and ingredients I shan't even mention! But those are the witches who believe that power comes only from evil. My magic is that of nature, and it requires no such sacrilege.

"Hold the broom high," she instructed me. "Whistle for the wind, and wait for the breeze to catch it, then speak these words."

And she whispered the magic charm to me. I would tell you, but I promised not to share it.

"You will feel the broom catch the wind, in return. That is the time to mount it and be gone. Do not be frightened, either by the ride or by what you find when you arrive—this particular clan of witches is a large one, and they enjoy a wild passion that gives the rest of us a dark name. Still, as long as you retain your soul and give it to nobody, not even your husband, you may yet prevail.

"But I must warn you, Faith Brown," said she. "You must bring the broom back to me before dawn. Your husband must come home in the same way he left it, to make his own peace with the night. Do you agree to this?"

"Aye," said I. "I do agree."

Esther gave me a quick kiss on the cheek. "Then

let your love for your husband and your faith in God guide you, and you'll not come to harm."

Too fearful for my husband to linger in amazement, I went out into the moonlit clearing behind her cottage. I raised the broom, as instructed.

I had no idea how late it must be by now. Past bedtime, I thought. Perhaps nearing the witching hour itself. The October night had turned increasingly chill, and a harsh wind sang through the crooked treetops. I pursed my lips, as my new friend had demonstrated, and did as neither my parents nor preachers would ever have sanctioned—

I whistled.

In a wink, the wind began to pull at the broom, tugging it like an invisible, playful dog.

Oh, I knew that, having avoided one kind of fire by marrying, I was now playing with another. But I sensed in my heart that it needed doing. So I spoke the words.

And the broom leaped in my hand!

Carefully I drew it to my side, tested my weight on it with my hand, then sat upon it. It waited for me, like the most gentle of ponies, then lifted me several feet.

I clutched the handle, my heart beating louder than the surf in the harbor. But the broom did not seem of a mind to toss me. It waited for my instructions.

I thought of Thomas, whom I'd loved so well— whom I thought I knew, though tonight brought dark hints otherwise. As I thought of him, the broom sailed higher, turned to the west, and gathered speed.

I held on, tight—

And I loved it. Does that shock you, Judge? It should not. I was soaring not through but above the woods of Massachusetts Bay Colony, farther and farther from the firelights of civilization, with but glimpses of the narrowing road beneath me. Likely I was flying over the hunting grounds of Mohawk and Mohicans, savages I'd been raised to fear . . . and yet 'twas bliss! Other than the joy I'd found in my marriage bed, 'twas the most fulfilling experience I'd ever known! Wind rushed past my ears, howling with the unfettered cries of animals and Indians, blowing back my skirts in a delightfully indecent manner. My cape flapped behind me and the ribbons of my cap whipped at my face, mingling with my now-loose hair.

I was momentarily startled when several other brooms, carrying women I recognized from our Sunday prayer meetings, flew to my side and kept pace with me. But my goal was too lofty to lose behind fear or doubt.

"Is this the way to the witches' sabbath?" I called, over the wind.

The women laughed at my naïveté, and I suppose 'twas a foolish question, considering our mode of transport. Still . . .

"I must find my husband," I pleaded, uncertain but determined. "Please, won't you tell me if this is the way to the meeting where he has gone?"

"We know only that there are several young people to take their first communion tonight," called a widow by the name of Hartson. "Your Thomas may yet be one of them, Goody Brown. Follow us!"

With a startling suddenness, they pointed their mounts downward and swooped toward a dancing flame on the distant ground. They laughed at my scream of surprise when my broom abruptly followed.

Was it my imagination, that I thought I heard my husband's voice, far below, calling my name?

In but moments, we had reached the ground and dismounted. My legs trembled, glad to be on solid ground again. I could tell that my hair was a wild mess, and I had lost my cap—pink ribbons and all. So I pulled up the hood of my cape, in a futile attempt at decency, and looked around me, increasingly shocked by whom I beheld.

Not my husband, praise God. But Goody Cloyse. Deacon Gookin. The minister. Many, many more.

Easily half the town, all supposed to be good and decent Christians, were in attendance, so deep in the wilderness that even the road had ended some way back! Hand in hand they stood or danced with some of the most wretched of the town's sinners, counted even less respectable than poor Esther herself! Along with them mingled numerous men and women whose fine clothes showed them to be city dwellers, perhaps from as far as Boston, at that. People of power and good reputation.

'Twas enough to make a person of less faith believe that they represented all of us, that there is no good on this earth.

I could see them quite clearly, by the red light of a towering bonfire in a forest clearing, though their faces fell into and out of shadow with the twisting dance of flame.

Several of them waved to me. Most of them were singing. I recognized the hymn's melody from the meeting house. But the words, in praise of licentiousness and greed, were far darker. It seemed as if the wind and the forest joined the song.

At one end of the clearing, a large, flat rock rose like an altar, framed by four huge torches made of burning pine trees. 'Twas there I recognized the elderly man whom I'd seen before, in the enchantment of Esther Prine's scrying bowl.

The man I knew was the devil, here in New England.

I had been raised a good Puritan, Judge. Perhaps a bit wild, with my pink ribbons and my coy ways, but good enough to know that even a married woman ought not walk right up to a man and speak before being spoken to. Especially not if that man were Old Nick himself! But I had already gone out alone at night, and kept company with a town outcast, and gazed into an enchanted bowl, and ridden the winds on a broom.

I suspected that a little unladylike vehemence would not damn me too much further. I held Esther's broom safely beneath my cape, and I confronted him.

"So glad that you could make it, Faith," said the old man, dignified and smooth of speech. "Did you have an enjoyable ride?"

"Where," I demanded, "is my husband?"

The devil smiled politely. "He should be here shortly."

"Or perhaps he has turned back. Perhaps you have lost him, as you should!"

"Possible," he agreed. "But he did not turn back the last, oh, five times he threatened to do thus."

Perhaps the devil was willing to feign good manners, but not I. "How dare you draw him away from me and into this depravity!"

"Goodwife Brown," said the devil, "You are new to Salem Village and, despite your quickness in learning it, you are new to magic. But I suspect even you know that nobody can take another's soul or another's faith. Not even I. It must be given away."

Then he turned toward the crowd that had amassed. He raised one hand high, somehow coaxing the bonfire's flames to shoot reddishly upward. "Bring forth the converts!"

He walked with slow, despicable majesty toward the altar rock.

And out from the woods, sweated and in disarray, stepped my beloved husband.

Thomas' eyes were maddened with grief and resignation. From his hand dangled one of my cap's pink ribbons.

No! Fearing what he might believe, from even such slim proof, I tried to go to him. But hands caught my arms, holding me back. Goody Cloyse and Mary Carter, one to each side of me, wrestled me toward the devil's large rock as if they were pushing me rather than holding me back.

Still, I saw Deacon Gookin dragging Thomas to the

same destination. I took some small bit of peace in that, despite the damnation that seemed to be circling us. Had he himself not bid me to trust that nothing dark could touch us, lest we allowed it in? Surely we could take strength from one another, and defeat the fiend.

"Welcome, my children," announced the devil, "to the communion of your race!"

I tried to reach for Thomas, to explain my presence, but the devil's servants turned us to look at his seeming congregation, an immense crowd of faces both familiar and foreign to me. They all had a similar look about them, I saw. 'Twas a look of yearning, of desperation.

And the devil, to feed that desperation, spoke lies.

He said that all men were evil, so that we need not fear or fight the evil within ourselves—was it not common? He spoke of women murdering husbands and babies, of sons murdering their fathers, as though 'twas the rule among the human race and not its ugly exception. I could see among his followers that they longed to believe his lies, longed to believe that if they had not committed a crime so heinous as the murders he described, they were in fact morally superior to this grotesque specter of their neighbor.

I thought, *Dear God. If we truly believed such horrors of our fellow man, how could there be trust, or mercy, or tolerance?* Virtues, Judge, which you must admit were horribly absent in 1692.

I thought that, and I nearly despaired. From the moment I sat upon Esther's broom, I'd felt fear.

Standing before these people, people who would prefer to believe the worst of man instead of the best, did naught to comfort me. Within the altar rock lay a natural basin filled with some kind of red liquid—was it blood, or mere water colored by firelight? Either way, it hardly seemed a positive turn of events! Only one thing comforted me—the one person that the biddies who'd imprisoned my arms would not let me turn to see.

Finally, as I thought the devil might continue his sermon for as long as Deacon Gookin can, the fiend said, "And now, my children, look upon each other."

And I could turn to my beloved husband. He was here with me. He was safe. Surely, together, we could stand against anything.

The devil continued. "Depending upon one another's hearts, ye had still hoped virtue was not a dream. Now ye are undeceived!"

I thought, what foolishness! *Are my husband and I not together? Have we not proven our hearts, and do we not stand here proving our virtue at this very moment?*

The old fool went on about evil—the nature of mankind, our only chance at happiness, on and on.

And yet . . . now that we'd been turned to each other, why would Thomas not look at me?

"Welcome again, my children," said the devil at last, "to the communion of your race!"

And the crowd chanted, "Welcome."

The devil dipped his hand into the red liquid, as if he meant to baptize us. I tightened my grip about the handle of Esther Prine's hidden broom, ready to beat the creature away by force if I had to, to keep that from happening. Nobody could take Thomas' or my soul without our permission, I reminded myself. Not only had the devil said that, but Esther had. That much, I believed.

To doubt it could prove far too costly.

"Thomas," I called over the chanting crowd, wanting to reach to him, hoping he could see how I loved him, how I believed in him. "Thomas!"

Finally, he met my gaze—but his seemed strangely unseeing. Surely—

He could not have believed that horrible sermon, could he?

When he shook off his strange paralysis, I saw in his countenance not trust but desperation.

"Faith!" he cried. "Faith, look up to Heaven and resist the Wicked One!"

Then he slumped, unconscious, in Deacon Gookin's arms—safe from the lies at last.

True, he'd lied to me in order to come here in the first place. True, he'd never quite summoned the willpower to turn back. But at least he'd fought the unholy baptism—for me, if not for himself.

Why did that not comfort me more than it did?

The devil waited for me, his hand cupping blood. "And your choice, Faith Brown? Will you come over to the ways of the wicked?"

I looked him in the face—and said something so rude, Judge, that even as a former ship's captain, you would blush to hear it.

The devil shrugged, smiled—and vanished. So did his congregation. Only I remained, I and my unconscious husband.

The night was ending, and neither of us had been baptized into evil.

I fell to my knees beside Thomas, gathered him into my arms, kissed the scratches on his handsome face where the forest's thorns or branches had whipped him. To my blessed relief, his eyes cracked momentarily. "Faith . . . ?"

"I am here, dear heart," I murmured, kissing him again. "I am here."

"I did not mean for you to know . . ."

" 'Tis all right, my love. I understand."

"I promised to come," he tried to explain. "When he gave me the power to find you, I promised to come back. . . ."

And he fell unconscious again or perhaps, hopefully, to sleep. He had walked the whole distance, after all, that I had magically flown.

I felt cold, of a sudden. Had the devil in any way been behind Thomas' and my marriage? Quickly, I dismissed the idea. We had married under God and nobody else. At worst, Old Nick had made it seem to poor Thomas that he'd orchestrated our meeting. But all Puritans of true faith know that the devil lies.

I cannot say I admired the idea of my husband being so duped. But 'twas better, I thought, than him becoming one of that awful, desperate congregation.

By then, the moon had set. I hated to leave Thomas alone, but I was well aware of Esther's warning to me. I had promised to bring her broom back, and it must be done before dawn. Thomas would need the long walk home, alone with God, to make his own peace with what had transpired that night. So I kissed my sleeping husband once more, and turned up his collar against the damp. I took my pink ribbon from where he still clutched it in his fist. Then I held the broom upward, whistled up the wind, said the magic words—and I flew home.

"Did you do it?" asked Esther, once I knocked on her cottage door to return her broom.

"I did," said I. "Neither of us was confirmed into that demons' evil congregation. We stood strong together, and 'tis all over now."

She gazed upon me for a long time, seeming troubled, as if she doubted me. But surely she'd been able to watch the whole thing, and knew I spoke the truth!

"I hope that is so," said she. "I hope that is how you stood strong."

I did not understand.

Not until my husband arrived home the next morning.

5.

I was watching anxiously for him, of course. I had been out into the street three times. 'Twas no longer deserted, and familiar faces hailed me and smiled. Had they truly been at the devil's meeting, the night before, or had their presence been as illusory as the fiend's lies?

They had all vanished, after all, when Thomas and I rejected those lies.

Knowing which possibility I preferred, I chose the most probable of the two and smiled back.

Finally, late that morning, Thomas wearily rounded the corner by the meeting house. He looked both angry and oddly bewildered. It mattered not—he was home, and safe, and oh, we had so much to discuss together! I skipped down the street to him, embracing him, almost kissing him before the whole village.

'Twas not propriety, Judge, that stopped me.

No, 'twas Thomas himself. He showed no gladness to see me. In his eyes I saw none of the affection or even the fire that had bound us, that three months previous. Instead, Goodman Brown looked sternly and sadly into my face, and passed on without a greeting.

I followed him, of course, bewildered but still hopeful. When I went after him, into the house, he sat where you sit now, staring into our fire.

"Thomas," said I, and he turned slowly toward me, like a man asleep.

"The ribbons," he said, as if to himself, beholding the pink ribbons I had laced back through my second best cap. "Then was it all a dream?"

What? He did not know?

"Last night?" I asked—

But he slammed his hand forcefully onto the table, startling me back a full three steps. "No, Faith!"

You can imagine my distress, to be spoken to so sternly. "But, Thomas, last night—"

"No!" He stood and came to me, stood over me,

wrathful. "You will never speak of last night to me. Never!"

I searched his face and my memory, trying to understand how he could be so angry—and I lit upon a heart-wrenching possibility.

He did not know that I'd gone only to rescue him. He had fallen unconscious before he'd seen me refuse the fiend's invitation.

But surely he could not doubt me, his Faith, so sorely!

"But dear-heart," said I. "If you would but hear me—"

And he struck me. Full across the face, he struck me, and I fell to the floor, and he stood over me again, a stranger after all.

Turned by the devil, after all—not through baptism, but through doubt. Doubt in his neighbors. Doubt in his ability to love and forgive. And doubt in me.

"Never," he growled down at me, "speak of it again."

And, curling into a ball to weep, I did not.

'Twas the end of our happiness together. 'Twas the end of his happiness, completely. He became the stern, sad man you know now. 'Twas not only myself who brought on his wrath. He never again looked on another human being with aught but distrust, no matter how the minister or the deacon or his old family friends tried to intercede. Oft he would wake at midnight and, if I attempted to comfort him, would shrink from my touch, until soon we slept

on cold, separate pallets. Sometimes at morning and
eventide, when we knelt down at prayer, he would
scowl, mutter, gaze sternly at me, and turn away,
even once the children came. Even now, hearing the
minister speak on Sunday, he yet turns pale and
glances heavenward, as if fearing God's wrath shall
destroy the village—rather than trusting God's love
to save it.

*   *   *

Old Goodwife Brown sighed at her profound loss,
her old hands clasped in her lap. "That, Judge, is
why my Thomas sided with you and yours during
the late trials. He would prefer to doubt the goodness
of his neighbors, or even his wife, than to trust in
his or God's power to withstand any possible witchcraft. And that is why I say I would have preferred
he to be a witch. It is not because I prefer magic
users, though Esther Prine and I became great friends
before she and her son escaped to Rhode Island,
where she lives happily even today. I prefer the
witches because I so despise the doubt and hypocrisy
of their accusers."

"You speak harsh words," said her guest.

"Do I? The people you hanged as witches believed
in God and honored their souls so firmly that they
refused to speak false confessions, even to save their
lives. You, my husband, and the others like you will
have to explain to God why you took them. And if
it had aught to do with the lands that came available,

which those so-called witches had refused to sell before they stood accused, then surely the devil lingers in New England even now."

The judge shook his head, his old eyes filled with a distrust similar to her husband's. " 'Tis a wild tale you weave, Goodwife Brown. But you seem remarkably well, for all the trouble of which you speak. I cannot believe that a woman could remain of good cheer, in the face of so unfortunate a marriage."

He looked pointedly at the cradle, where slept her youngest grandson, the infant's face pure with an innocence only one of them truly believed. "I should wonder at the number of your and Thomas Brown's progeny, were it truth. But I thank you for the amusement of your tale."

Faith Brown watched him stand, her eyes narrowing. But she knew better than to further waste her breath on ears that could not hear. "Then wonder you must. Tell me, Judge. Do you mean to speak to Increase Willard in this quest of yours? As you know, he was accused and arrested during the trials, and escaped hanging only when the governor disbanded the court."

Her guest nodded as he donned his cloak. "Aye, Goodwife Brown. 'Tis my purpose to speak to all involved. Why do you ask?"

She reached into the cradle and lovingly adjusted the blanket that protected the infant in her care. "Tell him I have seen his grandson, of late, and that the child does well."

She turned to look back at the judge, amused to

see no comprehension in his doubting eyes. Even with the proof in front of him, the judge remained as blind as her Thomas.

Whom none of her beloved children resembled.

"You must be mistaken, Goody Brown," said Colonel John Hathorne, of late a judge at those awful trials. "I have known Increase Willard my entire life. He has never married."

"Ah." Faith Brown smiled at her own, happy secrets. "You must be right, of course, Judge.

"Never mind."

Author's Note:

I do love faux sequels.

The original "Young Goodman Brown" tells of a Puritan who warily journeys deep into the woods outside of Salem Village to attend a witches' meeting. His ambivalence turns first to dismay as he realizes how many people he thought were good Christians are attending the meeting, and then—when he finds his young wife Faith there— becomes horror. Although the whole experience could have been a dream, Brown's disillusionment turns him into a bitter man for the rest of his life.

Ah, literahtoor.

The more I thought about it (and I've taught the story for years), the more this story annoyed me. Brown (Hawthorne doesn't give him a first name) turns his back on his obviously loving wife on mere SUSPICION that she may have attended the same black mass HE did? Well, enough of that! Finally, Faith gets to contradict the tone of the original, complete with a dose of woman power and emphasizing the importance of trusting one's neighbor instead of always doubting.

FYI, I named the fallen woman "Esther Prine" in hopes it would sound familiar to you. As for Colonel John Hathorne—he really was a judge at the Salem Witch trials. He also was Nathaniel Hawthorne's great grandfather. Hawthorne added the "w" to his name to distance himself from the Trials. Luckily for me, my female ancestors needed only marry to escape that dark legacy.

DYNASTY

by Bill McCay

*In the course of his career, Bill McCay has been respon-
sible for some fairly serious books—and some not so
serious. His Star Trek novel, Chains of Command
(coauthored with Eloise Flood), spent several weeks on
the New York Times bestseller list. Pretty serious. The
Riftworld series, written with Stan Lee, has been described as a wild and woolly, comical look at the world
of comics. Bill's five novels carrying on what happens
after the end of the movie STARGATE mix comedy
with some stark portrayals of combat.*

*Bill himself admits that his pen seems to have only
two settings—grim or silly. It's easy to guess which direction he veered toward in presenting this sidelight to
the Sleeping Beauty story.*

S PECIAL To the International Enquirer
Dateline: Thuringia

A modest inn forms the present headquarters of Georg
II, recently deposed monarch of Pumpernicklia. His small
room stands in sharp contrast to his former domains, especially cluttered as it is with pieces from his suit of armor.

Display of this warlike panoply is undercut by news that his charger has been seized for unpaid debts. Already dealing with the sobriquet "Georg the Walker," the onetime sovereign discusses the awakening of Princess Briar Rose and his own reversal of fortune with our correspondent.

GW: My family assumed the crown a century ago, in all the legal forms. That we should be repudiated for a mere slip of a girl with a ridiculous botanical name . . .

IE: There is the young Prince Florimel—

GW: Even worse! And his apparent skill at governing is based on an ability to penetrate a briar patch.

IE: They were, after all, enchanted briars.

GW: And for this great feat, the people of Pumpernicklia turned from the proven leadership of our dynasty.

IE: Yours was always considered a cadet branch of the family.

GW: The only representatives of royal blood not struck by the Great Sleep. Is it my grandfather's fault that he was sixty-third in line from the throne? Had he not been at his manor, getting the potato crop in, Pumpernicklia might have faced a much greater succession crisis. Those ingrates might have ended up governed by some peasant nobody in seven-league boots.

IE: Questions were raised about the noble status of Reinwald I.

GW: My grandfather was a Graf, and we have the papers to prove it! He saved Pumpernicklia! He kept us out of the Cantalbutte war!

IE: Softly, your Majesty. The annals suggest—

GW: A pox on the annals! The press has always been antagonistic to our line. Your master, Ruprecht the Fox, could have sent a correspondent from *The Anglo-Saxon Chronicle* instead of your lowly rag. It's mere bias on the part of the annalists.

IE: Nonetheless, Majesty, Reinwald the Penurious was in no financial position to call forth the nation's array.

GW: With the royal treasury lost behind magical briars? Nonetheless, he kept the country stable. We faced no weapons of magical destruction financed by wild men in forests.

IE: Iron John turned out to be an ensorcelled king.

GW: Oh, indeed. Well is it said, "History is the chronicle of the victors." But none can doubt the achievement of my father, Georg-Herbert.

IE: Georg I, as he is known in the annals.

GW: Georg the Great, as he should be known! The first to enlarge the realm in centuries!

IE: We're not aware—

GW: It's in your precious annals! The River Vod, our boundary with Thunder-ten-Tronck, shifted course, gaining 150 square yards for Pumpernicklia. And yards were bigger in those days. My father had much longer arms than I.

If truth be told, scribe, Father could have done great things for Pumpernicklia had he lived. If he hadn't stopped at that fair to buy hosen when the peasants revolted—

IE: Leaving you in your minority, and your uncle Wilhelm as regent.

GW: Perhaps the annalists were correct to give him the eke-name "Geschikt Willi" or "Guilielmus Oleaginus." I didn't necessarily agree with many of his policies. But it still smacks of *lèse-majesté* to me.

IE: Wilhelm did manage to bring unprecedented prosperity to Pumpernicklia.

GW: By creating something much like the Dutch Tulip Madness, planting that oriental radish to supplement the potato crop.

IE: The Daikon Boom brought much-needed cash into the economy.

GW: So did his little maneuver of mortgaging the lost royal treasury—the one behind the briar wall—to the Medicis.

Still, if he had kept his Geschikt Willi in his hauberk instead of chasing the ladies-in-waiting, Wilhelm wouldn't have united the nobles against him. Even then, he tried to keep in control by naming my cousin Alberecht to the throne. I had to take my case to the Imperial Electors before I got the crown. Humiliating. And then, no sooner do I begin to make my mark upon the Mark when the Great Blight ends the Daikon Boom. And when I finally put down the peasant unrest, this Florimel comes along. What kind of king names his son Florimel, I ask you?

IE: The final birth-gift for Princess Briar Rose was that she would not die as threatened by the Uninvited Guest, but would sleep for one hundred years. Shouldn't this have warned you—

GW: I had more pressing concerns than ancient history! And then it was too late. The fairies were solidly behind Briar Rose. You know what they say: your fate is sealed once the fairies are against you—or rather, the "fey folk." Curse this Polemical Correctness. I always left a bowl of milk outside the castle door!

Well, we'll see if that flowery pair can run the country's finances on fairy gold! My last decree mortgaged both royal treasuries. We'll see if the fairies or the Fuggers have the last laugh!

IE: We understand that the resulting litigation has tied up your own funds. What do you plan, Majesty?

GW: I'll head for the setting sun—and somewhat south. My hope is to find a land where the leading minnesingers won't say they're ashamed to live in the same principality with me.

SERPENT'S TOOTH

by Susan P. & Bradley H. Sinor

Not too long ago a friend of Brad Sinor's commented that Brad wrote family stories. "Yeah," Brad told him. "If you're related to the Addams Family or Dracula."

Be that as it may, Brad has seen his short stories published in the last few years in such anthologies as Warrior Fantastic, Knight Fantastic, Dracula In London, Bubbas Of The Apocalypse, Merlin, Lord Of The Fantastic, and others. He will have several more coming out shortly. Two collections of his short fiction are also available—Dark and Stormy Nights and In The Shadows.

He ha also seen his nonfiction appear in Dark Zones, Starlog, Personal Demons, Enterprise, California Highway Patrolman, Top Deck and Long Island Monthly, among many, many others.

As for Sue, when she's not standing behind her husband Brad with a two by four to make sure he finishes his various writing projects, Susan P. Sinor performs in, and works backstage on, numerous community theater productions. With her husband, she is a caretaker of the home owned by two insane cats named Pewter and

Ashe, who at last report were planning to take over the universe. This is her first professional sale.

D EAR MOTHER,
Why didn't you warn me about the problems stepchildren cause? Not that I would have listened, of course. I know, I know, I was in love; at least I thought I was. After all, he had blue eyes to die for.

Okay, maybe I wasn't really in love, but I liked the man well enough. Look, good marriages have been made from worse beginnings. So he didn't have "that" much money, but then, you don't expect a second son to have much money. Not to mention he wasn't a drunkard, like my late lamented spouse. I do hope you hear the irony in those words.

Besides, I'd been a widow long enough. My girls and I needed someone to support us, and he had a daughter who needed a mother, too.

I thought it would be just perfect. You know, two broken families united to make one whole. It's just the sort of thing they talk about in all those books.

Now, there is no doubt in my mind that I did my dead level best to make this whole thing work. It was all her fault, that little brat of a daughter of his, Ella.

From the beginning I tried to treat her like she was one of my own. The girls tried to treat her like a sister. I think the idea of having a younger sister thrilled Drusilla; this way she wouldn't be the youngest.

But what did I get in return? Resentment! Nothing but pure unadulterated resentment! I just don't understand.

I'll give you an example. After the wedding I put all three girls in the same bedroom. I figured that if they were sharing a bedroom, that would help them share each other's lives; you know, Mother, the way my sisters and I did. I wanted them to be closer, like a real family. It could have been so perfect.

So much for my dreams of perfection. It only took two or three days before Drusilla came to me and said that it just wasn't working out. Ella just wasn't cooperative, would just sit and sulk and wouldn't get involved with anything the other two wanted to do. It was like she resented breathing the same air as Anastasia and Drusilla.

All they were doing was playing with their hair. You know how young girls like to play with their hair and clothes. Well, when I tried to talk to her about it, she complained that my daughters were being cruel to her.

My daughters are not cruel people! Okay, sometimes they may tease a little, but it's always just in fun.

I sat down and tried to have a heart-to-heart, mother-to-daughter talk with Ella, to make her understand that if she'd just try to get along with them, things would be so much better for us all.

Maybe I am an optimist, but when she walked out of my bedroom that night, I was sure things were going to work out. Yeah, right. I won't bore you with the details. Let's just say that by Friday night I knew things were not going to work with the three of them in the same room.

The problem was, the only room I could put her in was that little room in the attic. It certainly wasn't big enough for Ana and Dru! I hoped that she would be much happier up there, in her own private room. After all, it wasn't as if I could put her in the guest room and make any guests we might have sleep up there!

Then the complaints started. She was lonely; she was cold and she was becoming very annoying with all this whining. It was winter, after all; what did that ungrateful girl expect me to do, wave a magic wand and speed up the seasons! It was only a couple of weeks until spring, so I told her to wear something warmer to bed and gave her an extra blanket. As for being lonely, she had had her chance to make friends with Dru and Ana. I was certain that they would give her another chance if she learned to behave. The tears and screaming didn't faze me a bit; she just wanted her own way and was not getting it.

Now you know I try to run my household efficiently. A place for everything, and so forth. Dru and Ana know that and always get their chores done quickly. I expected the same from Ella, too. I explained her responsibilities to her when I took over the household. I said I knew she wasn't accustomed to cooking and cleaning, but that we all had our own jobs and that was hers, so she would just have to get used to it.

Well, she argued with me, said there were servants

to do that. But I told her that I'd had to let some of
the servants go. We couldn't afford them any longer,
and besides, I'd caught them slacking.

She didn't like that at all, said that I was picking
on her and her *own* mother would never have treated
her that way. So I had to remind her that her *own*
mother was dead, I was her mother now, and she'd
better get used to it and hold up her end.

Lord knows I tried to accommodate her and not
sully the memory of her mother, who, looking at that
house, seemed the most disorganized person I have
ever seen. I have no idea what John saw in her. I
tried to make friends with the people who had been
friends with her. But some of them! Mother, you will
not believe what bizarre people they were.

One afternoon this very common looking woman
showed up at our back door and said that she was
a friend of the family; at least I think that is what
she said. She had such a thick accent and seemed to
mumble every other word.

Truth be told, she could have been saying she was
anything from being a good mother to maybe being
a godmother. I suggested that if she were a friend of
the family she should come calling some time when
John was at home. That way he could set the Watch
on her, in case she was a lunatic or something.

Add into this the half a hundred things that it
takes to keep a household running. So did I have
any spare time? No, but I took some and tried to
work with Ella. Yet all I got from her were snide
remarks and looks that would have ripped my heart
out if it were possible.

One afternoon I was inspecting a new batch of vegetables that had had been sent over from the market. I asked Ella to help me. While I was deciding on the menu for the coming week, Ella was supposed to be bringing in the baskets of vegetables from the cart and putting them away. Now, this was an easy task; it wasn't as if I were asking her to master some complicated recipe for dinner. Did she do it; did she pitch in and try to do her part in this project? No!

She came into the pantry, sulking about having to do "servants' work," carrying only one basket when they were light enough to carry two or three at a time, Then she had the nerve to throw that basket down, scattering the small pumpkins in it all over the floor, and run out of the room. When I confronted her later, she tried to claim that she had seen a mouse and it had frightened her. I mean, really, as if I would allow vermin in my house, you know I can't stand them. If I thought there was even the slightest chance of mice having invaded our property, I would definitely get a cat, even though I find cats almost as disgusting as mice.

I tried not to be mean about it, but I had heard all I wanted to from her. It wasn't easy for me, either, taking someone else's home and husband; having to retrain and rearrange, and get things into the way that they need to be to run right.

John kept saying that this wasn't the way that he was used to doing things. Why are husbands so difficult to train? You'd think they'd want things to run smoothly and easily, but every time I made the tiniest suggestion for a slight modification in behavior, he went off the deep end and sulked for days.

I am not that hard to get along with; I just have a firm sense of responsibility, and I expect everyone else to feel the same. But I was going to tell you what happened last week.

John had announced several weeks before that he was going to be away on a business trip to the provinces, so the girls and I were up early to watch him ride off.

The trip was supposed to take no more than a month, but he had told me there was a chance it might take longer if several business deals that could be worth a lot of money to us worked out.

I don't mind these long trips, I know he is working for the betterment of our family; besides it gives me a chance to get things done around the house without interference and without having to hear, "But this is the way we've always done it."

The big problem developed three weeks into that trip in the form of an invitation to the Governor's Ball. In this province that is the key social event of the season. So there was no way in the world I was going to miss it. All right, I know it was a social no-no for a married woman to attend without her husband, people looking down their noses at you and all that, but what kind of choice did I have?

Besides, there would be plenty of eligible young men at the ball and this would be the chance to get the girls properly introduced into Society. I would attend as their chaperone, a fitting role for a married lady.

But, by all that was holy, the girls would not let their chores go by the wayside while we were getting ready. After inspecting our wardrobes, I came to the conclusion that we had nothing suitable for the occasion. Therefore each of us would have to make a new dress for the ball. Drusilla, Anastasia, and I got busy right away on our outfits, but apparently Ella hadn't learned the basics of needlework and was having trouble. I don't want to horrify you by describing that "thing" that she created. It would not do, not do at all.

We each offered to help her when we had the time, but she acted as if our offers were insults to what little ability she had as a seamstress. So, with so much to do, her dress was barely half finished when the day of the ball came. There was no way that it could be completed in time for our departure, and we told her so. She would have to stay at home.

After all, it wasn't our fault she didn't have anything to wear; we had time to finish our dresses, she should have had enough time for hers, especially with our help. I did feel sorry for her as we dressed. For once, she didn't throw a tantrum. She actually helped us fix our hair. We were grateful for the effort and told her we would try to bring her something from the party. Our coach came and we waved goodbye as we rode off.

Well, the ballroom was breathtaking. There were flowers everywhere, and fountains of champagne. Uniformed servants discreetly appeared with hors d'oeuvres and disappeared with empty glasses and plates. We were treated like royalty. We were presented to our hosts and their son, Richard, who had been away at school for several years. The young man was very handsome, I would say in his early twenties, just a few years older than my girls.

Richard seemed rather taken with Anastasia. I was hoping they might spend some time together, getting to know one another, you know. I could definitely see possibilities in those two as a couple.

Then a new guest showed up, an unescorted young lady. Needless to say there were tongues wagging before she managed to walk ten feet into the ballroom.

She seemed somewhat overcome by all the pomp and didn't quite know what to do, when Richard spotted her and practically ran over Ana to get to her. I never got a good look at her, but there was something familiar about the new girl.

The two of them spent the rest of the evening dancing in the garden. Richard seemed to have totally forgotten not only my Ana but also every other guest in the place. I have to say, that school he attended obviously did not teach him all that he needed to know about manners and how someone in a political family is supposed to behave.

I happened to have stepped out on one of the balconies and was listening to the big clock tower tolling midnight, when I noticed the girl who had been with Richard running out into the garden and toward the street gate. I stepped back inside and heard a lot of people chattering about how the girl had just abruptly turned and run away from Richard without an explanation. The thing was, no one seemed to know exactly who she was. This sort of thing would never have happened in the social circles you raised me in, Mother. I mean, really, a party crasher like that and no one had the nerve to throw her out.

We got home just after two; Ella had obviously gone to bed, since she had certainly not stayed up to greet us, which I thought was very rude.

The next day we heard all over town that the unidentified girl at the ball had lost a shoe while running down the steps, and young Richard had found it. He swore that he would search all over town until he found the girl the shoe fit.

When he came to our house, I told Ella to stay in her room since she hadn't even attended the ball and there was no need to just come in to gape at the young man. But did she listen to me? No!

She sneaked down the back stairs, the ones that she seemed to prefer most of the time, and into the parlor; wearing the oldest dress she had. At least the girls and I had dressed up for the governor's son. Look, he may have been behaving a little nutty, but I figured there was always the chance he would get interested in Ana or Dru. Okay, it was a long shot, but it never hurts to try.

Mother, you'll never in your life guess what happened next! The world turned totally upside down! Richard took one look at Ella, and before I could turn around or get a word in, he had put the shoe on her foot and whisked her into his carriage and away to the mansion. He was chattering something about marriage.

I wasn't sure if I was going to faint or have a

heart attack right then. There were obviously some mistakes that needed correcting. I went straight after them and demanded to see the governor about his son's behavior. This was just impossible. I told him that Ella couldn't possibly be the girl his son was looking for because she hadn't even been at the ball.

About that time Richard and Ella appeared. I wanted to take Ella off in private; she had embarrassed herself enough as it was. But neither Richard nor the governor would hear of it, so right in front of them I asked Ella what had possessed her to try to pass herself off as the girl being searched for. She was obviously trying to take advantage of this poor deluded boy.

That was when Ella told me that she *was* the girl. She spun a really strange story. Apparently, after we left, her "fairy godmother" had appeared. I mean, really a "fairy godmother!" This figment of her imagination apparently magically dressed Ella for the ball, turned vegetables and mice into a coach, horses, driver and footman, as well, with the warning that the enchantment would last only until midnight.

The girl was obviously lying. How was I, or anybody, supposed to really believe as ridiculous a story as that? Richard seemed to believe her, though, or not really care; he was still determined to marry her. So what was I to do? This could have some very bad repercussions for our family, socially, as well as for John and his business. Trust me, you don't want to get on the bad side of the governor.

I had one trump card left: Ella's father. I insisted that no marriage could take place until he returned.

After all, Richard still had to formally ask John for his consent before they could be married. Well, I was sure that my husband would never consent to his daughter marrying at such a young age and that would be that. If necessary, I was sure I could persuade him.

Actually, I hoped that they would get tired of each other and that Richard would take an interest in Anastasia again. I really think that my daughters should marry before Ella does; after all, they are the eldest, and one should have respect for tradition.

John finally returned, ten days later than he had planned, with news that he had made a fortune off this trip. But that was a moot issue. When I told him everything that had happened while he was gone, he got mad at me! According to my dear husband I should have made sure that Ella was able to go to the ball with the rest of us, as if he thought we were supposed to wait on her hand and foot. I gave him a piece of my mind about that idea.

You know, Mother, in the long run, this marriage might turn out to be a good thing. It's not what I wanted, but you always taught me to make the best of whatever happens.

Of course, there are some advantages to having Richard in the family. He and Ella aren't even married yet and we've already started having gentleman callers at the house for Anastasia and Drusilla. Even my future stepson-in-law's younger brother has come calling, not to mention more than one highly placed government official who has started making noises about steering some very lucrative business possibilities John's way.

One odd thing happened recently. The other night I happened to look out in the alley and saw Ana talking to someone. It was that plain looking woman I mentioned earlier, you remember, the one who said she was an old family friend, but I couldn't understand a word she said. They seemed to be talking so intently that Ana didn't even notice those mice that were running around her feet.

As soon as the wedding date is set, I will send you all the details. We have so much to do before the wedding that the girls and I just won't have enough time to make dresses for the wedding, so I had to find a dressmaker. I'm sure the dresses won't be nearly as nice as they would be if we made our own, but I guess we'll have to get used to it. After all, the wives and daughters of wealthy businessmen, not to mention the parents of the governor's son's wife, do not make their own clothes.

Your loving daughter,
Harriet

MIRROR, MIRROR

by Jacey Bedford

Jacey Bedford lives in Birdsedge, a tiny village high on the edge of the Yorkshire Pennines, in the north of England. She's been a librarian and a postmistress but now she's an unashamed folk singer—performing all over the world with vocal harmony trio Artisan, (www.artisan-harmony.com.) When she's not on the road—and even when she is—she's hardwired to her laptop keyboard, writing science fiction and fantasy. This is her third story for a DAW anthology and she's currently working on a fantasy novel for young adults, based on the Tam Lin ballad.

M Y MIRROR had a special kind of magic. It always told me the truth.

I sat at my pedestal table, opened the filigree door across the front of the wall-mounted mirror, and stared into the reflective surface of the glass. My face was lit by the natural daylight from two long narrow windows in the granite wall—a relic from when the residence had been a fortress and needed arrow slits. Now the residence was protected by a strong curtain wall and had taken on some of the comforts and pretensions of a palace.

I examined my reflection. Another mirror might have shown my skin fairer, might have masked my blemishes with its own imperfections, might have favored my figure by showing me more slender than I really was, but this mirror, precision engineered in the Eastern Islands, showed me as I really was. It helped me to find my flaws and cover them up, quickly, before Henri saw them.

I put the pewter flask of black hair dye back into its secret drawer in my table and stared into the mirror to make sure I'd completely covered the gray wisps at my temples. How cruel to begin to gray before the age of forty, especially as the whole plan to save Alba, and my own survival, depended on my beauty.

My face was still beautiful—though there were the makings of fine lines at the corners of my eyes. Laughter lines or crow's-feet, it was all the same. Whatever you called them, they were wrinkles, and though Henri had plenty of wrinkles himself, he liked his women young and beautiful. I'd been queen of the pack for fourteen years—longer than any of the others—but I could feel the younger bitches snapping at my heels. It was a battle to the death and time was my only weapon. If I could just hold on a few more years. . . .

At sixty-eight, Henri was an old man, gout-ridden and mean-tempered, his prowess as a hunter, a sportsman, and a lover long past. Unkindly, age had bled him dry of his youthful attributes and had not replaced them with wisdom, so he ruled Alba now with an iron hand, unthinking and not mellowed by kindness. Daily, I saw him make decisions which showed his willingness to surrender long-term stability for short-term gain. Decisions I would not have taken, and decisions that I would make damn sure his daughter did not take when she stepped into her father's shoes.

For Blanche was the future of Alba.

Henri had no notion of education, especially for women, and so I'd taken on young Blanche. By the time she was twenty-five, I intended she would be ready for the role of queen, with me as her mentor, of course. In the meantime, Blanche was barely sixteen and Henri's death—soon, please—would give me a period of grace as regent, to set right some of the wrongs of his reign.

I sighed and twisted up a strand of my hair. When Uncle Martyn and I had originally devised this plan, we had thought to put a dynasty of Devereaux on Alba's throne, to rule wisely for—we hoped—generations, but, of necessity, the plan had evolved and adapted with circumstances. We neither of us thought that Henri would be impotent, or that he would live this long, but surely it must end soon.

Marrying a lustful and greedy king was a dangerous business; he'd already done away with five wives before me. Despicable man! He was ailing now, with a wasting palsy that had taken away his manhood, but—I shuddered—it didn't prevent him from pawing me and demanding base attentions that even a whore would blush at. Ah, yes, I was playing a dangerous game. If I couldn't hold on to Henri's attention, I'd get what the other queens got—a short walk to the execution block.

Of the five wives before me, only one still lived.

Maria had been the first. His dead brother's widow, married to secure his succession, but eight years older than Henri, then twenty-seven, Maria did not prove fecund. After four years, with his kingship of Alba indisputable, Henri had cast her off to depression and suicide in order to marry a strumpet who, at twenty-two was already pregnant with his child.

Anya had given Henri two daughters, only one of which lived. The plain-faced Lizabet, now thirty-four, was indisputably his, but legally disowned, and he had not seen her since the day he beheaded her mother for the adultery he'd driven her to.

Janet had been next. Some said she was Henri's only soul mate, but even a king's love could not keep her on this earth, and she had died bearing him his only son, a sickly child who had not lived beyond his fourth year.

Annike was the pawn in a political marriage, who came to Henri, already handfasted but sight unseen from Zeederland, across the northern sea. Though by no means ugly, she neither fulfilled the beauty that her portrait promised, nor did she have any personal charm. Henri met with her once in public, and then sent her back home with all her dowry and the treaty torn in twain. To my knowledge, she still calls herself the Queen of Alba and resides in her father's palace with her house dogs and her serving maids.

That was the point at which I had hoped to make my move, backed by Uncle Martyn, who had the king's ear; but only two weeks before my court debut, my plan fell apart, for Henri took a childish passion for Kate LaLanne, a slip of a thing no more than sixteen. Against her will, he married her outright. His fifth queen.

She bore him a daughter scarce eight and a half months into their marriage, but ugly rumor—actually whispered in Henri's ear by my uncle—told of Kate's earlier romance and her longing for her childhood sweetheart, Philip Parr. Furious, Henri seemed to forget that he had pronounced his young wife to be a virgin bride and had proudly showed the bloodied sheets. He accused her of an affair with Philip and, though the young man fled for his life, Henri pronounced Kate guilty without a trial and executed her, casting her child, Blanche, out of his household.

And then it was my turn at last. Better three years late than not at all. Already twenty-four, but still a beauty and claiming to be twenty-one, I charmed Henri right out of his crown with my wit and my splendid looks, and, once we were married, with my body. And with each day and night that passed, I hated him more and more; but I was trapped.

Once you're on a runaway horse, it's safer to ride it to a standstill than to try and get off in midflight. So I watched my husband every day, wondered how much longer he could survive, and vowed to outlast him.

I looked in the mirror again, saw myself in the

clear light from my windows, and patted my throat with the back of my hand. No sign of a double chin. I touched the glass. It never lied to me. I was as beautiful as ever, and I would hold Henri's favor until the day he died. Please, God, let it be soon.

With Henri's first child, Lizabet, legally disinherited and now gone to the Church as one of the sexless, black-robed Brides of God, I needed a baby to secure my position. Had Henri once managed to bed me properly, I might have risked all and found some anonymous man to ensure a child, but not once in fourteen years, with me naked in his bed every night, did he get close enough for any pregnancy to be believable, so I reworked my plan and turned instead to Queen Kate's forgotten daughter.

It took all my powers of persuasion to get Henri to openly admit that he believed Blanche to be his true child. In the end I persuaded him to it on the grounds that it strengthened perceptions of his virility. Though the little girl, strangely pale to look at, was not the child of my flesh, she became the child of my heart. From her sixth year, I tutored her myself, not just in her letters and in mathematics, but in history, politics, and ethics as well. On Henri's death, Alba would have an educated and enlightened monarch.

I smiled at my reflection. Much as I loved Alba, I couldn't pretend that my ambition was entirely selfless. My precious mirror showed me that.

"My Lady." Saskia, my maid, bobbed a curtsy to me as I stepped out of the alcove.

"I'll wear the blue today." I pointed at one of the

three court gowns that had been laid out for my choice and Saskia helped me into it lacing it tight across my breasts to show a delicate amount of cleavage. Childless as I was, my breasts were still firm and full—one advantage to the embarrassment of My Lord Husband having to take my maidenhead with his fingers on our wedding night to bloody the sheets.

I shivered at the memory.

Saskia tut-tutted at my feeble attempts at hairdressing. She unfastened what I had done, combed my hair again, and pinned it up. I patted her hand in thanks, for truly, without Saskia to fetch me my hair dye, in secret, I might have had gray streaks by now and a swift and deadly departure from the king's favor. I would never have been able to go tripping off, unnoticed, across the town that nestled at the foot of the curtain wall.

There was a knock on my door and a steward announced my uncle.

"Lord Martyn Devereaux."

Uncle Martyn didn't wait for my permission; he marched in and, with barely a deferential nod, he began to give me a list of the petitioners who would appear before the king this morning.

"Simmons claims a further five hundred acres across the river from his holding at Maisery, but the abbott contests it. With the extra five hundred acres, Simmons can hold the water and bleed the Church dry if they want fishing rights."

"Who holds the weir above?"

"The Abbess of Wednesbury."

The church, from its heart in Hierenia, was too demanding. "Then let Simmons take the land, it keeps the power out of the hands of the church."

"And Simmons?"

"Make sure he knows whose decision it was and take some recognizable bauble from him as a pledge of fealty."

Uncle Martyn smiled. "I've taught you well, Catherine."

I glared at him. He needn't think I would be his puppet when the time came, but for now I would not pull him up for his familiarity.

"Anything else?" I asked.

"The Hierenian ambassador wants to present Prince Charles, the youngest son of the House of the Hierene. He's been here for two weeks and the king has not granted him audience yet."

"Why doesn't he present him at the proper time?"

"He's pledged to the church before the next diplomatic mission."

"All right. I expect Henri would grant him this one favor, even though I would like to see the Hierenians sent far from this court."

My steward knocked gently on the door again and opened it. "My Lord King is leaving his chamber, My Lady Queen."

I nodded. That gave me two minutes to get into position at the foot of the grand staircase, ready to enter the receiving room on King Henri's arm.

As he descended and took my arm, Henri smiled at me and patted my hand. "You left my chamber early, last night, my dear."

"My Lord, I thought you were sleeping. I know that Doctor Fallarian made one of your draughts, and I didn't want to be the cause of it not bringing you a peaceful night's sleep."

"Such a thoughtful wife, Catherine, but come to me tonight before I take the draught, and bring some more of that oil you had mixed."

"With the greatest of pleasure, My Lord."

We walked into the audience chamber together and the king sat, allowing me to sit also. His subjects and petitioners remained standing and I could see, behind the crowd, Blanche's snow-white hair. She was doing as I had instructed and observing the petitions and the way each was answered. Our lesson this afternoon would be to analyze them. She would tell me what decision she would have made and why. Mostly, her answers were good.

The petitioners came before us, heads bowed, eyes cast down in supplication. On the subject of the river, I managed to intervene with a suggestion, and the land went from out of the control of the church—a small personal triumph.

Then it was time for the Hierenian ambassador to present his prince. There are some proprieties that we must observe for even the youngest princeling, so a fanfare sounded and the doors at the far end of the audience chamber opened with a certain amount of ceremony to reveal a dark-haired and well-formed young man.

He walked forward, eyes straight ahead, but someone moved through the crowd, close to his side, someone with white hair. For a second his attention

was diverted and I saw a look pass between him and
Blanche that set my heart hammering in my chest. If
she'd developed any attachment to this princeling,
then she could just forget it. Alba was not going to
be sacrificed on the altar of a political marriage. Hierenia had too much ambition, so a move to put a
Hierenian prince on the throne alongside Blanche
was out of the question. I glanced at Henri, but his
eyes were on the prince and he didn't seem to have
noticed his heir.

The audience over, Henri declined lunch and retired to his chambers. I was too distracted to eat,
even though my cook sent word she had prepared a
chiffon of cheeses. Instead I marched up to the solar
where I tutored Blanche daily. My soft slippers made
little sound on the stone floor and I entered the room
with no ceremony. I hated to have door-openers attend my every move, and had long since dismissed
them to more useful duties except on formal
occasions.

I found Blanche looking out of the window, down
into the central courtyard and, crossing quickly over,
I saw that she was watching the cavalcade from Hierenia readying for departure. The young prince—
handsome enough to turn any girl's head—looked
up at the solar window, saw her, and waved. She
started to raise her hand, and I grabbed her wrist
and squeezed until she yelped and turned from the
window.

"What have I taught you about propriety?" I
dragged her into the middle of the room and then
let go of her wrist. I could see blood trickling where

my nails had dug in. I took a deep breath to calm my temper and sat down on the wooden high-backed chair by the trestle table.

"I was only waving good-bye."

"Are you sure you didn't mean, 'Until we meet again'?"

"What if I did?' She tilted her chin up at me in defiance, her delicate cheeks flushed and her blue eyes sparkling with unshed tears.

"Such a pretty boy to be given to the church," I said. "I fear he will turn some lecherous old abbot's head and find the religious life . . . most interesting."

She started forward and then realized I was goading her. She's not been my student these last ten years for nothing. She gave me a level look and said, quite calmly, "He's not going into the church. He's going to ask his father if he might go into the army instead."

"Ah." I nodded my head. "He's going to be a noble warrior."

She nodded.

"And which way do you think the Hierenian army will be marching as soon as your father dies?"

"I . . ."

"You know they would like nothing better than to annex the Rowan Territories, and from there, our border is too tempting. Unless, of course, they don't have to go to the expense of waging war, they'll just marry Alba instead." I slammed my palm flat on the table and Blanche jumped visibly. "We've talked about this. Your father has given in to Hierenia too many times. They think we're a soft target. You, my dear, are a very soft target."

"Should I not use marriage as a tool?" She leaned forward onto her hands on the other side of the table.

"Ah, now you're thinking with that part of your anatomy that you sit on. Yes, dear girl, use it by all means, but your virginity can only be used once, unless you save it."

"Save it for how long?"

"Forever. Be the virgin queen. Play them all off against each other. Hierenia against Lascaux, and the both of them against Zeederland."

"And how should I get an heir?"

"In the dead of night and in secret, and once you have got your heir, the man must die. No one must have claim to your love or to your children."

"That's inhuman, My Lady."

"Yes, inhuman, but royal. You'll be a woman in a man's world. Human is not an option."

"But Charles and I . . ."

"Whatever passed between you must be forgotten . . ." I looked at her face and I felt the blood drain from mine until I was probably as pale as she was. "You didn't . . . *do* anything you might regret, did you?"

She glared at me, defiant.

"Answer me, girl, or I'll get a surgeon to check your maidenhead."

She sighed, knowing I was not bluffing, and slid on to the stool on the opposite side of the table. "We did nothing except hold hands in the moonlight. But if he had asked me to, I would have done more, and we promised each other that there would come a time."

"A promise you must break. Let him go to the church, for you will be Alba's virgin queen and you will make her strong once more."

"I'm only sixteen. You ask too much of me."

"I ask no more than I am prepared to give, myself. To save Alba, I will die a virgin if I have to."

"But the king . . ."

"Has no courage in him, else I would have been teaching children of my own instead of bringing you back from banishment to be his heir and my protégé."

"Lady, I . . ."

"And if you ever say anything, I will personally rip out your tongue and eat it, braised. Understand?"

"Yes, My Lady."

"So we'll say no more today. Go to your room and meditate on duty."

She stood and bobbed a curtsy to me; but even though she seemed to give in, I was troubled. Blanche's spirit was independent. There was more than a strong streak of her father's "*I want*" in her.

I watched Blanche closely after that, and I had Uncle Martyn's spies keep a sharp eye out for whatever might be happening in the court of Hierenia. My first clue that something was amiss came when I had news that Charles had not taken holy orders, but had taken a captaincy in the army instead. Martyn assured me there had been no messages between

Blanche and Charles, but I couldn't trust he was right. As I said before, Blanche was my student, and, young as she was, that made her dangerous.

During the course of that summer, Henri sickened. His gout became unbearably painful and his palsy visibly worse. Doctor Fallarian dosed him with a painkiller that all but made him insensible for most of the time, and, at long last, I came into power, ruling in Henri's name, with Blanche beside me.

Now, at last, I could begin my work.

I sent for Merianas, an old general who had the running of our army. Recruit, I told him. Train. Defend. And to Rufaldo, captain of our raggle-taggle navy, I gave permission and money to build two new war ships and a promise of more next year. The money I diverted from Henri's pet project, a new and very splendid house of worship right here in the city. The church could wait, maybe forever.

Uncle Martyn became my eyes and ears, and he gave me a handful of men who swore their allegiance and knew the value of staying in shadows.

Then, as the summer started to mellow into autumn, a messenger came from Hierenia asking if a deputation might come to propose a union between our two countries. I sent back to say that with Henri's health failing, now was not the best time. They replied that there couldn't possibly be a better time and that Alba might need their protection from incursions on our Lascaux frontier. I kept the first letter from Blanche, but she heard about the second and came to my room just as Saskia was pinning up my hair.

I saw her face, red with rage, reflected in my mirror and it told me the truth once again; that, despite all my teaching, Blanche was still her father's daughter. My heart sank to my boots.

"Why didn't you tell me?" Blanche asked.

"Tell you what?"

"Of what amounts to a marriage proposal from Charles."

"It's of no consequence."

"I say it is!" She stamped her foot.

I sighed and closed the door across my mirror. I didn't need to see any more.

"You cannot marry with Hierenia, Blanche."

"I will be queen one day. I can marry where I will."

"When you are queen, but, until then, I will keep Alba free. You will thank me for it when you still have a country to inherit."

She made a sound that might have been frustration, or might have been disgust, then flounced out of my room slamming the door so hard that my mirror, my precious mirror, dropped from its hook on to the pedestal table, teetered and fell forward. Only my dear Saskia saved it from falling all the way to the floor. She set it on its back on the table.

Trembling, I opened its door and saw, to my horror, that the glass had cracked diagonally and that the pieces had moved, so that where I had seen one reflection, now I saw two.

And yet, my precious mirror still told me true, for once I had been a whole person and now I must tear myself in twain. There would be the Catherine who would rule with an open heart and an even hand, and a second Catherine who would do whatever she had to do for the good of her country and the safety of her people.

Without my mirror to tell me the truth, I might not have had the courage to do what I must. For though I knew what must be done, even I quailed at the enormity of it. But trusting to my mirror, I devised a plan.

I could see no way around it. Blanche, child of my heart, was doomed—or else Alba was. But she must be got rid of in such a way that her going was open-ended. If she died, a new heir would have to be chosen. If, on the other hand, she ran away to join her lover and disappeared from all knowledge, I could continue to hold the regency for her against her return. And if, in his dying days, the king should get an heir on me. I would be totally secure.

Using the courtly writing of Hierenia, as a scribe would, I wrote a note on parchment which said, simply, "We will never be together unless we make it happen. Leave a note to make it known that you have come of your own free will. The fellow who carries this message will bring you to me. I yearn for your presence." Then I signed it, simply, C.

I called Cato to me, my favorite of my uncle's shadowy men. He came at dusk, and I swear no one saw him move along the corridors of the residence. I was alone in my rooms, having dismissed even my faithful Saskia.

"You have sworn allegiance to me and me alone, Cato."

"I have, My Lady."

"And thus to Alba."

"Lady, I swore allegiance to Alba in my cradle."

I looked at the man, he was maybe thirty-five, tall and robust in a military kind of way, with square capable hands and a lean, angular face.

"Have you a wife?"

"I had, My Lady, but she died in childbirth before I took service with Lord Martyn."

"And your child?"

"Lived, My Lady. A strong son, now nearly twelve. He lives with my sister and her family."

A son; that told me what I needed to know.

My life at court had been one long risk, and now I was about to take a series of them, each one more daring than the last. Each one could be the death of me if I was found out.

"Cato, I know you can keep your own counsel, for that's entirely why my uncle pledged you to me."

"Yes, My Lady. I'm no loose-mouth."

I nodded and began to unhook the bodice of my dress. "Good, then help me off with this, will you?"

If I could have captured his face in a painting I would have liked to hang it beside my mirror, for it was truly a mask of genuine surprise and, I like to think, delight. I took his hand and laid it on my breast to confirm my meaning. For a moment, it was still and then he began to caress me as though it mattered that I should have pleasure from our encounter.

"My Lady, what if I should get you with child?"

"I'm counting on it. For the king has not been capable of that in all the time I have been wed to him. My monthly time is right. You shall come back to me every night for a week and we shall see what we can make between us. And after that, you will forget it happened. You will tell no one and you will lay no claim to me or my baby."

"My Lady." He picked up my hand and kissed my fingers in acquiescence. "It shall be as you say in all things."

There is nothing like the vigor of a man setting out to make a son. Though I was nervous, after my experience with Henri, Cato was a revelation. His body was clean and his lovemaking—yes, I can call it lovemaking—was honest and straightforward and I reveled to have him inside me with his strength and his seed. For seven nights we made our sport, but I knew that the seventh night must be our last, even though he held me, naked and trembling in his arms, and with rare and simple eloquence professed his love.

"If you truly love me, Cato, you must do one more thing, exactly as I ask it."

"Of course."

I sat up and slipped out of the bed, draping a robe across my shoulders. I opened the secret drawer where I kept my hair dye and next to it was the rolled parchment I had written a week ago.

"Take this to Princess Blanche tonight, in secret. It is an invitation to a tryst from her lover. It tells her to trust you to take her to him." I looked at him and he nodded. So far, so good. "Then you must take her into the forest—far into the forest—and kill her."

"My Lady?" He took a step back from me and I saw the horror on his face. He was a good man—even a gentle man in his own way—and I had asked him to kill a child.

I touched my fingers to his face. "For all the love you bear me, and for all the love you bear Alba, Cato, I ask you to do this. Would you see Alba governed by Hierenia?"

"Never, My Lady."

"When King Henri dies, and Blanche comes to rule, she will wed the young Hierenian princeling who turned her head with his pretty smile." I found genuine tears rolling down my cheeks. "Cato, if there was another way, don't you think I would take it? Blanche is like a daughter to me. I persuaded the king to bring her back to court and legitimize her claim to the throne. I nurtured her like my own and I taught her all I could—but it wasn't enough. She'll give Alba to Hierenia as a dowry. I can't let that happen."

"Of course not, Lady." He pulled on his pants and shirt.

Could I trust him to do it? Was he too kind? Would he relent at the last moment when she screamed and sobbed and threw herself on his mercy?

"One more thing, Cato." I pulled the robe tight around me and belted it. "You must bring me her heart. Kill her clean and easy, but when she is dead, cut her heart from her breast and bring it to me before you bury her body."

He stood still for so long that I began to count the

seconds. I got to five before he exhaled suddenly and nodded. "It shall be as you say, My Lady."

"For Alba."

"For Alba."

Then he picked up his boots, took the parchment, and left.

Within a couple of minutes, the outer door opened and Saskia let herself into the room. I'm pretty sure she'd guessed what had been happening for the last week; the rumpled bed and the man-smell on my skin gave me away better than words.

At my command she ran a bath and put out my nightdress and formal robe, the one I wore when Henri called me to his room at night. I bathed and dressed and, taking a shielded candle in a glass case, I walked down the corridor to Henri's rooms. Doctor Fallarian was in the outer chamber.

"Doctor."

"My Lady Queen." He bowed low, his gray whiskers brushing the back of my proffered hand.

"My Lord Husband has always been a vigorous man, and I'm minded to think that his vigor has not been extinguished by his illness. Though he finds it hard to speak, on my last visit he asked me to come to him again in the night, and I think it only right and fitting that I perform a wife's duties to the end."

"My Lady, I think he is not . . ."

"He needs me tonight, Doctor, and I would thank you to leave us in peace."

"I have not yet administered his nighttime draught."

"I'll give it to him afterward. You may go."

He bowed and did as I asked.

Henri's bedroom smelled stale and, as I listened to his wheezing, I wondered if I could go through with this, but it was too late to back out now.

First I opened a window and let in the balmy autumn night air. Then I put my arm under his shoulders, raised him up and gave him the sleeping draught. He mumbled at me as if he thought I was Fallarian. When he dropped back to the pillows, insensible, I pulled back his bedcovers and stripped off every last stitch of his clothing, save for the bandage on his left foot, throwing garments to one side as if it had been done in passion. My own clothes I dropped at the foot of the bed and then I mussed my hair and tumbled the bedcovers. I snuggled close to him as a true wife might, shuddering at the coldfish feel of his flesh, and wrapped us both in his quilt. Then I raised myself on my left elbow and with the palm of my right hand I covered Henri's mouth and gently pinched his nostrils together with my forefinger and thumb.

He didn't even struggle.

When I let go, his last breath sighed from his lungs and he lay very still.

Doctor Fallarian found us in the morning. I played the grieving wife, holding Henri's cold body to my naked breast. Through tears which I didn't even need to fake, I looked up at the good doctor and said, "He was just like himself last night, Doctor, lusty as a youth, but I fear the excitement was too much for his heart."

Back in my room, I breathed deeply once again and put my hand on my belly, wondering whether it held new life or not. If it did, and if I survived the birth, then the kingdom was secure. I had done all I could do to keep Alba safe from the Hierenians, though at a cost. The sacrifices I had made, and had still to make, would be worth it. The only two, now, who could play me false, deliberately or otherwise, were Cato and my sweet Saskia. As a woman I so wanted to let them live. As a queen, I knew I could not. Both their parts in my plan were over.

I opened the door and looked once more into my mirror. Saskia had tried to mend it. She'd managed to line up the glass so it no longer showed two images, but across my face was an ugly crack like a scar running from brow to chin.

I stared at it and, for the last time, the mirror told me the ugly truth. I was now just one being, no longer half ordinary person, half queen. I was now all queen, but I was, and would remain, damaged to my very soul by what I had done and what I might yet do.

I closed the door on the mirror, not liking what I saw, but I knew I could live with it if I had to— for Alba.

AFTER THE BALL

by Pamela Luzier

Pamela Luzier is a voracious reader of science fiction, fantasy, humor, and romance, and her stories usually include two or more of these elements. Three of her short stories have appeared in other fantasy anthologies, and she has published two romance novellas and ten novels under the name Pam McCutcheon. A former industrial engineer for the Air Force, Pam now lives in Colorado where she writes and co-owns a bookstore. You can find her on the web at www.pammc.com.

"CINDERELLA is a witch," Griselda declared in ringing tones. She ought to know, she was the ungrateful wench's stepmother.

Unfortunately, her announcement dropped with all the elegance of a dull thud in the silence of the glittering throne room. Perhaps if there had been more people present, her accusation would have had more effect, but the king had insisted on privacy for this interview. Only he, the queen, Cinderella, the prince, and a few of the king's advisers were present to hear

Griselda's defense. And none of them seemed inclined to be sympathetic.

Griselda would have liked to think this semiprivate audience was out of concern for her own reputation, but she suspected the king and queen simply didn't want anyone else to hear the truth about Cinderella.

Luckily, Griselda had it on good authority that one of the advisers was a magic-sniffer—the tall, lanky one named Bern. She would keep his abilities in mind in case events went against her.

The king, looking regal with the golden crown on his equally golden hair, stroked his beard and frowned down at Griselda from his throne on the raised dais. "Cinderella, our son's future bride, is not on trial. You are."

Griselda seethed in silence. She and her poor, mistreated daughters were forced to stand humbled before the few members of the court while her stepdaughter was allowed to sit in the royal presence. It was so unfair. Cinderella had captured the prince's heart with her evil, deceitful spells, and Griselda's daughters were left with nothing but ashes. Worse, they had to stay mute behind their mother and watch as she was unjustly humiliated.

Griselda raised her chin. "I have done nothing wrong. What am I accused of?"

The elegant dark-haired queen, who still retained the beauty she had been famed for in her youth, frowned. "You are accused of being a bad parent to an orphaned child left in your care, of treating a gentlewoman like a servant, and of being cruel to a gentle soul."

Griselda almost snorted in disbelief. Cinderella, a gentle soul? The conniving chit was more wily and crafty than anyone she knew. And being a bad parent was no crime, or half the parents in the kingdom would be in the dungeons.

"She has bewitched all of you," Griselda said scornfully. None more so than the prince, who stared, besotted, at Cinderella's glowing beauty. And where, pray tell, did they think she had acquired her good looks? She certainly hadn't looked like that before the ball.

Besides, since when was it wrong to treat poor relations like servants? It happened in all the best families.

The king raised a condescending eyebrow. "You persist in these accusations?"

Griselda curtsied, trying to appear humble. "I must, Your Majesty . . . if you would hear the truth?"

The king and queen held a whispered consultation, then the king nodded. "Very well. Let us hear your tale from the beginning."

"Don't listen to her, Father," the prince cried. "She is the wicked one, and she is trying to turn you against my intended bride."

"Cinderella will have a chance to explain herself," the king said. "After we hear her stepmother's story." He glared around at the people present. "And I will brook no interference until it is told."

Griselda cast a triumphant glance at Cinderella, but the silly girl didn't even have the intelligence to appear afraid. She would soon regret underestimating her stepmother.

Casting her eyes down in an attitude of despair, Griselda said, "My dearly departed husband, bless his soul, was sadly deceived in his first wife, Cinderella's mother. He saw only her beauty and did not realize that the heart of a cunning witch lurked within her bosom."

Satisfaction filled Griselda as she glanced up and saw distress on Cinderella's face. The witch was right to feel so, for soon Griselda would unmask her true nature.

"You have proof of this?" the king asked.

"Yes, Sire. The village priests found Cinderella's mother guilty of practicing witchcraft and burned her at the stake." There—let Cinderella explain that away.

The queen turned to look at Cinderella. "Is that true?"

Cinderella's bowed head told it all, but at least the girl had the grace to nod and confirm the truth.

"I see," the king said slowly. "Well, being put to the torch is no guarantee of evil intent. We fear we have many overzealous priests in our kingdom, especially in the west, who have tortured and killed innocent women whose only crime was being at the wrong place at the wrong time. It is possible Cinderella's mother was one such.

Blind fool. But Griselda dared not utter her accusation aloud. Instead, she merely bowed her head, and said, "I am certain the record speaks for itself, Your Highness." She didn't know exactly what Cinderella's mother had done, but like mother, like daughter. It must have been heinous.

He waved that away as if it were inconsequential. "Well, we don't have the records available, nor the priests to question. Go on with your story."

"I met her father not long after. He was shocked and dismayed at learning of his first wife's true nature. Fearing his daughter would follow in her mother's footsteps, he moved as far east as he could and sought a sensible woman who would take Cinderella in hand and ensure she never indulged in such foolishness."

"You?"

Griselda bowed her head in modesty. "Yes, Sire. He hoped I would raise his child in piety and decency, as I have my own two daughters." And it hadn't hurt that Griselda had still been a fine figure of a woman. "But the child was inconsolable at her mother's death."

And, indeed, Cinderella looked greatly saddened now at the memory. Griselda almost gagged when the gullible prince put his arm around Cinderella and clasped her to his chest. If he knew what a viper she could be, he would not hold her so near.

The king nodded. "So I understand. And that is why you gave her nothing but rags to wear and made her sleep in the ashes?"

"I did no such thing," Griselda said in indignation. "It was Cinderella's choice."

The queen looked skeptical. "It was *her* choice to look like a beggar?"

"Yes," Griselda declared. "Their western customs require mourners to rend their clothing in grief and cover themselves in ashes. The child took it to extremes and persisted in mourning her mother for many years beyond the customary time. She even chose to sleep on the hearth to ensure she was always covered in cinders, then demanded we call her by the new name she had chosen—Cinderella. Indeed, she used her evil magic to make us forget the name she was born with."

When the queen continued to look skeptical, Griselda said, "I tried to coax her away from the hearth, to no avail. Cinderella stubbornly refused to give up her bereavement, no matter how poorly it reflected on the rest of her family. In fact, she resented me so much for taking her mother's place that I think she *wanted* to make me look bad to the other villagers. And it became much worse when her father died." She shook her head sadly. "He was stolen from us far too young by a fever, his last wish that I continue to watch over his daughter."

"So you honored your dead husband's wishes by working Cinderella's fingers to the bone to slave for you and your daughters?"

The poor, deceived queen appeared to be as enamored of Cinderella as her son was. "It wasn't like that at all," Griselda protested. "Idle hands mean idle mischief, and no one can get into more mischief than my stepdaughter. Just look at my own daughters." Griselda made a sweeping gesture that encompassed Edda and Solvig, standing behind her. "Before Cinderella arrived in our household, my daughters were the fairest in the land, bidding fair to rival you, my queen, in their beauty."

The queen didn't seem flattered by the comparison, so Griselda continued, wondering what would convince her of the truth. "Now, as you can plainly see, my ungrateful stepdaughter has enchanted her stepsisters so that none will find them fair."

Indeed, they had been called downright ugly— Edda with her skinny beanpole frame, spotted complexion, and teeth like a horse, and Solvig whose girth had become such that she had problems fitting through most doorways.

"Are you saying my son's betrothed did this to them?" the king asked in disbelief.

What else could explain why her sweet angels had turned into such homely spinsters? "Yes, she did it out of spite, because they still had a parent, and she had none living. Plus she envied her sisters' beauty and wanted to spoil any chance of happiness for them. To keep her from plotting further harm, I had to keep her as busy as possible."

The members of the court didn't look convinced. "It was for her own good," Griselda explained. "I feared that if she had idle time, she would continue to practice her evil tricks. And if our neighbors had realized I harbored a witch child in my household, they would have ensured she met the same fate as her mother." Griselda sighed, righteous in the knowledge she had done her best. "My plan worked, and I kept her safe and the kingdom ignorant of her true nature."

"Oh, really?" the queen drawled. "If you are so concerned about maintaining your promise to your dead husband and keeping Cinderella safe, then why are you revealing this 'true nature' now?"

Raising her chin, Griselda declared, "Because there is a greater need at stake—the fate of the kingdom. As much as it pains me, I must tell the truth for your sake."

"If she was such a danger," the king said, "why did you not reveal this before?"

"Because she had done no real harm . . . until the ball was announced."

She stole a glance at Cinderella, but her face was still buried in the prince's shoulder—no doubt to keep the guilt in her expression from being seen by the king and queen.

Looking doubtful now, the king asked, "What happened then?"

Griselda hurried to follow up on her advantage. "Suddenly, Cinderella was seized with the conviction that she must attend the ball, ensnare the prince, and marry him."

"And what is so wrong with that?" the queen asked. "After all, your daughters had the same objective, did they not?"

"They did. What young girl would not? The prince is charming, kind, and fair of face and form. Of course they wanted to catch his eye." It couldn't hurt to pour on the praise for the royal pair's only child.

"Then Cinderella did just as they did," the queen said in triumph.

"I fear not, Your Majesty." Griselda shook her

head sadly. "It was then that Cinderella finally gave up her mourning and turned calculating. Though Edda and Solvig were content to be themselves in hopes that the prince would see their natural sweetness show through the appearance Cinderella had doomed them with, my stepdaughter was determined to shine brighter than any maiden at the ball. And the only way she could do that was through . . . magic." Griselda whispered that last word, fearing the taint would stick to her if she said it too loud.

"How so?" the king asked.

"She rose from the ashes, washed herself for the first time in many years, and demanded that I provide her with a sumptuous gown." Griselda still felt indignation at the chit's boldness. "I refused, of course."

"Why?" the queen asked. "You dressed your daughters in the best money could buy, and said you had tried to coax Cinderella from the ashes. Why would you refuse to give her a gown when she finally did as you asked?"

"Because she made it quite clear that she was out to trap the prince and bend him to her will. I feared what would happen to the kingdom if she succeeded . . . and to Your Majesties, since you would be the only impediments standing between her and the throne."

The queen gasped. "You are accusing our future daughter-in-law of treason?"

Wary now, Griselda spread her hands. "You be the judge." Especially since Cinderella continued to hide her face.

"So we shall," the king said with a frown. "Explain this use of magic."

Griselda hid a triumphant smile. She'd be happy to. "After years of stubbornly living amidst the ashes on the brick hearth, you can imagine how awful and rough her skin and hair were." Seeing the queen frown thoughtfully at the obvious truth gave Griselda hope that she might listen to what she had to say. "None of the mundane remedies I tried would bring them to any semblance of beauty, so she did the unspeakable." Griselda paused and let foreboding enter her voice. "She used her black arts to call upon her mother's help."

"But her mother was dead by then," the king said, looking puzzled.

"Yes, that is why the act was so despicable. She brought her mothers' shade back to help her. Oh, she said it was her fairy godmother—trying to make the apparition seem harmless and inoffensive—but I know better. From the description the servants gave me, this so-called 'fairy godmother' was, in fact, her mother, who taught Cinderella the dark arts."

"That's a very serious accusation," the king said. Even the magic-sniffer looked alarmed.

"Yes, Your Highness, I know. But I feel it my duty to warn you of Cinderella's true nature."

The prince shot her a murderous look as Cinderella moaned piteously and snuggled into his arms. *Well, when I'm through, you won't be so loving anymore.*

"She prevailed upon her mother's shade to use her ill-begotten power to make her beautiful, so radiant that she would eclipse any woman at the ball. When I saw what she had done, I was frightened."

Griselda hung her head. "I knew then and there I should have gone to someone and explained what happened, but I had grown fond of the girl and didn't want to see her hurt. So, I tried to keep her home instead."

"How?" the king asked.

"I set her impossible tasks, telling her if she accomplished them, she could attend the ball."

The queen scowled. "If she is as powerful a witch as you say, why would she agree to such a thing? She could just thumb her nose at you and your demands and do as she pleased."

"Because I threatened to reveal her secret if she didn't do as I requested. I felt bad about holding it over her head, but it was the only way to keep her from using her magical wiles on the prince." Griselda gave a rueful smile. "But I wasn't entirely cruel. I even let her believe there was some hope I would let her attend the ball. Unfortunately, she took full advantage of that."

The king stroked his beard thoughtfully and motioned for her to continue.

"I threw a bushel of lentils into the ashes and told her if she picked them all out, she could go with us."

"And did she?" the queen asked.

Griselda sighed. "I fear so. She brought them to me faster than humanly possible."

"So you gave her permission to attend the ball," the queen said in satisfaction.

"No, I—"

The queen leaned forward, as if pouncing upon her words. "You went back on your promise?"

Ignoring the queen's question, Griselda explained, "I wanted to know how she had done the chore so quickly. So, I threw two bushels of lentils in the cinders, saying she had to sort and clean them before she could go. Then I hid and watched to see what she would do."

"I imagine she picked them out of the ashes very fast," the queen said dryly.

"So I thought. But to my surprise, she called a flock of birds. They swooped in through the window and pecked all the lentils from the hearth then put them back in the baskets for her." Just in case someone didn't catch the significance of her story, she spelled it out for them. "Only witches have the ability to call animals and use them as familiars."

The queen sniffed. "It sounds to me as if the birds felt sorry for her. I know I would."

Griselda shook her head sadly. Cinderella must have put a spell on the queen for her to continue so adamantly in the girl's defense despite all the evidence against her. But it would be folly to contradict the queen. Instead, Griselda said nothing and glanced at the king and the magic-sniffer, who were deep in consultation. Good—it appeared they had not yet fallen under the girl's spell.

The king gestured at her to continue. "So, *then* you let her go to the ball . . . ?"

"No, Your Highness. Seeing her use her powers in so audacious a manner, I feared she would balk at nothing to bespell the prince. And the queen," she added boldly. When the king raised an eyebrow but didn't say anything, Griselda continued in a more urgent tone. "I forbade her to go, and tried to keep her so busy helping Edda and Solvig with their preparations for the ball that she wouldn't have time to get ready herself." She sighed heavily. "I thought it had worked—when the coach carried us off to the ball, Cinderella was still at home in her unkempt rags. The only way she could have made it to the ball on time is with the aid of unholy magic."

"Aha," the queen exclaimed. "But if you didn't see what happened after you left, you have no way of knowing if she used magic or not."

"Oh, but I do. The cook told me all after the ball, quaking with fear for what she had seen."

She paused dramatically, but the king filled the silence with an annoyed, "Get on with it."

Disconcerted by his apparent lack of sympathy, Griselda said, "Cook described how Cinderella was white with fury, and called upon her mother to help her in her hour of need. This 'fairy godmother' appeared and with a single wave of her hand, made Cinderella and her complexion beautiful. Then, with another wave of her hand, she fitted my stepdaughter with a gown of spun gold and sparking glass slippers."

There—let the queen explain *that* away.

The queen tried, tossing her head. "I imagine your cook had been imbibing too freely of the cooking sherry."

"Cook is a teetotaler, Your Majesty."

"Then she was crazy with fever, or imagining things. Or, more likely, she's a liar."

Not wanting to call the queen herself a liar, Griselda said, "I've never had any problems with her before. But . . . how else would Cinderella have acquired these items? And it gets worse. Seeing that Cinderella had no way to get to the ball, her mother changed a pumpkin into a coach, white mice into horses, and lizards into footmen."

"Utter nonsense," the queen declared.

"I might have thought so, too," Griselda explained. "But your own servants will tell you she arrived in a grand coach and four. The girls and I had taken the only coach our family possesses. How would she have been able to acquire such a lavish equipage with no money and very little time . . . save for magic?"

"There must be some explanation."

"Perhaps," Griselda conceded, not willing to offend the queen too much. "And I might be convinced of that . . . except for the other evidence of magical usage."

The queen looked wary now. "Such as?"

"Those glass slippers, Your Highness. Think about it. How could anyone possibly dance as Cinderella did without breaking them? Glass is a very fragile substance, and the dance figures were strenuous. Had you or I worn those slippers, they would have shattered instantly. Yet Cinderella wears them still, with nary a scratch on them. How could that be . . . unless they were enchanted?"

Everyone turned to look at Cinderella's feet which she tried unsuccessfully to hide beneath her gown. The truth was obvious.

Following up immediately on her advantage, Griselda added, "Luckily, the magical spell had a limitation. Didn't you wonder why she fled so precipitously when the clock struck midnight?"

"I assumed something had happened to upset her," the queen said. "Or that she was urgently required at home."

"Neither was the case. The magic was due to run out. To avoid being caught in her rags with nothing but a pumpkin and vermin to see her home, she had to flee." Griselda arched an eyebrow. "But wasn't it convenient that she managed to leave a souvenir behind with which the prince could find her?"

"Convenient?" the king repeated with a barking laugh. "It was damned inconvenient if you ask me— riding all over the land, being inundated by desperate spinsters, and inspecting every dirty, smelly foot in the kingdom. If she was so intent on being found, why didn't she make it easier?"

Griselda managed a graceful shrug. "I can only speculate. But Cinderella was well aware of the maxim that says a man prizes the reward he has to toil for far more than the one that falls into his lap." She gestured at the prince who still clasped Cinderella to his breast. "Apparently, it worked."

"Aha," the queen exclaimed. "If you knew the shoe belonged to Cinderella, why did you insist your daughters try it on?"

Griselda hung her head. "I'm ashamed to say I

was afraid to admit I knew it was hers for fear she would be found out, that we would be reviled for harboring a witch in our midst. It would have looked suspicious if my daughters were the only two in the kingdom who weren't eager to try the glass slipper on."

"And you?" the queen demanded. "Why did *you* try it on? Don't you think you're a bit long in the tooth to be my daughter-in-law?"

She wasn't *that* old. "Of course," Griselda said soothingly. "But I never expected to wed the prince. I simply wanted to see if the slipper would fit. You see, Cinderella and I wear the same size. If it didn't fit, I knew it had to be enchanted so that it would fit only one person. And so it was."

Before the queen could interrupt with another objection, Griselda said, "I knew how unlikely it was that, out of all the women in the kingdom, the glass slipper would fit only one person. Sooner or later, someone else would have realized it, too, so I confined Cinderella to her room, trying to keep her from claiming it and making her witchery obvious to one and all."

Griselda sighed. "Unfortunately, she used her black arts to escape, made herself beautiful once more, and caught the prince wholly within her thrall when she put the shoe on her foot." She gestured at the two lovebirds, inviting everyone to see the truth for themselves.

"Have you anything more to add?" the king asked.

"Just one more thing, Your Majesty. Once she had thoroughly conned the prince, Cinderella knew that all she had to fear were the people who knew her for what she truly was—me and my innocent little girls. That is why she made up this story and accused me of mistreating her." And just in case her logic hadn't convinced them, Griselda added, "If you don't believe me, have your magic-sniffer confirm my story. *And* hers—don't let her use magic to bespell you as well."

The king nodded in decision. He gestured the magic-sniffer, Bern, to his side, saying, "We shall ensure no magic is used in this room without our leave." He turned to Cinderella. "Please come forward, child."

The prince looked stricken. "Father, you can't—"

"Quiet," the king ordered. "There are some grave charges here, and Cinderella must be allowed to speak in her own defense."

The prince bowed and sat back down, and Cinderella stood to face the king and queen. If Griselda didn't know better, she might have been fooled by the girl's demeanor. The picture of injured innocence, Cinderella managed to look stunningly lovely even as copious tears coursed down her face. If that wasn't magic, what was?

"What have you to say?" the king asked. "Is what she says true?"

Cinderella wrung her hands in such an obvious bid for sympathy that Griselda was surprised the entire assemblage didn't immediately condemn her.

"Some of it," Cinderella said in a small voice.

Surprised by the girl's admission, Griselda narrowed her eyes, wondering when the lies would come.

Cinderella gave the prince a nervous glance. "My mother's gentle spirit did use magic to reverse the effects of my mourning, but it was good magic, not evil. And she did it because she loved me, because she wanted me to look nice for the ball and the prince. You see, she knew how much it meant to me to win his heart . . . because I love him so."

What sheer, unadulterated pap. Why weren't they all gagging on this syrupy treacle?

"And your stepsisters?" the king asked. "Did you . . . alter their appearance?"

"No, Your Highness," Cinderella said with eyes cast meekly down. "They did that on their own. Solvig cannot pass by a sweet without putting it in her mouth and I understand Edda resembles her father."

"Ridiculous," Griselda declared. "How could my precious cherubs have grown into such hags without magical intervention? It is obviously a lie."

The king gestured at the magic-sniffer. "Your verdict?"

Bern descended from the dais and approached Edda and Solvig. They shrank back at his approach, but he did nothing more alarming than peer at them and sniff a bit. It was true, then. He really could smell magic.

Bern then went to Cinderella and took a whiff of her and the prince as well. But nothing showed on his expressionless face as he walked back to the king and stood by his side to whisper in his ear.

Griselda held triumph close in her breast. Now everyone would hear the truth, and she would be vindicated.

The king rose and perforce, the queen and prince rose as well. Drawing himself up to his full height, the king said, "We have made our decision."

Griselda's heart leaped in her breast. Finally.

"Bern has tested all three girls and has found no residue of magic anywhere on Edda or Solvig. Their appearance is unfortunate, but is not due to magic." He glared sternly at Griselda. "I suggest you do as Cinderella said and look to your first husband's features and your daughters' habits for the culprits."

"Nonsense. Cinderella must have bewitched—"

"Nor has the prince been enchanted," the king continued inexorably, not letting her finish. "Furthermore, Bern has determined that Cinderella is, in fact, a witch."

Murmurs filled the room and Griselda turned smug. Finally she would have justice.

"However," the king said, his voice rising above those of the court, "her magic is benign, not dark. There is no evidence that she has violated the law of three or that she has wished harm upon others."

"The law of three?" Griselda repeated in confusion. "What's that?"

Bern explained. "It is the law all witches abide by. They take a vow to harm none, for they know anything they do for good or ill shall be returned to them threefold."

"What? So you're saying she *is* a witch?" Griselda wanted to make this very clear.

The king answered. "Yes, but from your own testimony, it is obvious she used magic only to contact her mother's spirit, not for any personal gain. Her mother is the one who performed the rest of the magic, and benign magic at that."

Very confused now, Griselda could do nothing but sputter, "B–but she's a witch!"

The king nodded. "Indeed she is, and a very good one. Tell me, what made you imagine we would object to having this talent in the royal family?"

"But all witches should be burned at the stake," Griselda protested. "Everyone knows that."

The king shook his head sadly. "Only the ignorant believe so. And we have been working hard to stamp out this sort of misconception in our kingdom."

The queen glared at her. "This wicked woman's accusations against the future princess pose a danger to Cinderella, my family, and the kingdom. We cannot let her continue to spread her lies throughout the land."

The king pondered for a moment then nodded. "The queen has the right of it. Therefore, we find you and your daughters guilty of treason."

"Treason?" Griselda repeated in disbelief. "But—"

She broke off as she realized the king paid her no heed. Instead, he was listening to Cinderella who was now whispering urgently in his ear.

Nodding, he said, "Your stepdaughter has pleaded for clemency. As our wedding gift to her, we shall not order your execution. However, to ensure you are not allowed to spread your venomous views, you are banished from the kingdom immediately."

No, no, this couldn't be. Was she in the middle of a nightmare? "But, Sire, I——"

"Enough," the king thundered. "We have spoken. At Cinderella's request, we shall send you to join your sister in the land to the west."

The king waggled his fingers at them, and Griselda abruptly found herself and her daughters yanked out of the throne room and plopped into another place . . . a place with a strange-looking yellow pavement surrounded by low bushes and very short people.

The king is a witch as well? Why had she never suspected?

Suddenly, she heard Cinderella's disembodied voice, sounding concerned. "Be careful, Stepmother. Watch out for flying houses."

As Edda and Solvig ran screaming down the road, Griselda folded her arms and scoffed, "Flying houses, indeed. As well I might believe in flying monkeys."

"Mama, run," Edda cried as a shadow blocked out the sun.

But it was the last thing Griselda heard before the house landed on her head.

PEGGY PLAIN

by Devon Monk

Devon Monk lives in Salem, Oregon, with her husband, two sons, and a little dog, too. Her fiction has appeared in Year's Best Fantasy 2, Realms of Fantasy, and Black Gate. "Peggy Plain" is the third story set in the nursery crime world of Las Fables. The other two, "Nursery Crimes" and "Sugar n' Spice," appeared in Amazing Stories and Talebones, respectively.

IT WAS SUMMER in Las Fables, and hot enough that the weasels were popping. I'd just gotten a job as the community events reporter at the local newspaper, the *Six Pence Slinger*. Not exactly glam, but a girl has to take what she can get in this town. My name's Peggy Plain, and I'm a gal without a rhyme.

Of course, I planned to change that. All I had to do was be in the right place when something exciting happened. Then I'd have a rhyme, maybe even have my name added to The Book where anybody who's anybody in Las Fables is listed. And I'd be remembered.

Isn't that what everyone wants? To have their name remembered?

I'd gotten a lead that there was a new up-and-comer in town—a gal by the name of Bo Peep. I was on my way to interview her, maybe find out what she had that I didn't that got her noticed so quickly. I hurried down the yellow brick streets, dodging the monkeys chasing weasels. Overbaked gingerbread men crumbled as I passed. I rounded the corner at Paddy Cakes' Diner and crashed into someone.

"Sorry!" a male voice said.

A strong, callused hand reached out for me.

"Let me help you up. Are you okay?"

I looked up at the most handsome man I'd ever seen. He was tan and had green eyes. His hair was sun-tipped brown and a little mussed. He wore a white shirt, dark slacks, and loafers. When he smiled, he looked a little guilty, a little uncomfortable, a little shy.

My heart tumbled harder than Jill down a hill.

I put my hand in his. With a gentle tug, I was on my feet again and standing close enough I could smell tobacco and something sharp and pleasant, like pickling spices, on his breath.

"My name's Peter," he said, turning our handhold into a handshake. "Peter Peter, son of Peter Piper."

"The peckers?"

"Best peckers in Las Fables. And you are?"

"Peggy Plain." I couldn't seem to take my gaze off his face. But then, he wasn't looking away either.

He leaned closer and said, "I think I lost my heart—I mean hat. Hat. Right there on the bricks."

I knelt. We still didn't let go of each other's hands. I stood back up and looked at his hat before giving it back to him. "Oh. Are you a policeman?"

There was that shy smile again. "Just joined the force, but I hope to make detective someday."

"Will that take long?"

"Not if the right case comes along."

"Well, if I see anything out of the ordinary, I'll let you know." Three blind mice screamed and scampered down an alley, a mittenless kitten right behind them. "I'm a reporter for the *Six Pence Slinger*. I can use a contact person in the police department."

"I'm your man," he said.

"Everything okay, Peter?"

Peter Peter nodded at the man who stepped out of the diner. "Peggy, this is my partner, Jack. Horner, this is Peggy Plain."

"Pleased to meet you," Jack said. "We have to get back to the station, Peter. Paperwork."

Peter put his hat on, nodded, and walked away.

Forget about Bo Peep. I spent the rest of the day planning how to get Peter to ask me to marry him.

Over the next month, I found out everything I could about him. He had no rhyme, just like me. He was trying to make his name in Las Fables, just like me. And through the course of lunches, coffee, and eventually dinners and long walks, I knew he was in love, just like me.

Our marriage was a small affair. Our picture was in the paper, but not on the front page— just a little photo in the community section that read: *Peter Peter has a wife.*

They didn't even use my name.

We rented a house of sticks from the larcenous Pig brothers. It wasn't much, but it was home, and I was happy.

But Peter wasn't. At night, he'd stand out in front of the house, staring at the empty street that edged the Dark Enchanted Woods.

I put away the leftover pumpkin casserole, and went out to stand next to him. The woods were dark, and still as death.

"What are you looking at?" I asked.

"My future." He crushed his cigarette in the dirt and turned back to our shabby stick house. He tugged the door. Our dishes and spoons ran out of the house with a triumphant yell. Peter didn't even try to stop them.

I went to bed that night and stared through the cracks in the ceiling. A cat fiddled in the distance, and the lonely figure of Bessie crossed the moon.

"Is it me?" I asked Peter.

"No. Not you, Peggy."

"Is it work?"

He sighed and turned onto his back. "Maybe there isn't room in this town for a cop like me. All I do is shuffle paperwork and run background checks on flying monkeys. Maybe I should just go back to being a pecker. At least I was good at that."

I put my hand on his shoulder. "It's just that nothing exciting has happened yet. Your big case will come along soon."

Peter slid out bed and shrugged into his shirt. "I

don't need your pity, Peggy. I'm going for a walk."
He didn't come home that night.

I got out of bed before the cock a-doodled, and
made Peter poached pumpkin popovers. He came
home just as the sun rose over hill and dale. Without
a word, he ate breakfast, drank a cup of coffee, then
changed into his uniform. He didn't even kiss me
before he left for work.

I knew I had to do something to help him. While
I dried and tied our remaining dishes securely into
the cupboards, I had an idea. All Peter really needed
was a crime.

I was a reporter. I was smart. I was resourceful.
I just had to get a juicy story and send it Peter's
way.

I put on my shoes and coat and grabbed my official
Six Pence Slinger notebook. The notebook was a
sturdy wooden binder, made to hold up to any re-
porting situation. Time to go see that Bo Peep gal
who was causing such a stir among the royalty. I
hoped she had a shady past.

And who knew? Maybe on the way to Peter's big
break, I'd make a name for myself, too. Get my name
in a rhyme, my rhyme in The Book.

It took longer than I thought to track down Miss
Peep. The editor at the *Slinger* had no leads, and
neither did any of my contacts at Paddy Cakes'
Diner. Near as everyone could tell, she had moved
a lot since first coming to town. It was a little boy
who lived down the lane who told me he thought
he'd seen her up by the Charmings' castle. He said

the prince had taken a shine to her and was letting her use one of the royal meadows.

By the time I walked to the castle, I was tired and hot. Over in the meadow where the green grass grew were at least two dozen fluffy white sheep, munching away. I crossed the open field and nearly ran into Peep. She had a crook in one hand, and her bonnet was tossed back, revealing waves of shining golden locks. Her dress was so tight and cut so low, I didn't know how she moved in it.

She looked at me. Limpid blue eyes, perfect skin, pouting red lips. She was gorgeous, glamorous.

She was everything I wasn't.

Not that I was jealous.

"Bo Peep?" I asked.

"Yes." Even her voice was beautiful. Alto with a hint of an accent.

"I'm Peggy Plain—Peter. Peggy Peter. I work for the *Six Pence Slinger*, and I'd like to interview you."

"How sweet," she murmured. "Why don't you come sit in the shade of the haystack?"

I nodded, uncomfortably aware of what a sweaty mess I was after tramping around all day looking for her. I was also aware that she wasn't sweaty at all. She smelled like lavender.

On the other side of the haystack was a chair, a table with a pitcher and glass of lemonade, and a basket of yarn and knitting needles. She sat in the chair. Like a queen on her throne. Like she was used to being worshiped. Like she was somebody.

Like I wasn't.

I took out my heavy notebook and leaned against the haystack. "How long have you been in Las Fables?"

"A few months. Everyone's been wonderful. Especially the men." She picked up the tall glass of lemonade.

"Men? Like the prince?"

She took a drink, licked her lips. "Absolutely yummy," she purred. We both knew she wasn't talking about the lemonade. "Oh, but I don't suppose you understand that kind of thing, do you, Peggy Plain?"

"Peter," I said with a forced smile. "Peggy Peter." Truth was, I'd never even met the prince. I'd seen the king once or twice, just like I'd seen the rest of the royal family, his horses and men, during big events.

Already hot and tired, now I was getting angry. I decided to change the subject. "What exactly do you do with sheep? What are the hazards of sheepherding? Static cling?"

"Hardly," she said with a throaty laugh. "They have the finest wool—soft as silk, strong as a witch's curse. If even one sheep is lost, my customers—very important people you wouldn't know, Peggy dear—won't get the wool they need. This is a business," she added. "A real job. Not like writing silly stories for a tabloid."

Everything became very still. I could still feel the wind, could still hear boughs breaking and babies crying in the distant trees. But all I could think of was wiping that condescending smile off of her face. I lunged forward and knocked her over the head with my wooden notebook.

Her eyes rolled back in her head and she slumped to the ground.

But while I stood above her, my triumph faded to shock. What had I done? I knelt and checked for a pulse. She was still alive, just unconscious.

The sheep bleated. I glanced over at them. One was shuffling off, heading into town. What was I going to do? If I couldn't wake Peep, the sheep would wander off and get lost. That would be terrible. Her important customers wouldn't get their wool, it would hit the news, everyone in town would know, the police would investigate.

The police.

I took off Bo Peep's dress. Then I tied her hands and feet and used her handkerchief to gag her perfect mouth. I dragged her to the edge of the haystack and covered her with hay. I shucked out of my own dress and put on Peep's. It didn't fit me the same as it fit her, so I pulled the yarn out of the basket and stuffed my bodice. At the bottom of the basket was a jar of *Beautiful Thee* magic makeup powder and a mirror. I applied the powder to my face, my hair, my bare skin. I put on Peep's bonnet and looked in the mirror.

That magic powder was incredible. No more Peggy Plain. Looking back at me from the mirror was a gal who could give the fairest in the land a run for her money. My hair was gold, my lips soft, my skin perfect. I was glamorous. And now I knew Peep's secret. I smiled and hid the mirror and makeup. With one last check on the sleeping shepherdess, I strode out into the field.

It wasn't hard to lose the sheep. Once they were spooked, they took off in all directions. I could barely contain my excitement. All I had to do now was report the crime. I called the paper and left an anonymous tip that something big was happening in Charming's field.

Then I strolled to the police station, out of breath, and I hoped, prettily mussed.

Jack Horner came over from the corner. "Can I help you, Ma'am?"

Perfect. Not a glimmer of recognition on his face. Hopefully, this getup would fool Peter, too. "I need to report a crime," I said in the softest alto I could manage.

"Come right this way."

"No. I want to talk to Peter Peter. I'll wait here." Horner looked confused, but went off to fetch Peter.

Peter strode into the lobby, his strong, concerned face showing absolutely no clue that I was his wife. The magical powder was amazing!

The deception sent a delicious tingle under my skin. I batted my eyes and tried to look like I was in distress.

"Oh, Detective Peter," I breathed.

"Just Officer Peter, Ma'am," he corrected. "I haven't made detective yet."

I pouted. "Well, that can't be right. I heard you are the best police officer in Las Fables. Can you help me?"

"I'm here to serve, Ma'am. What's the trouble?"

"My sheep are lost. They ran away. Without them, I'll be ruined." I managed a sniffle, and Peter pulled a handkerchief out of his pocket.

"There, there, Miss . . ."

"Peep. Bo Peep."

"Miss Peep," he said. His voice had changed. It was softer, deeper. "Come into my office, and I'll help you fill out the sheets—sheafs. Sheafs of papers. Reports."

"How dare you—I mean there isn't time for that." I couldn't believe it! He was flirting with me—I mean with her—with Bo Peep. "Paperwork will take too long. My sheep might never be found. I need you to give me—I mean give this your personal attention."

I looked up at him through my lashes. *Come on*, I thought, *This is your big chance. Take it, Peter.* I leaned forward, showing a little more cleavage. "Please?"

That did it. Peter told me to wait while he got his hat, then he opened the door for me.

"Why don't you take me to where you last saw the sheep."

Just what I'd hoped for. While he was looking for sheep tracks, I'd run away home and wait for him to tell me all about his big case. But as we walked to the field, I began to sweat so hard, the powder was coming off. Peter kept glancing at me, his expression more and more troubled.

Luckily, there was quite a commotion at the field. All the king's horses and all the king's men were searching for the sheep. A crime-scene brick wall was being erected by the H. Dumpty Construction Company.

Reporters from the *Slinger* were nosing around and asking questions.

Peter didn't even pause. He took it all in, then, being the good cop he was, walked straight toward the haystack.

Where I had left Bo Peep.

Time to fly away home. I turned to make my hasty retreat.

"Hold on, Miss." One of the king's men put his hand around my arm. "Aren't you Little Bo Peep?"

"Uh," I stammered.

"Majesty. I found her!" he called out.

Charming himself, resplendent in ermine and red velvet, broke out of a crowd of horses and walked my way. I looked over and saw Peter kneel down at the edge of the haystack. He brushed hay away, and gently touched something there—Peep's hand!

I kicked the king's man in the shin. He yelped, and let go of me. I had to get out of there, get away, get rid of this disguise and get back home, before Peter found out I was me.

I headed for the opening in the brick wall. There was a worker on top of the wall, troweling mortar. I dashed by just as he swung his legs over the side of the wall to sit.

I collided with his legs and fell flat, knocking off my bonnet.

The worker yelled. I looked up. And saw Humpty Dumpty take the longest, slowest fall I had ever seen. He shattered on landing.

The rest was a blur.

The sheep showed up, wagging their tails behind

them. The real Bo Peep got a carriage ride with Charming up to the castle.

Humpty Dumpty couldn't be put together again, though all the horses and men were called over to try.

Peter took me in his arms before handcuffing me.

"Peter? What are you doing?" I asked.

"I have to take you in, Peggy. You're going to shell."

"On what charges?'

"Eggravated murder."

He threw me in the shell like a common criminal. Me, his wife, Peggy Plain.

He came by the next day, with a copy of the *Six Pence Slinger* under his arm.

"Why did you do it, Peggy?" He looked as if he hadn't gotten any sleep.

"I did it for you, Peter. To make you a detective. To give you a name, a rhyme."

He winced and looked out the triangular window carved in the side of the pumpkin. Somewhere down the row of gourds, a harmonica sang the blues.

"We wanted the same thing, right, Peter? Names? Rhymes?"

"No, Peggy. I just wanted happily ever after." He tossed the newspaper onto my cot and walked out of the shell. The warden locked the bars behind him.

I picked up the paper and read it with growing excitement. *New rhymes added to The Book. Peter Peter Pumpkin Eater had a wife. . . .*

I sat on my cot and smiled. Not exactly glam, and they hadn't used my name, but, hey, a girl has to take what she can get in this town.

HEATHCLIFF'S NOTES

by David Bischoff

David Bischoff studied English Literature at the University of Maryland, College Park—and then swerved into Radio, Television and Film. He worked for NBC until he started doing better financially as a novelist—and immediately switched media, although he's been known to dip back into script and production work at times. He now lives in Eugene, Oregon, with his wife Martha Bayless, an English professor at the University of Oregon, and their young son Bernie. Gothic motifs have often figured into Bischoff's fiction (The Selkie and The Judas Cross with Charles Sheffield and Mandala), but he's never gone so close to his literary sources before!

Whether it is right or advisable to create beings like Heathcliff I do not know; I scarcely think it is.

—Currer Bell

CALL ME Heathcliff.
  Captain Ahab does.
We were down at the Hellfire Club one night, hav-

ing a smoke and a laugh, and after a game of snooker, he clumped on up to a great big leather bag by a club chair and pulls out a slim volume.

THE NATIONAL HARPOON
My Story
Captain Ahab

"Heathcliff, my boy," he said, in that New England salt accent of his. He patted my shoulder. "We're characters in two classic novels making a mint for publishers. Why shouldn't we profit a little ourselves?"

"Indeed, sir," I said. "My consulting business used to prosper, and there is still a little salt pork and hardtack laid up, so to speak, for Catherine and me in CloudCuckooLand."

"Aye, and, alas, I hear that Catherine has been taking in washing from Virginia Woolf and the Bloomsbury snobs lately. She's a proud lass. Can't be likin' that much, eh?"

I admitted as much.

He stomped his peg leg emphatically. "Aye! So what you'll be needing to do is to write yourself a book. Mebbe a commentary on *Wuthering Heights*, then."

"There's more than a few dozen of those."

"Aye, but none with the true story, eh?"

"No. You're in the same boat with me, Heathcliff. You die at the end of your novel. No sequels for us!"

So I think.

I think of a slim volume for some college class somewhere, some dry crib sheet.

WUTHERING HEIGHTS DIGESTED
by Heathcliff, Esq.

SYNOPSIS

In the eighteenth century, a wonderful Yorkshire farmer and owner of the house called Wuthering Heights, Mr. Earnshaw, brings a cute waif home after a trip to Liverpool. The waif, called Heathcliff, immediately is loved by Earnshaw's daughter Catherine and loathed by Earnshaw's son Hindley (the bloody bastard!). Catherine and Heathcliff run wild in the moors and hide behind bushes and play doctor. When they reach puberty, they play lots of "toad in the hole." However, Mr. Earnshaw and his wife die (sigh!). Then true calamity strikes. Catherine suffers an injured ankle and is tended by the Linton Family at the hoity-toity Thrushcross Grange for five weeks. Catherine gets all polite and civilized, decides to social climb and ditches Heathcliff to marry Edgar Linton. Angry, Heathcliff storms off.

When Heathcliff returns three years later, looking rich and well-garbed, Catherine is pregnant with Edgar Linton's child. Catherine realizes the bad mistake she has made. Heathcliff realizes he can't forget his dearest soul, his Catherine. Alas, Catherine dies giving birth to Edgar Linton's daughter, Cathy.

Vowing revenge, Heathcliff encourages Hindley to drink himself to death. He marries Edgar's sister Isabella and

*has a son, Linton. Heathcliff tries to marry Cathy to
Linton . . . but . . . but . . . oh, drat.
I forget.*
   THEME
   *Emily Bronte achieved revenge on millions of adolescent
males in high school, forced to read her book.*
   SETTING
   *Thunder. Lightning. Mist. Fog. Heather. Moors. Sheep
dip. Porridge and French-fried Mars Bars.*

"No, I guess not, Ahab. No retelling." I smiled
grimly. But if there's to be a book by me with the
truth about *Wuthering Heights*, it would have to be
about that romance novelist from the future."

Now, being a literary character for quite a time, I,
Heathcliff, know my way around a few literary
terms. The most useful in the telling of this, my tale,
is the term "thesis."

Now, what thesis has to do with, say, old Ahab's
prosthesis (ie, peg leg in place of limb bitten off by
Moby Dick himself), I can't say. I can say that thesis
(ie, statement of intent at the beginning) is useful to
understand the gist of what I have to relate here.

My thesis is that this, dear reader, is the relating
of Heathcliff's missing years.

Now mind you, I hadn't a clue and supposed I'd
just gone off poaching in the woods for those many
seasons. Ms. Bronte certainly would have you believe
I was in no good spirits and had more than one mean
streak in my Yorkshire body. In fact, if you may re-

call, I disappeared from Wuthering Heights when I learned that Catherine had feelings for Edgar Linton and saw him as a ladder into social climes unavailable to her through me, with my limited funds, education, and breeding. The fact that I preferred to be dirty and disheveled most of the time perhaps assisted her decision. For years in the moors when she thought she smelled a foul odor, I told her it was sheep dip. In fact, it was always me.

Churlish, nasty, and extreme of temper as the weather itself in the north of Blighty, I was booted hence from the novel, only to reappear when my cue was called three years later.

This gap did not go unnoticed by the exceedingly ambitious novelist, Barbara Carthorse.

"Heathcliff."

"Yes, Catherine, my soul."

"You haven't paid the lightning bill. And the thunder department called the other day to say that unless their requests for funds are met, we'll have no booms and rumbles ever again." She leaned over the breakfast meal of toast, marmite, and heather tea, her hair wild and her beautiful eyes flashing. "How's a stormy romantic heroine to roam the moors without the proper elements accompanying her immortal dance?"

Needless to say, Catherine's a drama queen. But then, so am I, especially on cross-dressing day in the Hellfire Club. (Lord Byron in a tutu, Shelley in a camisole, Keats in a prom dress—oh, what a sight!)

However, the figures upon the paper were clear enough. Heathcliff and Catherine, Yorkshire Moors, 9121, England UK . . . were broke.

"A shame, my dear heart, that we did not save the money from our consulting in those boom years of Gothic paperbacks."

"Aye. When those thick historical romances came along, Heathy, it wasn't only bodices that got ripped."

It was really a pleasant day in our part of Cloud-CuckooLand. The graves on the hill were properly moldering, the kirk in the glen was shining like a Thomas Kinkade painting on acid, and with a few morning ales in me, and my dogs snarling at my shins, I was ready for a proper good slog through some ripping muck. Ah, let me tell you, there's nothing like being a virile romantic male riding on the back of the North wind with a cask of brew in your gut and a good-lookin' lass pulling her knickers back up and smiling at you gratefully.

Too bad this wasn't totally that sort of day, what with the bills fluttering on the plank table.

"Have we ever heard back from the Copyright Office?"

"There's no hope of that, Heathcliff."

"Perhaps a guest star shot in a Dickens novel?"

"He's suffered the same fate."

"A musical, perhaps. Surely that would put us back into clover. I'll give Andrew Lloyd Webber a call. He was 'round the Hellfire Club t'other day, sniffing about."

"Hmmf. You'd think so. Well, I suppose I'll have to take in some washing again from the Bloomsburys down the road." She held out her hands toward me. "Look at these poor mitts. Och! I'm working my bones to the nubs, Heathcliff. At least Edgar knew how to provide for a girl properly."

I reached for her with one arm and started unbuttoning myself to give the lass some good Yorkshire comfort.

She slapped me away, the spirited wench. "You'll get no more of that, Heathcliff." She pounded the bills. "Until we're in proper thunder and lightning!"

I went down to the pub, got a pint, and used their phone to call my agent.

"Lou. How's the pastrami today?"

"A little fatty, but some nice rye. Heathcliff! Haven't heard from you for a dog's age. How's Cathy?"

"Passionate. Broke. We need some money, Lou. How's the romance market consultancy?"

"Bad. Bottom's dropped out of the book market and every other romance is written by Nora Robots."

"Gods! Is she the one who thought *Wuthering Heights* was a section of San Francisco?"

"Nah. Look, come to think of it, Armageddon's big these days. Think you might be able to help inspire some brooding AntiChrists?"

"The Great Hereafter sure isn't Hereafter money problems, Lou. Sure. I'd appreciate anything you can dig up for me."

"Call me in an hour."

An hour and a couple pints later, I put my shillings in the coin slot again.

"Heathcliff, I got something for you."

"Excellent, Lou. What?"

"Ever hear of "para-abnormal romances?""

I had to sober up some and go back to the Heights to get my corporeal form. It was hanging in a closet and hadn't been laundered for a while. I didn't figure Cathy would want to clean it, what with her own heavy laundry work, so I just buffed it up some, sprayed on some Right Guard, and rubbed some fresh dirt on the face.

I never liked going to the United States much, but that was where the Gothic business was for two decades, so I pretty much got used to it. I did some business through Ouija boards and mediums, but I knew I always profited most through my brooding brow and my dark intense eyes.

Barbara Carthorse had a big house in northern New Jersey, outside Mahwah. She had a stable and horse and a pond and lived by a lake. Lou said she'd done big business with bodice rippers in the seventies and Judith Krantz-type romances in the eighties, but then she'd put her time and money into jetsetting, computers, and young husbands. Now she was back down to a few million dollars and was looking to break into the publishing business again.

"What I've got to do is to write books sharp enough and big enough to start their own subgenres. Let's face it, that's what Mary Stewart did in the fifties."

I sipped at my martini. "Mary's a dear friend."

"She ever use you?"

"No, but my close friend Merlin did all right by her."

"Whatever." She went and opened the French window. A breeze blew in from the lake. She was one of those sixty year olds who've had so much plastic surgery and Botox that they look like gorgeous twenty-five year olds from far away and dead twenty-five year olds close up. She was wearing a riding outfit and was eyeing my rough-hewn corporeal form the way all the old horny romance ladies always eyed it. With curiosity and no small amount of lust. I'm glad I put a few dog turds in my pocket. Excellent talismans to keep 'em away.

"When your agent called, I was brainstorming with myself and riding out by the river. Funny, it was dark and stormy down away and I thought of nineteenth-century romantic literature."

"You've read *Wuthering Heights*?"

"Of course I have. I've got a Masters in Classics from Smith!"

"I'm very happy to hear that."

I drank the rest of my martini down and held out my glass for another. The butler came by and filled me up. One thing you can say about the twenty-first century. The gin's gotten quite a bit better than the eighteenth.

"And so, here you are. Heathcliff. And you know what? I can use you in a novel!"

My impressive brow furrowed. "I don't understand. I generally just consult. And there've been no complaints. My type of hero has gone out of style, true. Mr. Rochester and I have had a long talk about this, and we agree that it's because of this feminist nonsense. Women just aren't afraid of men anymore. The mystery and allure are gone."

"Too true. But I'm thinking postmodern here, Mr. Heathcliff. And I think I can use you. The call from Lou on my cellular right in the middle of my musings on the classics gave me just the inspiration I needed from you. And so, here you are . . . Are you prepared for a great deal of money?"

I raised a ragged eyebrow. "Aye. Catherine would love that!"

"It will be work—but I promise it'll be an adventure.'

I scratched my head. "Can't say as I like work or adventures, much. But things are getting a bit boring about Wuthering, so maybe I could use a holiday. And as far as money goes—I could use a new set of Wellies."

"Good." She snapped her fingers. My martini glass got filled again, with an extra olive. "Now, then. We're in the twenty-first century, Heathcliff. We're postmodern here."

"Ah," I said, pretending to understand what she was talking about.

She pulled out a cigarette and the butler lit it for her. "Postmodern. Yes. In other words, we're having a damned hard time making up stuff of our own—so we steal from the past."

"Ah." I shrugged. "Well, you'll be paying me, then, won't you?"

"Exactly. Now there's been a sequel to *Gone With The Wind* by Margaret Mitchell."

"Right. Rhett Butler. We used to play cards . . ."

"Can't hold a candle to you, dearie, for moody heroes."

"Ta."

"There have been sequels and prequels to everything, from the *Forsythe Saga* to *Jane Eyre*."

"Rochester told me about that one."

I was starting to catch the drift of the conversation . . . and I was getting a little worried. Reader, I gulped the rest of my third martini.

"Movies and TV serials of course. Big money. But to my knowledge, no one's exploited--ah . . . pondered and used the blanks."

"Pardon?"

"Those three years you were gone from Wuthering Heights, Heathcliff. After Catherine threw you over for Edgar Linton. What did you do?"

I shrugged. "Moped and skulked, I suppose. Found some loot and breeding to boot."

"There's not a phrase or a jot of dialogue that would suggest that you didn't go to Mars, now, is there?"

"Mars!" I said and stood up, spraying spittle and martini.

"Oh, do calm yourself, you big ox," Barbara Carthorse laughed. "Sci fi is so out in the twenty-first!"

I sat down and happily accepted my fourth martini.

"Ah," I said. "But Lou mentioned something called "para-abnormal romances . . ."

"Exactly. They started as 'paranormal romances.' That is, they were romances involving spooks and supernatural stuff and maybe a touch of sci fi . . . Especially time travel."

"Time travel. Hmmm."

"Here's the high concept, Heathcliff. I write a blockbuster and you're the star. And here's what you're really going to like . . . it's going to happen in the years you were away from Wuthering Heights. And there's going to be a romance in it. . . . Your romance with a beautiful succulent young woman."

"Not Catherine? She'll kill me."

"Catherine's off having a baby with Edgar Linton!"

I nodded. "Indeed." I felt the old ire rising. I felt my nostrils flare and a snarl creep upon my lips.

"My! You are a fearsome one. And yet, incredibly handsome . . . underneath all that dirt."

I glowered at her. The martinis made me moody.

She clapped her hands with joy. "Oh, yes! *The Dark And The Passion* will be a one-hander romance!"

"One-hander?" I asked, a little taken aback.

"One hand holding the book, the other . . . well, never mind."

The appropriate image entered my mind. I promised myself to live more simply in the future and make the money earned on this job last.

When I got back home, Catherine was working out a new moss-dance routine. "I almost wish I could do morris dancing instead of moss dancing," she said as I crouched down by our dinner rock for a cup of tea to try to sober me up.

"God! Morris dancing! Those bells, those sticks—
they're enough to annoy the dead. They certainly
annoy this spirit."

"Moss dancing is quite a bit more quiet, but there's
not a lot of rules to it," said Catherine.

"Better than the lichen stuff they do up in
Scotland."

She shrugged and sat down to join me for the tea.

"I've got a job," I told her.

"Good. Consulting?"

"That's right." I'd already decided not to divulge
the whole story. I didn't quite understand it anyway,
so how could I explain something I didn't understand?

"You'll be away a while then?"

"Aye."

"What about the dogs?"

"It'll be the kennel for them, I suppose."

"Very well."

She glared at me.

I glared at her.

"Oh, Heathy!"

"Oh, Catherine! My life! My soul!"

We were in each other arms immediately, and we
rolled and moaned around the moors for a few days,
scaring the wildlife.

Who needed thunder and lightning, anyway?

When I awoke from my passions, the earth was
still moving.

Or the earth seemed to be moving. In fact, there
was a good bit of swaying back and forth, and the

smell of brine and body odor. I peered about me in the dimness, and determined that I must be in the hold of a ship.

After some moments of disorientation, I also realized I was in a hammock. Born in Liverpool, a waif and orphan, I was informally adopted by Mr. Earnshaw and so introduced into the Earnshaw family. My life was the land and the moors—and it would appear now, I was literally where I had spent so many years figuratively: at sea.

I managed to haul myself out of bed and clamber around sufficiently to find a wooden ladder in the dimness. Desperately, I needed some wind. Some wuthering would be nice, too. I climbed up and pushed open a door above my head. I crawled out upon a deck. I got a blast of fresh sea air, and I filled my lungs with its life. I pulled myself out onto the deck and took a moment to take stock of myself. Away from the dank and foul belowdecks, I felt much better. In fact, I felt marvelous. I felt a great deal . . . larger. I touched my arms and found that my biceps were much larger. I looked down and even from that viewpoint I could tell that I had a larger chest and narrower waist. I looked about and noticed that from a yardarm there hung a small shaving mirror. I went over and looked at myself. Ye gods! I was a handsome brute—and young again—in full arrogant prime.

And despite the days of rolling about with Catherine, I felt as randy as a ram in springtime. I had the taste of youth in my mouth and the touch of destiny in my bearing. In short, I felt a lot better alive than dead . . . and better than I'd ever felt when actually alive before that silly hunger strike of mine at the end of *Wuthering Heights*.

Zounds! This Carthorse woman could write!

For, dear reader, as you may surmise, I was now in this new novel. Again I was a character in a book—only this one looked to be a great deal more fun than the others. Indeed, it looked to be a nice thick pleasure-swamp of words, bound together cheaply and stamped with a lurid cover of a man and a woman in historical outfits, clearly clamped onto each other and about to embark upon the embrace that rhymes with "duck."

Yes, and look! I could see it clearly then in my mind! The hero, he of the dark brown and long romantic hair, and of a mighty hairless chest bursting through a shirt—it is me, Heathcliff! And lo, in his arms, is a woman so searingly beautiful and buxom as to make my own dogs howl. Aye, my Catherine is nothing to kick out of the moors, but then a lifetime of porridge, berries, and roots didn't put much flesh on her. These paperback vixens swell from their clothing like muffins of promise, begging to be squeezed and plundered. Ah, to think—Heathcliff in the clinch with one of these pneumatic wonders of feminine pulchritude!

I wondered when the lucky wench would show herself. Soon, I should think, for there were no masts on the horizon, no cutlasses peeking up from the forecastle, and no other promise of any other sort of action in this universe of page-turning.

Indeed, I did not have to wait long.

Soon there were the undelicate sounds of retching beyond the poop deck. I hastened forward to be of help. Young and eager Heathcliff, come to succor!

In fact it was a damosel! She stood against the rail, leaning outward toward the waves. She wore large skirts and a blouse of utilitarian design, and she was dabbing at her mouth with a handkerchief.

However, instead of long and lustrous and blonde, her hair was dark and wiry—though certainly comely enough, I suppose, for those who like that sort of thing. She was slender--in fact, not at all of the luscious form on most romantic paperback covers.

"Good morning," I said. "May I be of help?" I said, eager to do my duty. It occurred to me too late that it would be more in character to make some nasty remark. Or in fact, was I even in charge of what I said, seeing as presumably Carthorse was writing the dialog here?

The woman spun around. She had a long, plain face. Narrow brown eyes regarded me s suspiciously from behind spectacles. "Can't a person have any privacy on this ship? I shall have to complain to the captain!"

"It looks as though you are seasick, ma'am." I said. "I am told that a bit of rum and sodomy help."

"Who are you?"

"My name, madam, is Heathcliff."

" Heathcliff? You're Heathcliff?"

"At your service, madam!"

"You'd better believe you're at my service!" She smiled, looking as though she felt a good deal better. "My name is Lady Folderol. We are sailing for the colonies, and you, Heathcliff, are my indentured servant for ten years."

I felt the bottom go out of my bowels. "Indentured servant? I assure you, madam, my teeth are quite real!"

"Ha! Snappy comeback. You are an arrogant one, Heathcliff." She swept up to me and looked at me with great ferocity. Then she pulled her arm back, fisted her hand, and punched me in the mouth.

Reader, I saw stars.

The next thing I knew, I was on my foundation, looking up at Lady Folderol, fingering my jaw. "Ah, madam. You are a saucy wench."

"And take this, too, you scum." She kicked me with a boot in the midriff. I grunted. I confess, it hurt, but it was not a kind of pain that wasn't easily borne. I felt as though I were playing a role, and as actor, it was my duty to fulfill my part.

"What is this for?" I asked.

"For Linton and Edgar and Hareton and even Mr. Lockwood and Nelly Dean and all the people you harmed and abused, Heathcliff!"

"But I've harmed no one—I mean, this is the 1770s, correct? All that hasn't happened yet."

"You are trying to escape your full due, you scoundrel!" She swirled around. "Captain. If you please. You are needed above decks. With your men."

Suddenly, sailors sprouted willy-nilly from everywhere, and a man with a tricornered cap and a patch over his eye appeared.

"Captain! You will have my servant kneelhauled for his crimes," cried Lady Folderol.

"That be a bit nasty, ma'am," said the captain, clumping down beside my mistress.

"Why?" demanded Lady Folderol.

The captain whispered in her ear.

"Oh, my. That's keelhauling?"

"Aye, and there be plenty of nasty barnacles 'neath this barge!"

"Well, let's flog him, then."

"Aye, that's a bit better."

The next thing I knew I was being manhandled by a bunch of sailors and tied to the yardarm. My shirt was ripped, exposing the rippling muscles beneath. I heard a little gasp from my mistress, and for a moment I thought I'd have mercy. But, no, the next thing I knew, she was demanding a cat-o'-nine-tails and started personally laying into me.

Again, I felt pain, but it was bearable. I felt no particular stripes or cuts in my back, but I grimaced and howled enough for ten men, and that seemed to gratify Lady Folderol no end. She gave me two or three lashings for each of the characters that I'd wronged in *Wuthering Heights*—that is, *all* of them— one for my dogs and other animals, and then a couple more for good measure.

I gave one more cry, one more gasp, and then pretended to faint away from the pain.

She stopped immediately.

"He's not dead, is he?"

"That's hard to say, ma'am."

"Oh, no! I didn't mean to kill him. I'm supposed to have him for another ten years."

From squinted eyes I saw the bos'n come over. He grabbed my neck and felt for a pulse. The next thing I knew, I was being untied and then taken to the ship's doctor. My wounds were covered with stinging astringent—aaugh!—and then I was placed in a comfortable bed. Not seeming to have had a pleasant night's sleep previously, I took the opportunity to immediately fall into a deep, dreamless sleep.

I was awoken by the sound of someone crawling into the bed.

"Oh, Heathcliff!"

I felt lithe arms and naked legs twine about me. A luxurious and languid perfume invaded my nostrils. The arms tightened emphatically.

"Oh, Heathcliff, I am so sorry. Are you alive?"

"Yes. I think so," I said. I became aware that the body pressing against me was quite naked and not at all unpleasant.

"Oh, Heathcliff, you are so bad, but you are so powerful! You are a very bad apple in the orchard of literature."

"I thank you. I think. Lady Folderol?"

"Not really. Actually, I am Lydia Foursquare, graduate in honors from Wellesley, PhD in nineteenth-century literature, Harvard University. Oh, and, Heathcliff—I am here to save you!"

"Save me?"

"Yes, my darling. I have read *Wuthering Heights* over and over, and am convinced that it should be changed. And, by your redemption, so can nineteenth-century literature itself be transformed into a healing salve for the world, that there may be peace and joy and equal employment opportunity for women in the twentieth and twenty-first centuries!"

"Save me? From what?"

"From resentment and anger and torment. And thus when you return to *Wuthering Heights,* you will do good, not evil!"

"Ah—but how then can I be true to my true wild nature?" I said. "How can I be as cold as the winter blizzard and warm as the summer solstice sun? How can I personify the link between man and the earth?"

"Oh, shut up, you wicked fool, and kiss me!"

I was suddenly well overwhelmed with Folderol.

"And let me tell you, Ahab," I told Captain A. over a pint of bitter at the H. Club when I got back. "That woman knew her way around the sexual atlas."

Those bushy eyebrows rose. "Please, sir. I am a prude, and can quote the Good Book extensively." He glanced around to make sure no literary critic was listening in. "But please, do go on!"

"We went to the Americas all right, and we rogered in Boston and we rogered in Philadelphia. But, aye, what should come up but the American Revolution!"

"What? Washington, Cornwallis, that lot?"

"Indeed."

"Are the dates correct?"

"Fudged, in fact, I believe—but then, sir, I do not believe that Mrs. Carthorse means to have scholars for an audience."

"And so, what happened?"

"Well, we rogered some more!"

"No. I mean, at the American Revolution."

"The colonies won their independence."

He looked as though he wished he had his hands on a harpoon. "The plot. This infernal novel, man."

"Oh. It only covered a year of my indentureship. But after a year of service—in more ways than one, I assure you—the lady professor set me free, for I had saved her life and showed that I was no longer the evil and resentful Heathcliff of the moors, but the New Heathcliff . . . perhaps redeemed."

"And then?"

"And then, sir—I damned her eyes and bought a ticket back to Blighty."

"No."

"Yes."

"Excellent. A page right out of *Gone With The Wind*."

"Page 568, as a matter of fact."

"Good for you, m'lad."

"Well, there's two more years before I go back to the Heights, so I suppose there's any amount of sequels to be squeezed out of them by Carthorse."

"And plenty more rogering. Damn! And all I've had lately was an option from Disney for *Galactic Moby Dick*."

"Maybe you need my agent. Buy him a lean pastrami on fresh rye and a kosher pickle. He'll love you."

"Aye. Aye, m'lad. I thank ye." So Ahab clapped his hand on my shoulder and bid me Godspeed.

I sipped at my brandy until I saw Byron come in and head for the billiard table. I went over to get some tips on stamina. It looked as though the years away from the Heights were going to be the longest of my life.

"Heathcliff."

"Yes, Catherine, my life, my soul."

"I am very pleased."

I took her hand and gazed deeply into her stormy eyes. Ah, bliss.

"The bill is not merely paid, but the Wuthering Fund was a brainstorm."

"So to speak, my love. So long as the Fiduciary Celestial is solvent, the interest shall pay for not just the thunder and lightning, but the wind, the rain—and the bitter cold."

"And you, Heathcliff—the fire."

"And you, my soul, the sun itself."

We kissed and held hands and danced a heathery dance.

"So, Heathcliff?"

"Yes, my love."

"Exactly how did you come by all this loot? You were gone for a very long time."

"My love, let us just say—I exploited my literary prowess. I no longer star in just one great book. I star in many bad books."

She lifted her eyebrow. "Ah. Well then, you'll not be unhappy to hear that our fortunes have improved otherwise, then."

"Oh?"

"Yes, and I suppose it is time to show you something."

She took me by the hand. We swept along the blowing moors to the music of the winds, and down into a calm valley, where rested Thrushcross Grange. Instead of the old eighteenth-century house though, there was now a grand mansion replete with patio, swimming pool, and tennis court.

Catherine's eyes flared with challenge. "And my walk-in closet is filled with nice clothes and fashionable shoes. And there's a hot tub in the bathroom. The Heights and the moors are all very well, Heathcliff. But a girl's got to have some luxury from time to time."

I felt the old venom rise, but calmed it. In truth, the centuries had soothed me and my vintage was mellower. Besides, I fancied this sort of house had a wet bar, and I had grown fond of martinis and olives.

"Oh, my love—a series of novels with you as well? But you died at such a young age."

She shrugged. "Fantasy and imagination are such wonderful things—especially if there are sequels, prequels—or equals involved.

"Equals?"

"Alternate dimensions, my love. Did you know that somewhere out there in literary land, it is Heathcliff who dies in childbirth?"

I shuddered.

There was a chiming sound—Beethoven's Fifth, I believe.

Catherine plucked a cellular phone from somewhere about her person and answered the call. "Yes,

Lou? What? Scarlett O'Hara versus Catherine Earnshaw? I don't think so." She firmly clicked off the connection and turned to me. "Come, Heathcliff. Let us haunt these moors again a few years before we work."

"Aye, my soul. It is good to be dead!"

So, hand in hand, heart in heart, we strolled through the hills of eternity. We watched the moths fluttering among the heath and harebells, listened to the soft wind breathing through the grass and wondered how anyone could ever imagine unquiet couplings of the lusty departed in this wild earth.

CUCKOO'S EGG

by Jody Lynn Nye

Jody Lynn Nye lists her main career activity as "spoiling cats." She lives northwest of Chicago with three of the above and her husband, author and packager Bill Fawcett. She has published twenty-five books, including six contemporary fantasies, three SF novels, four novels in collaboration with Ann McCaffrey, including The Ship Who Won; *edited a humorous anthology about mothers,* Don't Forget Your Spacesuit, Dear!; *and written over seventy short stories. Her latest books are* Myth-Told Tales *and* Myth Alliances, *cowritten with Robert Asprin.*

THIS IS THE WORST day of my life. Standing in the aisle of Winchester Abbey Church, wearing a priceless, blue silk tunic imported from Ind, it was my duty, my father Count Sir Ector would say, my honor, to introduce the king to his subjects for the very first time.

As he rose from his knees with the crown on his head, I announced to the crowd filling the stone church and spilling out into the bright, thin winter sunshine, "My lords and ladies, I, Kay, Steward of His Highness, wish to present to you Arthur, High King of all the Britons." And along with all of those attending except the Christian bishop, I had to drop to one knee as he passed. I almost reached out and yanked the purple cloak from his thin shoulders, but even the decorous nature of the occasion wouldn't keep my father from beating me black and blue afterward.

Out of the church processed the knights and ladies, nobles from all over, the lesser kings, visiting royalty, the wizard Merlin in swirling dark blue robes spangled with stars, my esteemed father and, at the rear, the guest of honor, newly revealed as His Highness the king, lord of the isle of Britain, son of King Uther Pendragon and his queen Ygraine, my obnoxious little brother, Arthur.

Of course, he was not really my brother. Well I recall the night he was brought to our home, the castle of Joyous Gard. In the middle of a frosty, starry night, shortly after Christmas, a lone rider roused the guards at the gates and demanded entry, though the way was barred until morning to all comers. Certain statements by the visitor brought my burly, red-faced father out of bed and down to the causeway in the cold and wet, and made him open the doors. The visitor bore a burden, a prune-faced baby who began to wail as soon as he was revealed to my father and mother in their private chambers.

Having a small command of the Arts Magickal myself, I know now that no one was supposed to remember that it was the wizard Merlin who had brought the babe. I, five years old at the time, awakened by the hubbub, made my sleepy way into the room, my straw-colored hair tousled about my head.

"Has Merlin brought one of his bastards here to live?" I asked in my piping voice and my ignorance. My father clouted me without turning around. Wizards were supposed to have given all their vitality to their magic; none was meant to be left for family. In any case, I should not have voiced what was in my and everyone else's thoughts.

Mother, a slender, black-haired lass with huge hazel eyes, loved the babe on sight. I thought it must be wizardry, but I have since come to know that all women respond to babies so. It keeps them from drowning the pesty brats when they cry. Arthur, for such was his name, was put into the hungry arms of my mother, who had just lost another child, a baby sister who was given a name just in time to save her from the demons in the graveyard. Arthur took to my mother Olivia's nipple like a river pike attacking its prey. The sight sickened me, though I was already five and had no further need of her milk. He was a grasping, needy child. I couldn't stand him from the start.

But, come the morning, every soul in the castle accepted the babe as if he had always been there. Only my father and mother and I remembered how he had come to us, thrust into our peaceful lives. Mother loved him. Father hovered over him protectively. To me, he was no more welcome than a cuckoo's egg that had been laid in a songbird's nest. The troublesome chick that hatched out clamored for all the attention my parents had to give, leaving me, the real son of the house, without the proper love and guidance that they owed me.

And for what sorry scrap of humanity? Arthur was small, no bigger than a wart on a frog, and so we came to call him when my father was not around.

The Wart got in the way of every single thing I did. As soon as he could crawl, he started following me around. With a gleeful crow he'd lunge for me across the rush-strewn floors, falling over and fouling himself in the process, then rising eager to embrace me and smear me with whatever he was covered with.

As soon as Arthur could stagger upright, Father insisted that I include him in my games. My friends teased me about having a little shadow. I resented him with all my heart. How unjust it was that a lowborn, nameless brat should have so much influence with my parents! And when we did include him, he whined that we were running too fast or climbing too high or hitting too hard in our mock sword battles. Arthur was such a bore, always whining when he got knocked down. He followed me everywhere. I put up with it, patiently, I thought, until I could stand it no longer. I pleaded with my father for privacy, but he didn't listen. Arthur could do no wrong, and he got away with murder because of it.

He was such a weaselly little boy, afraid of everything. During thunderstorms he'd wet his own bed, then come and sleep with me because he was afraid, and then he'd wet *my* bed. I was cuffed if I complained.

One of the unexpected bonuses, though, was that when Arthur turned five years of age, Merlin came to live with us. He occupied the top of the northwest tower of the keep, and after my father built sturdy wooden shutters to block out the wind, it was nice and warm up there. Merlin liked to be up high because birds came and went from his rooms all the time, rooks by day and owls by night. I got to recognize some of them, including a big rook with an unusual white feather in his left wing. After Merlin had moved in all of his philosophical devices and books, he started Wart and me on magic lessons.

I quite enjoyed grinding herbs and chanting charms. It wasn't like cooking, where you got greasy and hot. I'd always been very precise, and it paid off when my potions got exactly the results that Merlin demanded. The wizard was pleased and surprised at my talent, all the more so because his bastard son (or so I thought at the time), the clear reason he was teaching us in the first place, fell behind me in lessons, even taking into account the five years between us in age. I could hear the birds' speech when all Arthur could distinguish was noisy squabbling. I saw the glint of fairy wings over the spring flowers, and Arthur even missed the butterfly flapping beside her. As a result, I was dismissed from the lessons by Merlin so as not to take time away from his golden child. That was the moment I decided I was going to have to kill Arthur one day.

But I didn't—quite the opposite, in fact. Gensa, my father's half Saxon steward, used to take us on hikes over our land, teaching us the woodland ways, showing us what a properly plowed furrow looked like, holding up sprigs of growing things so we could see how they were in every stage of development. A spicy smell in the air—not a smell, really, but a feeling inside my forehead—told me that Merlin was tagging along behind us. He could move as silently as a shadow even in heavy boots, something I learned to my cost when he would catch me teasing his brat and twisted my ear long before I knew he was there. If the magic lessons did nothing else, they gave me a beacon signal to know he was around.

Anyway, Gensa trotted across a log bridge that spanned the trout stream. I followed after him, and Arthur followed me. The log had been there a long while, and its upper surface had been worn flat by the passage of many feet. It was wide enough for a man's foot. Don't ask me why it wasn't big enough for those little pins Arthur walked on. He missed his footing and plunged into the fast-moving water.

"Help! Glub!" he cried, as the current swept him along. I spotted Merlin among the trees, his hawk's face alarmed. They say wizards can't cross water. I knew for certain that one couldn't swim. Gensa was too far away. With a groan I jumped off the log into the cold water and started kicking toward the boy.

Arthur wasn't doing much to save himself. He'd panicked, the worst thing one could do, and was swallowing water. With a stronger kick, I caught up with him and grabbed him by the collar. The wool of his tunic was slimy when wet. I squeezed hard so as not to lose my grip, then towed the struggling boy to the bank.

Both men were upon us before I reached it. They hauled Arthur out, Merlin exclaiming like a hen with one chick, and pounded the water out of his lungs. As usual, they all made a fuss of him, taking no notice of me until I sneezed. They bundled us home and put us in front of a fire.

"Kay saved me," Arthur croaked over a mug of sweetened chamomile tea as my mother fussed and my father blustered. "He jumped in and saved me."

But not a word of thanks did I get from anyone but him. My only reward was a bad cold.

After that Arthur stuck to me like a burr. He broke my things, including a real glass vase from Rome a hundred years old that I kept near the window for the way it caught the light. He borrowed my books and lost them. The crowning insult was that my mother got it into her head that he would be the better for a sunnier chamber, and swapped his room for mine one day while we were out hunting.

"But why?" I howled furiously.

"He needs a space of his own," Mother said. "The extra warmth will do him good. You're nearly a man. You're strong enough to face discomfort."

Not nearly a man; I was eleven. What was next, that he would take my place as Ector's heir? One day, I vowed, one day the little brat would serve me as my squire. No more warm bedroom to himself. He was going to sleep on the floor of the hall with my hounds until the day he died.

While Arthur was no good at magic, he was worse when he started swordsmanship. As every boy turning seven must do, he began to take lessons in how to defend himself. Giles, the tilting master, a veteran of the eastern wars, despaired of ever teaching Arthur to wield a sword without cutting off his own leg. Merlin did some magic on the bronze practice sword until it was more his size. I thought that was coddling him. I had to heft that big hunk of metal when I was his age, though admittedly I was a more normal size. Arthur was like a wren among raptors. Must be the Welsh blood.

Over time, though, that light build helped him to move quickly. As he built strength in his back and shoulders, he could whip that small sword in under my defenses before I could lower my buckler, then stick me again when my shield went down to cover the first strike. Even when I knew it was coming, I couldn't always defend against that double attack. Giles started showing him off to visitors, who invariably laughed when asked to take on the runt of the litter and ended up shaking their heads in admiration when they got skewered or slashed not once but twice. Arthur began to strut with pride, the little cockerel. By the time he was ten, he could take on grown men. But not me. I smelled enchantment in his defenses and took it into account. He had some magic after all. His was not the sorcery of potions and spells, but of arms and battles and victory. As a result I learned to see his pet move coming on.

My father and Merlin were both away from home one day when Count Pellinore, an old friend, came to call. As a lad rising sixteen I was the man of the house. Giles brought out Arthur to show him off. I was in no mood for the boy to steal my thunderbolts. His growing arrogance was getting to be as unwelcome as the plague. I meant to cure that disease now and forever.

In full view of everyone in the castle and Pellinore's entire retinue, I countered Arthur's doublestroke again and again. I didn't let him land a single hit on me. Every time I felt his magic gathering, I changed the tempo of my attack and plunged in. The amazement on his face made me laugh. I trounced Arthur so soundly that he ran off the field crying. Giles looked perturbed, but everyone else applauded madly. Pellinore looked puzzled.

"Why's everyone so surprised that a big boy can defeat a small boy?" he asked. I smiled. That was the way it was supposed to be.

When Father returned, I got a beating, but even he had to admit that the Wart was easier to live with afterward. And Arthur admired the man who had bested him. Alas, once again he took to following me around like a faithful sheepdog. I yearned for the day that Merlin would come and take the brat away again and leave our family the way that it had been, the way it should have been.

I missed my father's attention. When we went hunting, the best horse went to the boy. Father told me it was because the horse could hold him on its back even if his bottom was greased, and Arthur had to learn how to hunt. If you wanted to survive, you hunted. So, Arthur was coddled again, and I got the worst portion.

We went single file into the forest, me at the lead, and Father behind to keep an eye on Arthur. The boy kept a long-running stream of chatter going.

"It's a fine day, isn't it?" he asked cheerfully. "Are we after deer, or a boar, or coneys? I know these are deerhounds," he added, leaning precariously out of his saddle to pet one of the huge gray dogs that ran alongside him, "but are they versatile enough to know what to do if a boar charges?"

"Hush, boy!" Father growled. "You'll scare all the animals for miles around."

The boy was quenched, but only for a moment. "You've got a whole bunch of spears, Kay. May I throw one when we corner something?" I ignored him. He spurred his horse a little closer to mine, but not too close. Arthur knew to keep a healthy distance from my mount, who was bad-tempered. It even bit me occasionally, but I kept it in line through sheer force of will. The only good thing about this lump of horsemeat was that it could jump like nobody's business.

I knew we were hoping for deer. The White Hind had been spotted in the forest that spring. Father would never have killed the forest queen, but it meant that deer were plentiful. I considered it good luck to see her. It had happened only once in my life, and after she'd passed, I'd found a gold solidus beside a road.

I sensed magic that felt nothing like Merlin, who had stayed behind at Joyous Gard anyhow. Suddenly, a white cloud broke through the green leaves on one side of the path, sailed over the track, and plunged into the undergrowth again, almost under my nose. The White Hind had blessed us.

"O–oh!" Arthur exclaimed. I was overwhelmed by its beauty, and even Father and his men were awed. Around us the forest was as silent as a church. Then the peace was broken by, you guessed it, Arthur's tongue. "That was the most beautiful thing ever! Except rainbows and the way sunset is after there's been a big fire, and Mother's embroidery, o' course."

Another crash interrupted his flow. An angry squeal made me spin in my saddle. A boar! Arthur, panicked, kicked his mount toward it instead of away. The move infuriated it and terrified the horse. It turned off the road to run, followed by the angry porker.

"Father!" I cried, and spurred my horse to pursue. The spears shifted and pinched my fingers as I sought to free one from the bundle in my saddlebag.

The horse was now charging blindly ahead. Arthur had abandoned his reins, but the faithful horse kept under him somehow. The boar, a trebuchet-launched ball of muscle and knife-tipped tusks, ran after them. Boards were sprinters, I knew. They had only to stay ahead until it tired. The going was thick. I spat out hazel twigs and beech leaves as they smacked me in the mouth. I thanked God that we were not in the oak forest. Those branches didn't give way when you ran into them.

My father and Gensa rode behind us, shouting. The horse, hearing voices of home and safety, doubled around. The boar, seeing its chance, turned, blood in its tiny red eyes. I worked a spear loose and hefted it. I was too far away for a good throw. I maneuvered for position. Arthur's horse charged past twenty feet away. In between us was a fallen beech, its roots washed away by the spring floods. I kicked my mount toward it, raising its mouth by the reins. *Jump, you beast, jump!*

We landed on the other side nearly on top of the boar. It countered to go around me. I had but one chance, and let fly with the spear.

It struck! The boar let out a terrible squeal and began to dance around in a circle, shaking its head up and down. The spear, in a once in an eternity chance, had gone down its throat. Blood began to spout out of its nose. I was watching its death throes. Father rode up beside me, clambered out of his saddle, and dealt the coup de grâce with his ax. We looked at one another, breathless. He pounded me on the back, then embraced me. I had never been so proud.

The moment didn't last, of course. Gensa appeared through the trees in a moment, leading Arthur's horse. The boy clung to its neck, weeping, with blood on his face. That was typical. I had bruises where the branches had struck me and underneath, where the saddle had come up hard when I jumped, but Father fussed over the little cut on precious little baby's lip.

Not long after that, Pellinore came to visit again. Mother had her minstrel sing him the story of the boar hunt.

"Olivia," he told her when the song was done, "it's time that boy of yours is knighted."

"So soon?" she asked. "He's only twelve."

"Not Arthur," Pellinore said, with a laugh. He thought she was joking. I knew better. "Kay!"

"Is he ready?" Father asked.

"Time enough and past time. He's doing well in music and dancing. He's taking lessons from Merlin—doing well, is he?"

"When we have time to meet," the wizard confirmed grudgingly. It had been a long time since I'd been at the alembics, but I had personally heard an explosion only a week before that sent shards flying into the courtyard from Merlin's window and saw Arthur flying out the door not long after that.

" 'Zactly," Pellinore said. "He's surely got swordsmanship under his belt. He's up on history and the rules of chivalry. Reading and writing and 'rithmetic?" He peered at me sitting down at the end of the long table by the pages. Those were my weakest skills.

"I . . . uh . . . maybe Mother will help me find a literate wife, maybe someone convent-trained," I suggested.

"And willing to delegate responsibility," Pellinore concluded, smacking a hand on the board. "Well, he's a man I'd be proud to have in my retinue. What about it, Ector? You can't keep the chick in the egg forever."

"Very well, very well, Father said. He beckoned to me. "Come sit up here by us, boy."

I sprang up. The other pages were torn between envy and admiration. They patted me on the back as I passed. Pellinore himself made way for me to squeeze in between them. I sat with my back straight as a poker.

"Now, boy, you know it's a great responsibility we're talking of, don't you?" Pellinore began. "You'll have to do well at the Christmas tourney at Winchester to kneel before the king and get the accolade. I'll take you on at tilting and swordplay, so you know you're facing a fair opponent. I won't hold my blows, I promise."

"It would be an honor, sir," I stammered, hoarse with awe.

"Let me listen, too!" Arthur squeaked, scrambling up to the head table to join us.

"No!" I protested at once. "You're just a page." Father and Pelly looked at one another, as though considering. The unfairness of it all! But Father glanced at Arthur with a sheepish expression.

"Not this time, boy. You'll be a man soon enough."

I sat back, pleased. My point had been made.

"But if you're to be knighted," Pelly added, "you're going to need a squire, aren't you, boy?"

I didn't hesitate. "O' course," I said. Perhaps Kern. He was bigger than I, and knew horses well.

"Me!" Arthur chimed in at once, almost before my

mouth had stopped moving. He scrambled to us and all but fell at my feet. "Oh, Kay, please let me be your squire. Plllleeeee—eeeezzzzze."

"Well . . ." I thought about it. Most of the pages in the castle were quicker on the draw than Wart, and all of them were bigger. But how could I pass up the chance to give him orders that even Father wouldn't countermand? "You are, then. Does he kneel for me to dub him?" I asked Pelly.

"Did you when your father made you squire?"

I had to think. "No, sir."

"Then, no. O' course." Pelly's jaws snapped shut, as though he was a purse who'd dropped a gold coin into my palm and was loath to give another.

"Right, then," I said. A victory was a victory. "Squire, go get us some wine!" Arthur looked puzzled for a moment. "Go on. It's an honor to serve the quality, isn't it?"

"Yes, Kay, I mean, my lord, I mean . . ." The boy chattered as he ran away. He was annoying even while he was leaving a room. I got to sit up with Father and Pellinore, not even having to join the other boys at disassembling the trestle tables or sweeping out the rushes. Manhood, at last!

"Merlin always told me I was destined for great things," Arthur chattered, as he tied on my leather cruisses. "This is working up to it, I guess."

"Don't whine," I snapped nervously.

I had to give Arthur credit: he never complained about how much there was for a squire to do, but equally, he never got anything done on time. A count from the southlands near the Germanic borders came to visit my father. His son and I agreed to a practice tilt, both of us looking forward to London. His squire had him armored, armed, and seated at his comfort with a goblet of wine while Arthur was still trying to fasten on my greaves. I felt like cuffing him and sending him sprawling, but there would be a further delay while he picked himself up, sniveling, and gathered his wits before getting me ready the rest of the way. Besides, Merlin was hovering just at the other end of the courtyard, leaning on his stick, watching us.

I felt like doing it anyway. The wizard was doing the boy no favor by coddling him. If he wanted to be a man, by Jesu, he should learn to be one the way the rest of us had, by learning that life is hard on those who have not yet learned its lessons. Pretty deep philosophy for a noncleric, I thought, as Arthur, at great length, knotted my belt and set my helmet on my head The swordsmaster, called into service as the marshal, stepped between us, then dropped his hand. "Have at!" he shouted.

We were pretty evenly matched. It looked like the bout would be a draw, until I decided to use Arthur's double-touch. The visitor was stunned, and the entire household cheered for me, even Arthur. I couldn't wait for Winchester.

My dreams of knighthood were swept away from me with the news that arrived at the manor just before we were ready to leave for the south. The old king was dead. Uther Pendragon, king and conqueror, had died of a fever from an old wound. His body was carried to Glastonbury, where it was interred in the floor of the great Abbey beside his queen, Ygraine, who had passed away two years before. The tourney was to go on as planned. Even on his deathbed the king had insisted on it. " 'I'll be looking down from heaven on it,' " the troubadour who came to the castle told us Uther had said. " 'Strike a good blow for me.' "

All my heart went out of me. I was saddened that His Highness had gone, but could he not have waited one more month? He'd left no heir apparent, so the throne at the tourney would be empty. Count Pellinore had arrived early to accompany us southeast. He and Father talked of nothing else on the long journey along Dere Street.

Merlin must already have known something was about to happen. The rook with the white feather had arrived two weeks before. He had departed two days later, no doubt to help with arrangements. I'd come to think of him as our wizard, but he'd been Uther's man long ago. My guess was that Arthur had been begotten on a highborn lady whose husband had vowed to kill the wizard if he came back, and Merlin would rather care for his son than his king.

Winchester was a great city, compared with our tiny town of Joyous Gard. Hundreds of contestants and their families and retinues crowded the streets, all of them abuzz with the astounding news.

The king had died without apparent issue, but his sword, Excalibur, had been rammed through an anvil and into a boulder by Merlin, and placed in the yard of the great cathedral church. The king's heir was alive, and would be revealed by his ability to liberate the sword.

Naturally everyone wanted to have to a go. The old king's steward, Gallipas, announced that the essay would be part of the tournament. I stood in a line that seemed a mile long until my turn came. I put my hand to the hilt and felt the tingle of magic race through me. This was a mighty weapon, one I'd be proud to wield, or serve. I used all my strength, then all my magic, then both together. Nothing. The next knight in line nudged me, wanting his turn. I retired, chagrined.

Every single knight, lord, and chief tried their luck, and all failed. We all repaired to the site of the tourney, the old Roman arena. Still trying to maintain the shreds of glory of our country. I vowed to acquit myself well. With Arthur's help, now a gangly twelve year old, I robed and put on my armor.

"Pour me some wine," I instructed him, nervous about the upcoming bout. Pellinore promised to give me a good fight, not to hold back on me.

My mother had made me a gage. I tried not to be embarrassed about it, because none of the girls in the county had offered me one. A few of my fellows looked embarrassed, too, but one fellow was festooned with favors. We wondered whether he'd bought them all off a peddler, or if they were really all from different wenches.

Arthur buckled on my belt. I pulled the scabbard around to settle it, but it was empty. "*No sword?* Go get me my sword!" I bellowed, backhanding him. He knew better than to go whining to our father. He ran off.

And the rest, horribly enough, is already history, passing into the realm of legend. Running through the empty churchyard, Arthur made the fateful decision not to go all the way back to our lodgings, pulled the sword out of the stone and brought it to me. I stated that I firmly believed that Merlin fixed it so his by-blow would become king. Merlin, hovering around the royal box with the court officials, didn't even deign to correct me when I suggested it, but my father knocked me to the ground with one backhand slap.

"He's the son of Uther and Ygraine, and none other, you idiot!" Ector growled. "I've known since the beginning." I crawled to my feet, vowing to keep my mouth shut, but it was too late: everyone had heard me.

"What an infamous suggestion," Pellinore added, my last ally lost. "There is a portrait of Ygraine in the cathedral. He's her very image, lad."

The result was that everyone was now angry at me except Arthur, who still, amazingly, looked up to me.

The rest of the story trickled out over the course of the next very busy week. The child had been conceived when Ygraine's ancient and doddering husband Gorlois had still been alive, so Uther Pendragon couldn't acknowledge Arthur's birth at the time. He'd been brought to us to protect him while the child grew up. The Bishop of Winchester was silent on the subject of whether the brat was considered a bastard or not, but since he was son of both king and queen, king he was. And I was a rude, uncouth, ill-mannered, barnyard-minded backward yokel for thinking otherwise. I was roundly snubbed by one and all, except Arthur, who still insisted on having me by him.

"You shall be my royal steward," Arthur vowed. "You have been my brother, and saved my life so often, I can ignore a thoughtless outburst that came out of shock. We're only human, after all."

I said nothing. He would have been justified in exiling me. That's what I'd have done, if our places had been reversed.

Then came the coronation. And now, the feast.

Merlin took his place smugly at the head table, as though he'd planned the whole thing, which, of course, he had. My father sat on Arthur's other side as his protector. Kings came to bow before Arthur and swear fealty to their new High King. I had to stand there and watch it all in my place of "honor," as the feast began. It couldn't get worse.

"Wine!" my father shouted. "Wine for the king!"

"Wine for the king!" the heralds echoed.

A page the same age as Arthur came running up with a wineskin, and dropped to his knees beside him.

"Shall I pour, Your Highness?"

"No, Arthur said, smiling up at me adoringly. "Let Kay pour it."

The wineskin was thrust into my hand and I stumbled forward, splashing a gobbet of it on King Lot of Lothian's priceless silk collar.

Did I say it couldn't get any worse? I was wrong.

"Kay himself told me, my lords," Arthur said, with a glance that told me there was steel beneath the simper, "that it was an honor to serve the quality. He shall have his chance, now and forever."

RAPUNZEL—
THE TRUE STORY

by Robert Sheckley

Robert Sheckley was born in Brooklyn, New York, and raised in New Jersey. He went into the U.S. army after high school and served in Korea. After discharge he attended NYU, graduating with a degree in English. He began to sell stories to all the science fiction magazines soon after his graduation, producing several hundred stories over the next several years. His best-known books in the science fiction field are Immortality, Inc., Mindswap, and Dimension Of. He has produced about sixty-five books to date, including twenty novels and nine collections of his short stories, as well as his five-book Collected Short Stories of Robert Sheckley. In 1991, he received the Daniel F. Gallun award for contributions to the genre of science fiction. Recently he was given an Author Emeritus award by the Science Fiction Writers of America. He is married to the writer Gail Dana and lives in Portland, Oregon.

THERE HAVE been some enquiries made recently as to the true story of the legendary Rapunzel, my daughter, and as to my part in her story. The roles of myself, my wife, the prince, and the old witch have also been misunderstood.

I am glad of this chance to clear my name, and to straighten out various differences that have come up between the true story of what really happened and the story as received by our scribes and pundits.

I might as well begin at the beginning. I am Rapunzel's father. My wife and I lived at the time of the story in the woods near a small European village. My occupation has been variously given as shoemaker, carpenter, weaver. Actually at the time of the story I was between jobs, keeping my family going with a bit of vegetable farming. The notion that I was raising a herd of horses is entirely wrong. My wife's name was Lois and her occupation was housewife—an unchic pursuit these days, but vitally necessary for the preservation of the race.

We lived quietly, Lois and I. Often in the evening after reading the daily newspaper, we played our favorite game of "Slapsie," in which wrong answers to questions about daily affairs as reported in the newspaper are punished by a slap in the face. This had nothing to do with wife abuse, as some of our more excitable critics have claimed; Lois slapped me far more often than I slapped her. The inference of wife abuse is not only wrong, it is monstrous. Only the year before I had been recognized by our local chapter of the Idolatrous Husbands Society, a group which brings rewards and recognition to those among us who go the extra distance for our wives. Does that sound like a wife beater to you?

I might as well get to the incident preceding our daughter's birth, and answer the allegation that my wife demanded the herb rampion in response to her pregnancy desires.

Rampion is not popular in our region. It is a coarse relative of the grass family, growing to a height of three feet. It is extremely prolific, and is sometimes used for animal feed, but only when all else is lacking. The idea of humans eating rampion is monstrous. The thought of a pregnant woman desiring rampion is insane. The latter-day authors of the Rapunzel story betray at the start their propensity toward evil lies.

What Lois, my wife, craved were avocados.

The avocado, gentlemen, is a thick-skinned, pear-shaped fruit, its skin ranging from a smooth yellowish green to a wrinkled purplish black, its interior a fleshy yellow color. A tropical fruit, used in salads, and expensive if you live as far from the tropics as I do. My wife and I had no avocado trees. But the woman next door, usually referred to as the witch, had a single large avocado tree in the middle of her garden, and she had set up a system of mirrors and sponges so that the tree would get the necessary warmth and humidity it needed. Rampion, indeed! What man in his right mind would steal rampion, and what woman in her right mind would crave it? If you're going to listen to my story, at least grant me that I do not sound deranged, and therefore am to be presumed sane until and unless a jury of experts pronounces to the contrary.

Avocados, I say, not rampion. It is a small and unimportant point, but the lies and misinformation around this story of Rapunzel have so mounted that it is necessary to clear them up in order to give you an idea of what really happened.

The witch's garden was surrounded by a high masonry wall, tall enough and strong enough to serve a prison. The avocados could in a sense be considered imprisoned, since our neighbor never sold them in the village market, even though, being of the great Haas brand, they would have brought in a lot of money. No, she hoarded them.

Pregnant with Rapunzel, my wife's cravings began. But not for rampion, that common unappetizing weed, eaten by dull-witted cows but not intelligent ladies, as my wife was at that time.

"Aye, avocado!" she used to moan. "Ah, the Haas avocado, child of long and painstaking interbreeding, luscious and ripe, melting in the mouth, its mild unforgettable flavor evidence enough of its virtues—ah, how well it would go with a teaspoon of balsamic vinegar, on one of those lovely little Delft plates my mother left me . . . to eat with a small silver spoon thus increasing the number of bites I could take of this supreme fruit of fruits!"

It was pitiable to see Lois thus obsessed. She constantly mooned over our dictionary, taking some pleasure in just reading the word "avocado." And of course there was a black-and-white line drawing of the fruit in our dictionary, looking like a wrinkled prune to my eyes, but like the source of ambrosia to hers. She couldn't get the avocado out of her mind, couldn't dispel from her inner vision the image of that green-black wrinkled fruit with its creamy pale yellow interior. In her mind's tasting place, she undoubtedly exaggerated the taste of that rather bland fruit, turning it into a cornucopia of delights. I infer this, of course, but it would be very like her, so imaginative a creature was she.

A time was reached, late in her pregnancy, when she could bear the obsession no longer.

"Thoms," she said, "I must have an avocado or die. If I die, it would probably kill our baby, too. So I beg of you—do whatever is necessary, but get me one of those Haases—a nice ripe one, well wrinkled."

"I'll see what I can do," I told her. And the next morning I went to our neighbor's gate and tapped.

The witch appeared. I introduced myself. "I am Thoms, your next-door neighbor."

"I know," she said. "I have glimpsed you through the gate. You and your wife. I am Allura, the witch."

"It is my wife I have come about," I said. "She is in her final term of pregnancy. She has an unquenchable lust for a Haas avocado such as you have growing in your yard."

"Has she, indeed?" Allura said. "What a pity. I have just contracted to sell my entire crop to the Haas people. They will coddle the fruit in sealed containers containing carbon dioxide and, when they have reached the perfection of ripeness, release them to the markets of this region and others."

"Could you possibly sell me one of your crop?" I asked. "It would never be missed, and it would save my wife's life, to say nothing of our unborn baby daughter."

"I wish I could," she said. "But the people at Haas have made their preliminary survey of my tree and have counted each fruit, real or nascent. If I do not deliver the entire anticipated crop, untoward events are likely to happen to me. You must understand that the Haas people are very powerful, and vindictive in the extreme, and I would not answer for the safety of any person who cheated them."

"Perhaps you have kept one avocado aside as a souvenir of the harvest," I suggested. "If so, it would be a mitzvah of the highest order to give or sell it to me."

"The idea of keeping souvenirs of my crop had not occurred to me," she said. "It is impossible now, but I will start it up next year, before Haas has made their count. I have just the place for it. Come into my parlor and tell me your opinion."

I could see no sense in doing that, but agreed to step into her parlor just to be neighborly.

Her parlor was small and tastefully decorated in green and russet.

"My," she said as we entered. "You are a tall young man, and strongly made. Do not hit your head upon the chandelier. Sit on the couch and I will show you where I plan to keep next year's prize avocado."

She darted across the room, and came back carrying a small goblet made of dark gold.

"See," she said, how it glows even here in the subdued light of my parlor. Hold it in your hand, feel its weight."

She leaned over to hand me the goblet, and tripped over a small magazine stand on the floor, lurched, and fell into my lap.

"Excuse me!" she said. She struggled to get up again, and in the process wriggled so heartily on my lap that I felt a swooning of my senses. All of her seemed to present itself to my hands and mouth, a sudden feast of breasts and haunches and warm, moist mouth. The excitement I felt was immediate and overwhelming. I could no more resist her than I could an army of armed men. Clothing seemed to come off her body of its own accord. Rosy flesh opened before me, my own clothing seemed to vanish, and there, locked and tumbled on that diabolical couch, a love couch if there ever was one, we enjoyed each other.

At the end I was miraculously dressed again, and so was she, and we talked to each other in the intimate yet formal tones of two who have known each other for a long time.

"Lady," I said, "I hope I was not intrusive."

"Not in the wrong way, no," she replied.

I blushed as I realized the double meaning. "I only mean that my deed was not thought out beforehand, not premeditated . . ."

"Next time," she said, "Perhaps it will be."

Covered with confusion, I took my leave. There seemed nothing more to say. And nothing more to do, until that hypothetical next time, if it should ever come around again.

I had to confess to my wife that I had failed in my avocado-procurement mission. She wept herself to sleep that night, and, the next day, seemed ill indeed.

That night I could not sleep for her groaning, her moaning, and her pathetic little attempts to keep still, which always resulted in more noise as she squirmed uncomfortably on the bed. By midnight I could bear it no longer.

I dressed and put on my shoes. I went over to her. "You shall have your avocado."

She tried to smile, but I could see that she was far gone in what science has since termed Avocado Birth Mania. I leaned forward and tapped her on the cheek with one finger, in imitation of our games of Slapsie.

"I'll be back soon," I said, and left.

How this simple and gentle gesture of love could be construed by her as a slap, and a hard one, I do not know. It was lying testimony that she presented at our divorce trial. Don't believe it.

I went to the masonry wall and, with the aid of a ladder, climbed to the top. I let myself down on the other side, into the witch's yard. As the poet says, "The black bat night had veiled the skies." There was no sound, no glimmer of light from Allura's cottage. I crept forward, slowly, to the avocado tree. There, taking my courage in hand, I plucked a single avocado from its branch and put it in my shirt. Then I climbed back to the top by way of iron stanchions set in the wall, and so returned to my own property.

What a celebration we had when I came back into my house! My wife was awake, hoping against hope that I had succeeded. When, with a small flourish, I gave her the avocado, her gratitude was beyond expression.

"Ah, Thoms," she said. "Now I know you truly love me."

"I have broken the law," I replied. "And I would do worse to satisfy you."

"Sweet," she said, giving me a kiss before she turned her full attention to the avocado.

Never has a woman had a better time than Lois had with that avocado. Not for nothing is it called "The Devil's Fruit." I watched as she peeled it with her long thumbnails, not bothering to wait for me to bring her a knife. Then she ate the creamy interior bit by bit, with her fingers, in a kind of controlled ferocity that was beautiful to behold.

Our lives were better, happier and more cordial, in the days that followed. Lois' desire for avocados in no way abated. In fact, it seemed to grow stronger, as if a taste of the forbidden fruit had given her an imperious desire for more. Twice more that week I sneaked over the fence late in the night. And then a third time—our wedding anniversary. How could I refuse?

This time, with a sliver of moon glimmering in the sky, I made my way over the wall. I tiptoed up to the avocado tree. I reached out—and a hand took my hand.

I almost died of fright at that moment.

It was the witch, of course. Dressed all in black, with her white face like a full moon within her hood, stern and infinitely distant.

"My God but you gave me a fright!" I said.

"A fright isn't all I'll give you," she said. "You have been stealing my avocados! Explain yourself."

Well, there I was, caught red-handed, or green-handed, with the avocado in my fist. A thousand lies raced through my mind, but I saw that the only one that would do would be the lie of the truth.

"Look," I said, "I've got a situation here. My wife has been lusting for your avocados. She's been dying for them. I took one because I was pretty sure you wouldn't want her to just die for want of a simple avocado."

"Don't be so sure of that. I told you that I had already sold this crop."

"Yes, I know. But I didn't necessarily believe you. Or I believed you, but thought that one or two wouldn't be missed."

"If you had taken just one avocado, you might have an arguing point. But the fact of the matter is, you have taken several." And here she listed the times and dates of my thefts.

"Well," I said, "my wife's cravings got worse, and I got tired of listening to her piss and moan. And, due to the special relationship I have with you—"

"What makes you think you have a special relationship with me?" she asked.

"Well, you know, that first night I came over here, that night of our intimacy . . ."

"That argues no relationship," she said. "You were served better than I was, to tell the truth, so you were the gainer there. You gained me, and then, surreptitiously, you also gained an avocado. This is the fourth avocado you have stolen. Now you must pay."

I knew there had to be some rejoinder to that, but I just couldn't think of one. I was in the wrong. I didn't feel I was wrong—the avocados hadn't been for me—but I was definitely in the wrong, somehow, anyhow. What could I do now, what could I say?"

"I am terribly sorry," I said, deciding on humbleness. "What can I do to make things right?"

"Now that's more like it. What you can do is, you can give me your newborn child when she is old enough."

"My child? My soon-to-be-born child? No, I can't do that!"

"Then you'll have to suffer the consequences."

"What are these consequences."

"Believe me, you wouldn't want to know. The revenge of a witch is a terrible thing. You wouldn't want that."

"But my baby child—you can't be so cruel—"

"I can."

"Then I can't be so small and insignificant as to accept it."

"Then suffer the consequences. Have you ever heard Hamlet's lines, where he says that he could be bounded in a nutshell yet count himself a king of infinite space were it not that he had bad dreams."

"It seems to me I've heard those lines."

"That will be your first punishment. It will suffice until I think up a worse."

She raised her hands and started to make a gesture.

"Wait!" I said.

"What is it?"

"I don't think I have the patience to be bounded in a nutshell. I really wouldn't like it. And the dreams would haunt me. No, I really don't want to do that. Especially not knowing that you'll think up even worse stuff to happen to me."

"Then what do you propose?"

"I'll give you the kid. Will that satisfy you?"

"It will. And your presence in my home will also satisfy me. Because, with you having made amends, I see no reason why we should give up our pleasure."

It was on my lips to refuse her. But one look at her cold, beautiful white face told me that would not be a good thing to do. You don't refuse what a witch asks of you. I had been wrong to steal the avocados. I should have let Lois die rather than do that. Maybe that way I could have escaped the consequences.

Something I found out later, but need to mention now, is that a witch is never the viewpoint character. She may seem to be narrating in her own person, but actually she's a mask frozen into a certain attitude in which is combined a moral judgment. A witch does not even always know she's a witch. That's someone else's judgment. She is forced to take a moralistic view of herself. That's because she's actually the narrator posing as the witch and making the judgments on herself that she, in her persona of Stage Director, thinks appropriate.

Anything the witch does militates against her in the general moral summing up that she knows awaits her. Witches, real ones, fight against this judgment with all their available energy. They know that in some larger sense, what they're doing is justified, or at least not their fault. But they also don't know it.

To find a way out of this bind is a witch's earnest intention. The justification of the witch is the real story that's being told here—not how a pretty, rather dull-minded little girl named Rapunzel had very long blonde hair, and so on.

"I can hardly wait to see my blonde-haired baby girl," the witch said.

"Blonde hair? But she's a newborn baby—she doesn't have any hair yet!"

"But she will have! Soon, soon!"

"How soon?"

"When I snap my fingers," the witch said, "Rapunzel, as I will name her, will be sixteen years old with long blonde hair."

"I don't see how you can do that," I said.

"As a witch, I am a mistress of the time lines of Earth, and I can lengthen them or shorten them. I choose now to shorten Rapunzel's by taking out the uninteresting years between now and her sixteenth birthday."

She snapped her fingers. I felt a dizziness, which soon passed, and I was . . .

Standing beside the witch again.

"She is now sixteen years old," Allura told me.

"But how can that be? I am the same as I was before you snapped your fingers."

"That is because I didn't snap them for you. I shall do so now."

"Not so fast! What are you snapping your fingers at me for?"

"Just to bring you up to date on where we are," the witch said. "You wouldn't want to sit around for sixteen years waiting for Rapunzel to come of age for the next event, would you?"

"I suppose not. But what's going to happen?"

"You'll see . . . And she snapped her fingers."

Sixteen years! I could feel them in the additional weight on my legs, and a certain thickness around my waist.

I blinked. I said, "Now what?"

"Now we celebrate the birthday of our darling daughter."

Well, I wasn't too clear about the continuity of all this. But I realized I was not in charge of the continuity. My only duty was to report what happened as it seemed to me. The overall continuity was in Allura's hands. And even though she was having me narrate the story, it was really her story I was narrating.

We lived in this round tower, the witch, Rapunzel, and I. The ground-floor door had been walled in at the same time that they took the staircase out. We all lived on the top floor, which had a window. There was no way into the tower. To get in, the witch would come home after a day of gathering simples or hexing people—I was never too clear on just what she did. She'd come home in the evening and call out, "Rapunzel, Rapunzel, let down your long golden hair." And Rapunzel would appear in the window and smile and undo her hair and let it down from the window.

Rapunzel was magical only when she let down her hair. The rest of the time she was a simpleminded little girl. But you never saw such a world of hair. Blonde and fine it was, but tougher than horsehair, tougher than silk, or an equivalent weight of spiderweb, tough beyond belief.

After Rapunzel undid her hair and dangled it out the window, and braced herself behind the bed, which was bolted to the floor, the witch would proceed to climb up the hair, hand over hand, until she could come in nimbly through the window.

Once inside the room, the witch would make dinner, and Rapunzel would comb out her hair and coil it up and hum to herself. An easily pleased girl was my Rapunzel.

And where was I at this time? Well, not long after we all began living together, the witch threw me out. She explained that I had to sleep out of doors for the present. That was in order that I could be the viewpoint character of the next event from its very beginning. Continuity demanded it, she told me, and I had to bow to that iron demand.

The event came along quickly enough, which was good, because the damp ground was giving me rheumatism. I was loitering around the countryside, sleeping under a tree, eating berries and rampion, because the witch usually neglected making dinner for me. All of a sudden I heard a man's voice singing—

> "Where is my love
> O where is my love?
> My love, where is she,
> My love, my love!"

Not much on originality, I'll grant you, but delivered in a strong baritone voice.

Peering through the leaves, I saw a fine, tall, good-looking young man, dressed in expensive clothing. I followed him as he looked up at the tower, then watched him duck out of sight when the witch came into sight with her basket of simples and hexes. I watched him observe how the witch got in, how she called Rapunzel and Rapunzel let down her hair, and I could practically hear his thoughts, which were to the effect, "Well, if a fat old lady can do that, what about me?"

He stayed hidden in the countryside all that night, until next morning, when the witch left the tower, letting herself down by Rapunzel's hair. He waited until he was sure the witch was nowhere within sight and hearing.

Then he called out, "Rapunzel, Rapunzel, let down your golden hair."

As I have said, Rapunzel wasn't too bright. She heard the words, but paid no attention to the fact that it was a man saying them rather than the witch. She let down her hair, and, quick as you can say knife, the young man climbed up.

Consternation. Surprise. Each was entranced by how beautiful the other was, and in each other's eyes they saw their own beauty reflected. They fell in love on the spot with each other's view of themselves—a match made in heaven for shortsighted people.

I was outside, at the foot of the tower, listening. I couldn't hear much in the way of conversation. But the sighs, the moans, and soon, the little moans and the soft squelching sounds they made told me what they were up to.

I thought to myself, "My little girl has grown up."

I thought about letting Lois, her real mother, know about this. But I knew that Lois, after divorcing me, had gone to the provincial capital and taken a course in law, with a special emphasis on the special rights of women as opposed to the dubious and alienable rights of monsters like witches.

I didn't think Lois would be interested. And if she was, shame on her.

As for me, I listened, enraptured, to their night of making love. I was secure in the knowledge that, however perverted my behavior might seem, the witch would change it around or drop it entirely when she came to write her memoirs.

The prince left at dawn. He and Rapunzel had already agreed to marry. The witch returned that evening and made us a nice dinner. Everything was fine. But then Rapunzel gave it away.

"The young prince is much lighter than you are, Mother," she said in her artless way.

The witch had been feeling testy of late. She was worried about gaining weight. She was still a gorgeous woman, but now she was a Reubens rather than a sylph. Well, with age, weight comes to all of us—we're lucky to not do worse. But the witch still believed that being a witch entitled her to special privileges. The trouble was, she couldn't figure out how to take weight off magically. She could do everything else with magic, why not that?

Dare I state it now? My confusion? My feelings of inadequacy? Dare I say anything about it, even to go so far as to say I don't know anything about it? We are in the tower room where Rapunzel has just artlessly confessed about the prince who came yesterday to visit her. Poor Rapunzel! So simpleminded, so sweet, such a good-looking girl except for that air of bovine simplicity about her, which some men—the prince, for example—found so attractive. For here was a girl not schooled in the wiles of winning men, of deceiving her parents in order to gain a premature entrance into womanhood. No, here was a simple girl, who artlessly confessed that which she would rather keep a secret. But such deception was not to be, because in her artless manner she had blurted it out.

"A prince? What is this about a prince?"

Innocently, Rapunzel went on: "A very handsome young man, Mother. I was sure you must have sent him yourself, so delightful was he, and such delicious sensations he set off in my mind and my body."

"You don't say," the witch said. "Well, we'll just wait until he comes back, as I'm sure he will. Then we will see what we will see."

Rapunzel nodded and clapped her hands. There was no thought of evil in her mind. To wait for the prince—she'd be delighted. And sure enough, after some hours there was a sound of footsteps outside, and then a young man's voice—"Rapunzel, let down your golden hair!"

Rapunzel looked at the witch. Some intimation was beginning to reach her that all was not well. But the witch nodded, and Rapunzel let down her long golden hair. The prince mounted lightly, and in a moment he was in the tower chamber with Rapunzel, the witch, and yours truly, the narrator.

He stood in the window looking in. He saw what he hadn't expected to see—the witch, furious, Rapunzel, puzzled, the father, observing.

"So you'd have at my daughter, eh?" the witch said. She made a furious gesture at the prince. He startled backward, lost his balance, and fell from the tower window, arms cartwheeling wildly as he glanced once off the side of the tower, and fell into the thorn hedge that surrounded the tower.

Ah, the cruel black curved thorns! They clawed his arms and legs, they tore at his face, they reached up and pierced his eyes.

His single scream was as full of meaning as a deathbed soliloquy. Here was a noble young man, caught up in the bad dreams I had spared myself.

He lay there for a moment, dazed, then pulled himself to is feet. His hands reached out, trying to supply by touch what lack of vision denied him. He blinked, but only tears of blood oozed out of his sightless eye sockets. Slowly, sadly, putting one hesitant foot after another, he started his long trek to that outer world that lay in all directions from the tower.

"Oh, dear!" Rapunzel cries. "Mummy, you have blinded him! How dare you, Mummy? He was mine, and you have gone and spoiled him!"

"Don't worry so much about the prince," the witch says. "Save some of your worry for yourself."

"What do you mean?"

"I mean it's time for all of us to leave the tower."

This wasn't so easily accomplished. As I have told you, the tower had no egress except by way of the window and Rapunzel's hair. How was Rapunzel supposed to climb down her own hair?

The witch was not to be put off by difficulties. She instructed us. I climbed down Rapunzel's hair, then the witch climbed down.

Rapunzel, all alone in the upper room of the tower, cried, "What about me? I'll starve to death up here!"

"Don't be a silly little goose," the witch said. "Just do exactly as I say. Undo your hair and slip it over

the iron ring in the floor. Climb out on the sill holding the free end of your hair. Now, slowly, loosen
your grip, and let yourself slide down. Husband,
catch her as she comes down."

Rapunzel did as she was told. She managed to get
down. I caught her in my arms. I was still hoping
that things might work out all right. The witch would
apologize, say that she got carried away, that she
was prepared now to make everything right. She
would find the prince and cure him of his blindness;
she would make up with Rapunzel, she would give
me a kiss . . .

But no, I was wrong, it was only wishful thinking
speaking in me.

The witch said, "Come, Rapunzel, I am going to
find a new place for you to live. Husband, you come,
too, so you may witness this."

So that was my role! I didn't like it one bit. But I
was aware of my duty as narrator—not so small a
task for an uneducated man like myself, a man who
couldn't even remember his parents since they didn't
figure in the story.

I fell into step behind the witch, who pushed Rapunzel ahead of her. And so we walked into the
countryside.

We marched, and Rapunzel's feet soon grew tired
and sore, and then began to bleed. During our rest
stops, I bound them up with rags which I tore from
my own shirt. And we marched on.

The country grew more desolate and bare. Who

would have thought that such a wasteland existed just beyond the tower? We camped for the night at a dried-up little stream. The witch conjured provisions for us, and I cooked them. We slept poorly that night, and the next day set out again, the witch driving Rapunzel before her, with me following in the rear.

And at least we came to a region that had no trees at all, only a sort of gray-green leathery underbrush, and this was buried in the sand this region was composed of.

There was nothing to eat here, and nothing to look at, except for the sand dunes that marched endlessly to the distant horizons.

In the midst of this desolation, the witch came to a stop. "This will do very nicely," she said. "Rapunzel, we are going to leave you here. You will have ample time to repent your artless bad intentions. My husband and I will leave you now."

She tugged at my shirt. "Come on, let's get out of here."

"No!" I cried. "I can't do it! I won't do it! You may do with me as you like, but I will not leave my darling daughter in such straitened circumstances!"

"Fool!" she cried. "Don't you realize that this is part of your punishment, too? To leave your daughter, and to regret that leaving all your life!"

"I won't do it," I said.

"Who is the hero of this piece?" she asked.

That floored me for a moment. "You?" I asked.

"Of course. Through you, I am the viewpoint character. But who is this story actually about?"

"Rapunzel?" I hazarded.

"Try again, dummy!"

"The prince?" She nodded. "How could it possibly be about the prince!"

"Just because he wasn't in at the beginning of our story, nevertheless, he is our true subject. And your duty is to tell his story. How can you do that if you stay here trying in your clumsy way to take care of your daughter, and merely delaying her destiny?"

"Is something good going to happen?"

"Wait and see. You are her father. You are responsible for everything that has happened to her. You cannot undo it. You can merely report it."

"But the prince is not here! How can I report on his movements?"

"Come home with me. I will provide a way."

This appeal to my prime purpose, my function as narrator, undid my intention. Meekly I nodded. The witch made a gesture. And a moment later we were in her little parlor, in her little cottage.

I was seated in the comfortable old armchair. In front of me was a box with a glass window. "What's this?" I asked. "I don't remember seeing this before."

"There was no need of it before," the witch said. "The world was young when we were here last, there were no deeds to speak of, consequently no one spoke of them. But now it is later, deeds have been done, and you must learn about them through the magical pictures on this screen, as we call it."

As I watched, the screen became bright, as if some light were shining behind it. Colored figures appeared on it. I saw knights and men at arms, queens and fools, castles and oceans, mountains and rivers. As I watched, the images segued—I also knew the meaning of that word—into a high overhead shot of a young man, walking slowly with the aid of a staff (I wondered where had he gotten that staff)—across a sere and barren wilderness.

I bent to the controls of the little box. It was as if I had a prior knowledge of them. I touched buttons, dials, wheels. I zeroed in on the prince, went to a close-up. I saw his blind face turned up to the pitiless sun. I beheld the bloody tears that fell continually from his sightless eyes. I watched the advertisements that insinuated themselves between these images, and I found myself longing for a certain make of automobile, though I didn't know what an automobile was.

"Now watch the prince," the witch said. "And I will bring you a glass of milk."

I was dimly aware that more than one drama was being played out here, and that hidden cameras were recording them for an unseen audience.

"And now," the witch said, "I will adjust the time lines again so we do not have to wait forever for this part of the drama to change into something else. This is what we call the art of story editing, my dear. Watch and all will be revealed to you."

I watched. What else could I do? The baleful power of that television set seemed to pull all my attentive faculties into it. The picture faded, then came into focus again. I understood that a lapse of time was being indicated. I watched as the blind prince staggered up a sand dune, then lost his balance and rolled down the other side. I saw dust and sand fly in the air, reflected by the golden sunlight.

And then, suddenly, and unexpectedly, I saw a hand reach into the frame and take his hand.

The new hand was long and slim, the nails immaculately done.

"Who is it?" the prince cried.

"It is I, your poor Rapunzel," a voice said. Then we pulled back and saw Rapunzel herself, clad in a tattered gown which was nevertheless appealing on a young girl's figure. She bent over the prince, who had fallen to his knees, and her tears fell on his face. There was a rising chord of music, a flash of light and color. Then the screen turned black, and then it came to light again, and I realized I was looking at the miracle of vision restored. Who could have guessed that Rapunzel's tears would provide the simple antidote for the calamity that had befallen the prince?

I sipped my milk. I watched entranced as the prince, his vision restored, bent over Rapunzel. I empathized, as soon as I remembered the meaning of the word, with the tender kiss the prince gave her. I intuited the ending, or saw it, when he was restored to his kingdom, his father having died of a broken heart.

* * *

The prince became the new king, with Queen Rapunzel at his side, and due to her elevation she had become as bright and intelligent as she was beautiful, the most beautiful, as well as the most talented, girl in the kingdom. My daughter! I felt tears fall from my eyes as I saw this.

The witch came and sat down beside me. I felt her intoxicating warmth, her infinite allure.

I leaned toward her. I said, "You are Rapunzel!"

"Yes," she said. "And you are my prince."

I scratched my bald head. "Some prince!"

"It is only in our old age that we realize that we are the prince," she told me. "We spend the rest of our lives being everyone else in the story. It is only at the end that we know ourselves."

I didn't want to know what she was talking about. Her talk was woman's magic, making things so that weren't so. I recognized myself as an opposing principle.

I said, "Lois, is that you?"

She nodded. She said, "Rapunzel has done well."

My Lois! She had been through the changes of womanly life, and was restored to me in my decrepit dotage.

I held her tight. She touched my cheek with her finger in the loveliest imitation of a slap. Then she closed her eyes and purred. The scene held for a moment before collapsing into something else, as all the scenes of life are wont to do, especially if a witch is stage-managing them.

AMONG THE STARS

by Susan Sizemore

Susan Sizemore lives in the Midwest and spends most of her time writing. Some of her other favorite things are coffee, dogs, travel, movies, hiking, history, farmers' markets, art glass, and basketball—you'll find mention of quite a few of these things in the pages of her stories. She works in many genres, from contemporary romance to epic fantasy and horror. She's the winner of the Romance Writers of America's Golden Hart award, and was a nominee for the 2000 Rita award in historical romance. Her available books include historical romance novels, a dark fantasy series, The Laws of the Blood, science fiction, and several electronically published books and short stories. Recent books include the hardcover publication of The Children of the Rock duology, Moons' Dancing and Moons' Dreaming with Marguerite Krause. Susan's email address is Ssizemore@aol. Com, and her webpage address is: members. aol. com/Ssizemore/storm/home.htm.

A WAKEN. And speak."
She knew that voice as well as she knew her own. It would have made her heart light with joy to

hear it, if her heart had still been in her body. His passing had been hard on her. Somehow Hatshepsut had never expected to hear him again, or see him. And yet, why not? Just because years had passed since their parting, it was only proper that Pharaoh have a favorite consort by her side in the life eternal.

She had spent seventy days in dark silence, aware, and yet unaware, feeling some things, unaware of others. It had not hurt when her organs were taken for separate embalming, yet her skin had itched when her body was covered with the natron used to dry it out. There had been a taste of salt in her mouth, yet she had known no thirst. It was odd, being dead, but now that the spell of Opening the Mouth had freed her from this limbo state, the awareness of being dead was already fading.

She opened her eyes, and over her head were the stars, brighter and clearer than the stars that shone over the lands of the living. Yet they were the same stars. Her stars. She turned her head and saw Senenmut standing beside her. Her Senenmut, where he belonged. Yet he wore the uneadable face of a courtier, not the open expression she knew from when they were alone together. Instead of helping her to sit up, he stepped back, aloof, leaving her to make her first movements in the afterlife alone.

This was fitting, she decided, despite the small prick of disappointment that touched her womanly emotions. Her mouth had been opened, she lived again. She took a deep breath and rose to her feet.

"She arises in splendor," Senenmut said as she did so.

This caused her to give him a sharp look, for these ceremonial words had been used between them in other times and places.

"Follow me."

His tone of command shocked her. He knew she had always resented taking orders. When he turned his back and walked away, she was insulted. All this was so strange that she held her outrage in check, and followed after Senenmut.

The world of the dead was strange, but she had expected it to be. While it felt odd that her feet did not seem to touch the ground even as she moved up a pathway toward a hilltop temple, she was not surprised by the sensation. She found it interesting that it was as light as the Red Land at midday, but the stars shone brightly in the night sky overhead. Animal-headed gods moved in the landscape that also contained farmers, priests, and nobles all going about their business. The river was full of fishing boats, barges, and all the busy traffic that belonged on the great river. In the far, far distance, palaces and temples seemed to hang in the air, separated from the clear world in which she moved by a veil as thin as the finest linen. She knew without being told that she could not reach the beautiful city in the distance until she passed through the temple before her. There were tests to pass. She was prepared, having long ago memorized the transmigration spell in the *Book of the Dead*.

Hatshepsut smiled.

As though he felt her smug assurance, Senenmut turned to face her. He smiled as well, the expression deepening the long lines on either side of his mouth. "In life you made the world as you wished it to be. It is not so easy here. Not so simple."

"Easy?" she answered, outrage flaring. "Simple?

He turned and walked on. She followed, but all sense of serenity, of certainty, was shaken.

"This is the temple of Tuat," Senenmut told her when they reached the towering entrance of the many-pillared hall.

"Tuat has no temples," she replied. "All temples are Tuat's."

"Your answer is partially correct. All gods are manifestations of the one god, Tuat, so all temples in the Black Land are temples of Tuat. In the land of Tuat there is only one temple, and all gods are one with Tuat."

"That is not written in the *Book of the Dead*." She attempted to step around Senenmut, but there was no getting past him. He was *her* servant! Why was he behaving so strangely? "I will enter the halls of Osiris," she told him. "You will take me there."

"It is within the temple of Tuat," he said. And then they were there.

It was a dark place, and empty, an abandoned temple. That was not right. She recognized the two pools, and the scales on which her heart should be weighed against a feather. The throne of Osiris, god of the dead, was unoccupied. "Where are the forty-two judges?" she asked. "Where is Osiris? Where is Thoth?" Her voice rose in anger, and growing dread. Dread that grew stronger as she saw the blank expression on the face of the man who was her most trusted friend in the world of the living. "What is the matter here?" she demanded.

"*Ma'at,*" he answered "Harmony, balance, all that is just and correct. You, Great Royal Wife, may have tipped the world out of balance, out of *ma'at.*"

She bridled at this. How many times had this been whispered in life? She would not tolerate it said to her face in death. And not by him! "I am Pharaoh! I am *ma'at!*"

"You are a woman who assumed the throne of Egypt. This is not the way of nature. You are accused of many crimes. You are accused of evil deeds. You are accused of being unnatural."

Unnatural! She stood straight and proud to face this man who had claimed to care for her in life. "How dare you accuse me of even pretending to be *natural*! The child of a god—a child of the great god Amon is a god. I was born in a woman's body, as my father Amon willed it, but I was born to rule as king. As my father willed it."

"You speak of a dream of being the god's daughter—"

"The god's *child.*" You were there with me, she remembered, when the dream came to me. "Do you not remember the words that were barely adequate for the powerful knowledge the god put into my mind?"

He held her close, together in the bed in the house they shared whenever she could leave her own palace. He was her daughter's guardian and master of many offices in her household. They had been lovers since long before she wed her weak and foolish brother at her father's command.

Her father was the reason for the powerful dream that had woken her, to find herself sobbing and shaking in her lover's arms.

She must have cried out about her father in her sleep, for Senenmut said, "The great king is dying, and that is a fearful thing. It is all right to cry, for you love him above all others."

Senenmut knew her pride, how she would hate to show the weakness of tears.

Yes, she was afraid, but it was proper fear and awe of what she had seen.

"I dreamed not of death," she said when she got the sobbing under control. "I dreamed of birth."

The memory lived in her still, and she knew it always would. It gave her knowledge, set her apart.

"Whose birth?" Senenmut asked. "Neferure?" There was concern for her daughter in his voice.

"I did not dream of giving birth. I dreamed of being born. No—of how I came to be born. I was there," she said. "I saw how it was. My father is a god. My father is Amon."

"Your father Thutmosis is Horus, Lord of the Two Lands." The correction was gentle, but there.

It almost made her laugh, but there could be no laughter at such a serious moment. She put her fingers over his lips. "Listen! I will tell you. Remember every word I say. My ba spirit floated in above the bed of my mother, Ahmose, and looked down upon her union with my father Thutmosis. While my father was within my mother, the great god Amon flowed like a river of gold into my father's body. The god took the form of the king. It was the god's seed that my mother took into her womb. Thutmosis was

Amon, Amon was Thutmosis, and I was conceived. I was born child of the king, and child of the god. I am not as other women. I am god born. Only I of my father's children was born this way. It is a great thing. A holy thing. It sets me apart, above. Someday—"

"Someday has come and gone," Senenmut said now, drawing her attention back to the empty temple within the temple of Tuat.

She held herself very still, very sure. "In death as in life, I am still the child of Amon."

"You believe this is a true dream?"

Of course it was true! She knew it with her heart, and all her souls. "I have said so," was her answer to this *man* who dared to question her. "You are not a god," she reminded him. "I am."

He nodded his had, but showed no other sign of humility. "I speak for the gods in this place. And the gods have more questions."

She kept her resentment to herself, though she wore her pride and surety openly. She looked upon Senenmut with contempt. "Then ask, servant."

"There are those who have accused you of usurping power, even as Great Royal Wife. You have been accused of sowing discord and fear within the royal household of your husband."

"Who accuses me of such nonsense?"

"The Lady Isis. She accused you of causing her own death."

"Isis!" Now there was a woman who had had no use for her brain, even before the embalmers drew it out of her head. "Isis bore my husband the son he named heir. I gave her all the respect she deserved for having borne my brother-husband a child. I cared for the child. The woman was a plotting fool. I might not have minded her plotting, if she was any good at it. She was an irritant rather than a challenge. She was a gossip. She was the tool of factions within my husbands court. Those factions plotted against my husband's rule, they weakened the power of the king. I protected the throne. That was my duty. That was *ma'at*."

"You kept *ma'at* during the rule of your husband by any means necessary?"

"Of course. Protecting Pharaoh is the sacred duty of his sister, his wife, and his queen. I was all of those things."

"You destroyed Isis?"

"I curbed the threat she brought into my husband's household."

"You ended her life?"

"I was not kind to her in life," Hatshepsut conceded. "But I gave her a magnificent tomb."

"She is proud of her mortuary temple, and the number of lector priests who care for it," Senenmut agreed.

"Then Lady Isis has nothing to complain about," Hatshepsut said. "Not that the lack will stop her."

Senenmut cleared his throat. "There are graver matters you must answer for. Your existence is in jeopardy."

She heard the warning, but was she supposed to learn humility and prevarication at this stage in her journey from god on earth to god in the land of Tuat.

Hardly.

She tossed her head, swaying the heavy dark hair that fell to her shoulders. She was aware of the weight, and the jangling of the gold-and-faience beads woven into the well-oiled tresses. She also became aware that she wore no crown. Not the crown of the pharaoh, nor the crown of a queen. She had long ago rejected the queen's crown, but even that official mark of status would have been a comfort in this dreadful time of questioning. A wave of fear went through her, but she rejected it as she'd rejected being queen.

"Ask what you will," she told Senenmut. "Weigh my heart against a feather, and you will find it light with truth."

"You were not the first choice as regent when your husband died, leaving your nephew Thutmosis Lord of the Two Lands. Why did you step out of the role of contented widow in the harem and take the regency into your own hands? This was not a womanly act."

"It was the act of a mother!" she protested. "You were there. You know well what happened. It was you who brought the conspiracy to light."

"Speak, then, of this supposed conspiracy, and how you acted as a mother, rather than as an ambitious woman hungry for power."

Of course she hungered for power. Why should she not take power, when she was the only one who knew how to use it? She had needed power in those early days after the death of her husband. She had needed the power, to save her own life, and more importantly the lives of her daughter, and of the nephew who was a child set on the throne of the two lands.

"Lady Isis' meddling will bring us all down," Senenmut reported. The late king let her infest her household with the priests of Seth."

"Only in Seth's aspect as a love god," she reminded Senenmut. "They performed great magic for Lady Isis to keep her in the king's favor. They are of no use to her now."

"Do you think they will just go away? The priests of Seth have their hooks into the mother of Pharaoh. They're maneuvering the council through her to have their high priest appointed the boy's vizier."

Senenmut had come to her as she played with her daughter beside a garden pool. The coolness of the water had helped alleviate the afternoon heat. The scent of lotus and other water plants perfumed the air. This hardly seemed a place of danger, but Hatshepsut sensed its presence in the worried face of her lover and ally.

Neferure held her arms out to Senenmut, who took the girl from her mother's lap. Hatshepsut rose and began to pace. She had allowed Isis to play love games with the Seth priests, so she bore some responsibility for allowing the agents of chaos to enter the royal household. What would her divine father have said about such a foolish strategy on her part? That she'd grown lax. That she had failed in her duty to protect Pharaoh and the land.

"I will not allow Thutmosis to be surrounded by the priests of any god but Amon," she told Senenmut. "They are evil. Their poison will infect the king as he grows. Amon is the guardian god of my family. His light is the only guide we need."

Senenmut cradled Neferure. "Thutmosis is not the only child that will fall victim to the false teachings and sick ways of the Seth priests. Neferure is bound to Thutmosis to become his sister-wife. The priest will take her from you to raise as their tool."

She had walked restlessly away from him as he spoke, now she whirled back. "They will not!"

She would never entrust her child to the teachings of any god but Amon. She would not allow Thutmosis to be corrupted. She would protect the land of her father. She could not go into quiet retirement as the king's young widow. Nor did she want to, despite half formed visions of leading a quiet life with Senenmut openly beside her. She did not really want to retire from the court.

"I will do what must be done," she told Senenmut. She would do what a child of a god and king must. She would take power in the names of Thutmosis and Neferure. She would protect them. "I will go to the high priest of Amon," she said. "I will call upon him, and the aid of the god my father. I will become regent."

"It was necessary," she said now. "It was accomplished. With the god's help."

"So you say."

"So I know to be true."

"Your belief in yourself is strong."

Your belief in me used to be strong, she thought, but did not say. If Senenmut chose to be her enemy now, she would certainly not show him that this betrayal hurt her.

"Taking the regency was your first usurpation. Does the justification that it was the act of a desperate mother justify putting *ma'at* out of balance?"

"Yes."

He looked taken aback with her curt answer. "The gods may not think so."

"The gods are parents."

"But the gods do not act against *ma'at*."

"Seth does," she reminded him. "What more must I answer for?" she demanded impatiently. "Perhaps we have all of eternity to conduct this conversation, but I grow bored."

He smiled; the deep, dimpled smile she so well remembered. This broke her heart. "You know what is left to answer for."

Indeed, she did. She had been a queen who declared herself king. "You aggravate me." She looked around the dark, empty temple. "The gods aggravate me. Did I shock them because I wore a beard?"

"A king is necessary to perform the rites that renew and keep the land."

"I was king."

"You assumed the symbols of the king—the crowns, the crook and flail and false beard only a king may wear. You are a woman."

"The symbols are enough. Godhood transforms the symbols into reality."

"Godhood?"

"I was born of a god. Thus, I am a god."

"You truly believe you are a god?"

"Was I not pharaoh? Did the sun not rise to my prayers? Did the river not flood, and then fall, at my prayers? Was there famine, plague, or war while I held the crook and flail and throne? If my father Amon had not approved of my actions, would I have been able to rule in peace and prosperity?"

"Perhaps great magic held off inevitable disaster."

"I performed only the magic proper for a pharaoh."

"You took the throne from the rightful king. This was against *ma'at*."

"It was meant to be."

"Why did you commit this heresy?"

"It was no heresy."

"You were regent. It was enough."

"It was necessary. Egypt needed a king."

"Egypt had a king."

"He was not the child of Amon. It was not his time." It was galling to be accused of stealing the throne of the land she had been born to rule, especially by one who had supported her actions. Gods were not thieves! Gods accepted their destiny, and acted accordingly. She had taken from Thutmosis, but only what was hers. "The high priest of Amon knew the truth of my vision, and supported my claim to the throne."

"But is it not a high priest's duty to support the god he serves?"

"Yes. Of course. Amon was served. How could serving the god my father be in any way wrong? Whether one is a man or a woman," she added before the silly accusation that it was heresy for a woman to be Pharaoh could be thrown at her again. "I served Amon and the land. I built temples, and brought trade from afar. The land prospered. I am right. Anyone who claims otherwise is wrong."

"And what of the rights of your nephew, the king? You usurped his throne."

"Did I kill him? Did I send him into exile? Did I

harm him in any way? Does he not rule the Two
Lands now that I am come to the land of death? He
has what is his. While I ruled, he had what he
wanted."

"Everything but the throne."

"He was born to be a great warrior, like his grandfather who was my divine father. It was Thutmosis
who begged me to be allowed to train and serve in
the army. He learned well, and the knowledge he
gained strengthens his rule as king."

"You have answers for every accusation."

"Of course. And my answers are true."

"You believe them to be true. We will now see
what the judges believe."

The temple, already shadowy, now went completely
dark. A hot desert wind blew through the darkness.
It wound itself around her like the strips of embalmers'
linen. Once more, as in the seventy days before her
awakening, she was bound in darkness.

She had known no fear during that waiting period,
for she had thought she knew the way to pass
through the perils that preceded judgment in the
halls of Osiris. She thought this new imprisonment
was meant as another test. She was supposed to be
afraid, to worry, to know guilt for breaking *ma'at*.
Was this the time when she was supposed to shout
her confession into the darkness? Was she supposed
to beg forgiveness?

Instead, she recited a long prayer to Amon, and
waited with patience that surprised her. Surprised
her, that is, until she recalled that she was in the land
of eternity. She did not like that her fate was not in

her hands at this moment. For she had been in charge of her destiny since the moment of her conception. She had not always known this. It had frequently been difficult to see her way with all the men called Thutmosis in her life. Her father Thutmosis had been commanding. She reluctantly obeyed, and laid her plans. Her husband Thutmosis had been disappointing, she had ruled in all but name for him. She schemed and survived. Her nephew Thutmosis had been challenging. She took what was his by birth, because she could. She had outmaneuvered them all. She had triumphed in life. Would she be defeated now?

She was unaware of time, and heard nothing but a sound like the buzzing of flies. She supposed this noise was the distant sound of her judges debating her fate. Eventually the noise stopped. Then the blackness faded back to the familiar shadowy outlines of the hall of judgment. She still could not move, but at least she could see.

Before her, ibis-headed Thoth stood before the scales of *ma'at*, her heart in one hand, a feather in the other. Osiris was seated on his throne, awaiting the weighing of her heart. The beast of destruction crouched beside the god's throne, ready to devour her if the weight of her heart proved her unworthy. She had seen this scene many times, painted on tombs, drawn on papyrus, carved in temples. Now it was real, the figures moved. It was truly frightening.

Thoth placed the feather on one side of the scales. After a moment's pause, he put her mummified heart on the other side.

Though she was dead, Hatshepsut held her breath.

Then she was bound in darkness once more. She could not even scream.

Until a familiar voice said, "Awaken. And speak."

Oh, no! Must she got through that ordeal all over again?

Though she was weary, she reluctantly opened her eyes. She sat up and looked around. This time she found herself in a very familiar garden. This time when she saw Senenmut she was not filled with gladness, but with fury. She raised her hand to strike him.

He was laughing when he caught her by the wrist. He pulled her close and kissed her, even though she kicked at his ankles while he did so.

When he let her go she spat. "I hate you."

He laughed again. "No, you don't."

"You humiliated me."

"I saved you."

He sounded as calm and sure as he always had, and as lacking in respect for her rank. "Leave my sight," she ordered him. "Never approach me again."

"How many times did you say that when we were alive?"

"This time I mean it."

"You never mean it."

She crossed her arms. "Go."

"Such a temper. I counted on that temper and pride, and you did not disappoint me."

As always, he managed to pique her curiosity just when she thought throwing him to the jackals was the perfect way to deal with him. "Disappoint you?"

"I said you did not disappoint me. When I volunteered to question you, I knew you would triumph."

"Volunteered?" Hatshepsut shook her head.

"Dealing with the gods is the same as dealing with any court of ambitious, bickering nobles, my love. Even Osiris was reluctant to be involved with a case as special as yours. Amon would be offended if you were judged guilty. Other gods are horrified at a woman's presumption that she can rule. Isis and Hathor and others argue that you proved that a woman is worthy of ruling. What is *ma'at*? What is justice? It was a tricky case. It is the gods themselves who sit in judgment of the pharaoh, by the way, not the forty-two judges that other people face. When I stepped forward to become your questioner, the gods were glad to take a step back and wait to see what would happen. This way, if you passed the tests, none of them would have offended Amon, or Amon's child."

This information did nothing to alleviate her anger. "Why you?" she demanded. "Why did the one man I loved question the validity of all I hold dear and true?"

He laughed again. "Because I knew the right questions to ask, of course. I knew the way to phrase the question for you to give the answers that you believed to be truth. Belief is everything in the land of gods."

Hatshepsut's anger faded slowly as these words sank in. He was a clever man, her Senenmut. He always had been. She must have passed the test, her heart must have been light with truth, or she would have been devoured. "You risked my displeasure to save me."

"As I have before."

Yes. There had been many times they had clashed in the land of the living. It appeared that they would now have eternity to clash many times again. She smiled, and held her arms out to him.

He looked longingly at her, but put his hands behind his back. "There is one more thing. A decision you must make."

She looked around the garden where she had spent all her happy hours with Senenmut. It was peaceful here. This house would be a good place to spend eternity. She knew what decision she must make, but she waited for Senenmut to put the choice to her.

"You were a queen, and will be treated as a queen if you choose to stay here. But you were also Pharaoh. A pharaoh joins the gods, and performs the duties of the gods. Accept your divinity, and you will be among the stars. Yours will not be the joyous afterlife of mortals, but the lonely joys of the protectors of the Two Lands. Remain Pharaoh, and we cannot be together, not as long as your name is known in the land of the living."

Her spirits sank, her triumph faded. So the gods had found a way to punish her for becoming pharaoh after all. She closed her eyes for a moment, and smelled the earthly scent of lotus and sun-warmed water. She quickly resigned herself from these simple pleasures. She looked at the man she had loved all her life.

"I will go among the stars," she told him. "A pharaoh can do no less."

He nodded gravely. "I know. You are a god now."

So she was. For as long as her name was known in the land of Egypt. Perhaps there was something she could do about that. "Being a god has its advantages," she told Senenmut. Perhaps, in time, her name as Pharaoh could be forgotten, erased, made as if she had never ruled. But not yet. "Wait for me," she told her lover.

Then she lifted her arms and rose into the sky, into the sun, and took her place with Horus in the barque of the sun, protecting its daily journey across the Two Lands. As was the destiny of every Pharaoh of Egypt.

KING OF SHREDS AND PATCHES

by P.N. Elrod

P.N. "Pat" Elrod has written over twenty novels and twenty short stories and coedited two anthologies, and still can't seem to break the writing habit. She occasionally surfaces from communing with the keyboard to guest at SF conventions and scarf chocolate, preferably both at once. Her website is www.vampwriter.com.

HERE DO I set down for posterity, a true and exact record of the misfortunes that have lately beleaguered the court of Denmark. Whoever finds this, I ask and pray that you hold all knowledge of it from my beloved Queen Gertrude should I predecease her.

The death of my brother, King Hamlet, could not have come at a worse time for Denmark.

I was in my chambers, setting to paper a thorough report of all that I saw and heard in Norway while acting as his ambassador there when the news of the calamity came to me.

Rather than a soft knock from one of Elsinore's countless pages, I was startled from my task by heavy pounding from a hasty fist. It occurred to me that my fears of an invasion from Norway were about to be fulfilled. I threw down my quill and, being alone, unlatched the door myself and pulled it wide, interrupting a second assault. Old Polonius stood without.

"What is amiss, sir?" I demanded, for obviously something of great import was wrong. His face was as white as his beard except for two red spots high on his cheeks from recent exertion. His breath came hoarse and hard. I'd ever known him as a man well able to keep control of his emotions; now he was positively tottering from inner turmoil. I took his trembling hand and led him inside. "Is it war?"

"W—war, your lordship?" He gave me so blank a look that he might have been struck by one of those strange convulsions that takes a man's mind away. "There is no war."

"Then, speak, what is amiss?"

His lips quivered and, overcome by whatever troubled him, he bowed his head and groaned. I glanced at the open doorway, but none were with him who might inform me of the nature of this trouble. That was odd. He usually had no less than two pages in tow the whole of the day to run his errands. I looked down both ends of the hall, but all was quiet in this part of the castle. From one of my windows I ascertained the courtyard below was also peaceful. It was the end of the hot part of the afternoon, and those who had no duties would take rest while they could.

In a firm tone I charged Polonius to explain himself. That seemed to break through, and he slowly raised his head. His eyes streamed tears, and without knowing the matter, I felt a kindred ill-omened leadening of my heart.

"Speak, sir," I whispered.

"Oh, good lord Claudius, your royal brother is dead."

Let God Himself be my witness, I almost laughed, for it was clear the dear old man had indeed lost his wits and was ranting. "Impossible. I saw him take his walk upon the upper platform this morning as always. He waved to me and I to him."

But Polonius shook his head again, as though to dislodge a stubborn fly. "Would that I were a liar, your lordship, but he is dead and gone and nothing can change that or bring him back to us."

I still could not take it in. "How comes he to be dead? Was it a fall?" Elsinore was full of stairs, many very steep.

"A fall? No, he was asleep in his orchard. He lies there still."

"What? Have you sent for a priest?" He blanched even more, and I knew that he had not. If there was the least breath of life remaining, then my brother must give his last confession lest his soul needlessly suffer. Perhaps Polonius was wrong. His sight was dim now with age, and though wise in statecraft, he was often wrong in more mundane matters—not that the death of a king could be considered as such.

"Lord Claudius, King Hamlet is *dead*. For hours, perhaps."

"And no one sent for help or told me until now?"

"As soon as I saw for myself, I came straight from there to you—wait, sir! There is more!"

But I was striding swiftly away. I loved Polonius like a second father—he had taught me much of the wisdom of his craft that I could better serve my brother and thus Denmark as ambassador—but could not wait upon him. Impatience and fear engulfed me. Grief, too, though I pushed that roughly from my heart. I could not and would not believe it; Hamlet could not, *must* not be dead.

Those inhabitants of Elsinore I passed to reach my brother's apartments continued their normal business with the peace of ignorance. Apparently Polonius spoke the truth about seeing me first, and word had not yet spread. Only when I descended several flights and entered the arched hall leading to Hamlet's private orchard did I perceive signs of trouble. No less than six guardsmen stood clustered before the orchard door. As a man, they had their swords ready in hand, tardily prepared to defend their royal master, but against what? Death? When his dread hand falls upon your shoulder, what mortal army can turn his purpose?

"Let me pass," I said.

The tallest, Francisco, planted himself in my way. "I beg forgiveness, Lord Claudius, but Lord Polonius ordered that we arm and keep all from the enclosure until his return."

My flare of anger was reflected in their frightened faces. "Even the king's brother?"

"Even so, lord." He looked to be highly unhappy

with his lot. "I can send a man to fetch him here, though."

I could have bullied my way in, but chose to hold back. If it was true, if my dear brother was dead, then it would be best to follow the forms of custom and wait. "Do that. And quickly. He was last in my chambers."

Francisco nodded shortly to the youngest in his charge, who sheathed his weapon and hurried off.

"Do you know what has happened?" I asked.

"Only that at the telling of the last hour Lord Polonius went to rouse His Majesty from his nap as usual. I was on watch here. His lordship came out, seeming most stricken. He told me to bring more men, and when I did, he then instructed us to stand firm and let none inside."

That made sense. The unexpected death of a much-loved king was bad enough, but letting the news fly forth without consideration for its effect on the common people could cause disorder. Polonius was aware of the impending threat from Norway; the last thing Denmark needed was to be thrown into chaos and thus be seen as vulnerable by the rapacious Fortinbras.

"You did well," I said. "We'll wait for the lord chamberlain's return."

"Lord? Do *you* know what is wrong?" Behind him, his men cast uneasy glances at the closed door to the orchard, ominous in shadows. They would be guessing the worst, of course. In light of Polonius' odd actions and orders, of me here at this time of day, of the king not showing himself, they would guess rightly. If the worst was true, then this would have to be handled with great care.

"Be at peace. All will be revealed soon."

That did little to bolster them, quite the opposite. I curbed my impatience as best I could until Polonius arrived, short-winded and troubled. He must have known his orders wouldn't have gone well with me, but I put a reassuring hand on his arm to let him know I was not offended. He had done the right thing.

"Stand down," he puffed at Francisco, "and let Lord Claudius pass."

One of them thrust open the door and the yellow light of late afternoon flooded the dim hall. I blinked against the glare and stepped into it, looking around. There was a strong scent of apple blossoms on the sea-washed air. This was my brother's sanctuary from the cares of his crown. Few were allowed here: myself, his queen, their son, Polonius, and a gardener whose only job was to tend this great garden. He worked alone and was always gone when Hamlet desired its peace. Ever busy with other concerns, I'd not been here in decades, not since Hamlet and I played within its high walls as children and certainly not since he was crowned king all those years past.

I tried to recall childhood memories of this place, but they were of no use now. Whatever paths we played on then were changed. Trees had grown, died, been uprooted, and replaced with other growth. This space covered no more than an acre, but the plantings were high and dense, and one could easily become lost.

Polonius was at my side. "This way, lord."

"Have you sent for a priest? For a physician?"

"Both, lord. They will be here anon."

He took me on a twisting path that seemed to lead toward the center. It was a cunning design, giving the illusion of a goodly walk, and within a turn or two it felt like we were in a shady orchard miles away. The branches above were laced together in some spots concealing even the looming bulk of Elsinore Castle.

I recognized a landmark. Ahead, overlooked by an old apple tree, was a vast stone bench. It was part of the very base of the massive sea cliff that Elsinore rested upon. The upthrust of stone was larger than two beds pushed together and much longer. A master hand had, in ancient times, carved it with fantastical shapes and patterns on the sides. The top was smoothed to within a foot of the ground, and polished. It had served as throne, fort, feasting table, riding steed, and other imaginings in our childhood play until we outgrew it. Now it was covered with thick robes to lend ease to the hard stone and there would my brother find respite from his cares.

And there he lay in his last rest.

I'd seen battle, and knew death's countenance. At a dozen paces I recognized the stillness peculiar to its presence. That it had come for my brother was true after all, and I was no longer master of my progress. Halting, I leaned on Polonius as the certainty swept over me. With no mind to the words, a prayer fled from my lips, and I crossed myself.

"This is trouble enough, but a harsher, more evil woe awaits," he told me.

"What mean you?"

For once Polonius was unable to summon words for explanation and again would only shake his head. My curiosity became stronger than my anguish. Hanging on each other like two old women, we slowly approached my brother's final couch of rest, my heart filled with dread.

The cushioning robes were in disarray, tossed about as though Hamlet had fought desperately against a bad dream. His arms were flung wide over his head, hands turned onto grasping claws, his whole body twisted and frozen in a posture of extreme agony. As we came closer, more details revealed themselves to the eye, but the mind denies such awfulness as being too impossible to exist, and so we stare and stare and stare into overwhelming horror.

My poor brother's skin was crusted and splotched with some loathsome excretion, as though he sweated the puss of vile infection through each and every pore. Crusted also was his very blood, which had burst from his eyes, nose, and gaping mouth. A stench like that of a man dead for a week, not mere hours, rose from him to merge with the sweetness of the apple flowers. Flies buzzed in legions around him.

Grabbing up one corner of a robe, I drew it over his bloated face. Had he not been in garb familiar to me I should never have recognized him.

I had seen men die from paroxysmal fits when their hearts stop, and I'd seen what the ravages of contagion could do to a body, but this . . . a bitterly cold hand closed hard around my spirit. What had taken my brother away was neither fit nor sickness.

The fear I'd felt before was a pale thing compared to what seized me now, for now I was round full with terror.

And I dared *not* show it.

"Lord Claudius?"

I looked at Polonius . . . and wondered. Could *he* . . . ?

And so did he return my look. I saw my own thoughts running panicked behind his blue eyes.

"You remember?" I asked.

He nodded, his lips thin with the effort to compress them together, lest he speak anything aloud.

"And think you it was *I* who did this?"

"I think nothing, your lordship," he said most carefully.

I was too stunned to be angered. "I understand your suspicion, but . . . see me, good friend."

"Lord Claudius, I—"

"*See* me!"

He looked from me to Hamlet's shrouded form and back. Polonius seemed balanced on the very edge of a cliff.

I had to pull him from it. "Recall you the service of my *whole life* as I recall yours. You above all others know my heart and the honest love I bear my brother—a match to your own, is it not?"

He teetered for a long moment, then cast his gaze downward. "I am most desperately shamed, lord. 'Tis a wicked demon who placed doubt in my mind."

"And mine, too."

I took up his trembling hand, seeing truth and trust restored in his withered features and with each fresh tear that started from his eyes. "So, despite our knowledge of such dark matters we are guiltless of this deed. That leaves us to find who is responsible. Who and how."

"And why," he added, wiping his cheek with his sleeve.

"Then avenge ourselves and Denmark for this treason."

The physician and the priest, one for Hamlet's body, the other for his soul, both arriving far too late, came up the path. I withdrew as they each tended to their spheres of influence, notwithstanding their appalled reactions to the condition of the king's body.

While the priest continued with prayers, the physician approached us and bowed. He seemed very shaken, but who would not be?

"Your lordship," he said to me. "If it please you, I am most heartily sorry that—"

"What caused my royal brother's death, sir?" I said abruptly. "Speak plainly and quick."

"Sir, I believe it was poison that left him in so lamentable a state."

My heart fell. If word got out that the majesty of Denmark had been murdered . . .

"What poison?" asked Polonius, assuming an air of reservation.

"Most likely from an adder slipped over the wall."

What? My surprise was genuine. Was the man a fool? But perhaps his experience was insufficient to the task. He was very young, having taken over most of the duties of his father, who had taught him his skills. Not well enough, it appeared.

Polonius and I exchanged a look. A shared memory was the cause of our moment of shared distrust. We both knew no serpent's sting would bring about such a putrid sweating as to leave a body bloated and stinking in the space of a few hours. Only a powerful poison could do that—one crafted and distilled by an expert hand.

Twenty years and more ago, as a young courtier dispatched to Italy, it had been my lot to learn of a death by identical means of dispatch. A cuckolded gentleman, unable to give challenge because of his advanced years, chose to kill his wife's lover by poison. The artificial infection (it was found) was poured into the unfortunate's ear as he slept and shortly he succumbed to convulsions, sweat, and bleeding, passing in terrible pain from this life to the next. The husband was judged to be within his rights and was acquitted, and his wife took herself away to a nunnery, which, considering the nature of her marriage, was a much safer place to be than home.

I'd eventually brought the tale back to Denmark, telling it to Polonius, among others, but only he knew the particular signs of that concoction, which was called juice of hebenon, though it was made of many other things as well. Some might know the name, but not its nature or how to make it. And like myself, my old friend could not tell a henbane plant from rosemary.

Yet still we stared at one another, for he had memory of the story the same as I. But by that we each knew the other would have instantly known, therefore, neither could have done it. Only someone else . . .

"An adder?" Polonius questioned sharply. "Are you sure? What sort?"

"There are many," said the doctor. "I know of none whose bite would ordinarily cause such a reaction. However, just as one man may suffer the sting of a bee and move on while another falls and dies from it, I believe His Majesty may have had the same susceptibility as the latter wretch. If he was overly sensitive to the venom, then would he quickly succumb with great violence to it. Perhaps, bitten while he slept, he awoke too late to call for help and thus passed from life."

Polonius nodded and looked to me. The explanation was reasonable, and though we knew it the wrong one, we had no choice but to make it serve for the moment.

"Then the orchard must be searched from top to bottom," I said. "If such a serpent is loose here, none are safe. Perhaps it pleased God to take our king from us in such a hasty and terrible manner, but I am not pleased and would have the instrument of His use destroyed."

"Presently, your lordship," said Polonius. "That shall be seen to presently, but there are other necessities pressing. We must organize. The other lords must be informed, and dear God, the poor queen must be told."

This would destroy her, I thought. Gentle Gertrude

hung on my brother's every word as though her life came from him and not heaven. "I will have to do that. And it must be done softly. She cannot see her husband while he is in so abhorrent a state. Her ladies should be at hand, and you as well, Doctor. You will also be needed to see to the cleansing of my poor brother's remains and to stop any rumors of plague or pox so none may take alarm. See to it."

"I am at your service, my lord."

Polonius threw him a sharp look at the error. I was not king, and therefore not his or anyone else's lord, but the old man couldn't say so to him while I was in hearing.

I shook my head at Polonius, so he saw it was of small matter to me, which it was; we had greater things to discuss.

But not now. I could hold my grief back no longer. I turned quickly from them and walked a few paces into the trees to escape their sight, and there gave in to it. They would doubtless hear my sobs, but would allow me the necessary privacy for as long as it took until the first wave subsided. It was my lot to set things in motion, and in those days to come my public duties would intrude upon my private mourning. But for this hour I ached bitterly at this unexpected sundering from my onetime playmate, lifelong friend, and finally king. My brother was dead, and I felt his loss like a mortal wounding from a dull blade.

When my parents died, it had fallen to others to see to the forms and processions of grief. I was able to mourn for as long and as deeply as my soul needed. Now the heavy responsibilities were on me, and I had few friends to help with the burdens. But that dear old man, Polonius, proved to be my greatest ally, adviser, and most trusted support through the worst of it.

My position in Denmark's court had never been an enthusiastic one, for there were many lords who vied to be my late brother's favorite and thus was I mistakenly perceived as an interloper ready to subvert their ambitions. They were fools to think their links to him could prove stronger than my own constant link of blood. Certainly Hamlet found grim amusement in their antics. However, their ever-shifting games of vanity and power were nothing to me; I did not play. It was far better to watch than participate in such politic comedies.

There was also a most important detail that these strivers continually overlooked: I had *no* desire to increase my power nor did I possess designs on the throne. That sovereign seat was destined to go to my nephew, young Hamlet, and he was welcome to it. In the course of years, if I was spared, I fully expected to serve the Danish cause as his loyal ambassador in his turn.

But his father's sudden death at this, the worst possible time, usurped his anticipated succession. Within a week Fortinbras—who was clearly preparing to take back the lands his father lost to us—would hear of King Hamlet's passing; within a week after that the young firebrand's armies would be ravaging those border lands he wished to reclaim, shattering our long peace and prosperity beyond mending for years to come.

Fortinbras would not—with *his* aspirations to glory—stop at the disputed borders, though, but would continue from Elsinore to Esbjerg, taking everything between in bloody conquest. The Danish nobles would defend each their several lands but would not unite to effectively defend Denmark as a whole unless they had a king to lead them. Separately they would fall; only together could we triumph.

But Prince Hamlet was in Wittenberg, a full month's journey away for the fastest messenger. He couldn't hope to return in less than two months, and by then he would have no kingdom to return to; it would be too late.

Polonius and I discussed this thoroughly and with much pain and care as well as consideration for young Hamlet's position. Had we some way to acquaint him with the crisis, he would have approved the necessity of instant action to preserve the state. Above all, Denmark must have a sound king, but particularly now.

The solution, Polonius said, was for *me* to assume the crown and do so without delay.

I confess the prospect was not a desirable one; I preferred my lesser position. "Let another be elected from the nobles of the land."

"Who?" he asked. "Who of that self-serving lot would you trust? This such-a-one is more ambitious than Fortinbras, that such-a-one too rabbitlike in manner to defend us in need or another is so grand in his vanity that he would bankrupt the whole of the treasury for a single suit of raiment. No, Lord Claudius, none of them have your understanding of what it truly means to rule wisely and well. You stood at your brother's side through many years and before that witnessed and learned from your father's long term. Young Hamlet does not possess such experience, and he's not here to be advised by either of us. Anyone else will bring eventual ruin to Denmark."

"But the nobles like me not. They will never elect me to be their lord."

"A majority of them will, at a word from me. The rest will fall in with the vote to prevent rivals from rising above their station."

"It'd be better they were wholehearted in their confidence, not forced."

"There will be no force, only persuasion. Once I set the facts plain before them, they'll be willing enough to have you stave off the invasion. Your report on what is afoot there— "

"They'll say I'm creating a threat from Norway to further myself."

"That they cannot do. Think you that yours were the only eyes and ears for Denmark in that court? I know of a dozen nobles with spies in place there, and to a man they will confirm the ill tidings you brought. They all want Fortinbras stopped. If you present them with a plan for that—"

"I had a recommendation prepared for—for my brother's approval . . ."

"Too late now for him to hear it, but in life he

heeded your counsel more often than not, and your advice was ever sound—another fact to put before the nobles. Your lordship, you *must* walk this path for the state to live on preserved from strife, and it must be an immediate starting out."

I had other objections, but in my heart knew he was right. If we waited two months for Hamlet's return, it would be too late, and Fortinbras would have swept in.

Thus did Polonius persuade me to my duty.

But I nearly ran craven from it when he broached the subject of the queen.

"She is loved by the rabble," he said. "Win her to your side, and you win their hearts as well."

I did not take his full meaning, thinking he meant her support for my cause was all that was needed. "She will prefer her son over me for the throne, which is to be expected. But once she knows the seriousness of this difficulty, she will come around."

"Do not count on that, for she has a blind eye when it comes to the lad. However, if played gently and well, she will prefer her *husband* over her son."

This was a day of thick sight for me. "But my brother is gone."

"I refer to *you*, sir. Become her husband."

To that I responded with a staring eye, unsure if I heard him right.

He pressed on. "The advantage is obvious. The queen remains the queen—which to her is far better than being the queen mother. She retains her honors and respect and position in the court, you have gained her approval and with that the support of the rabble, which counts for much, and young Hamlet is *still the heir*. Denmark is made secure by keeping the crown within the stability of a long-established royal family, its care in the hands of an honorable and well-schooled lord who will hold and protect it most diligently."

A wily old fellow was Polonius, but he seemed to have overstepped himself with this outrageous suggestion. A marriage was quite absurd, though it was sound politics and nothing new to me.

Many years ago in my youth I'd been betrothed to a number of young ladies. My father's political maneuverings demanded such matrimonial alliances, and I took none of them too seriously. Sometimes the girl died, in others the contract was canceled as her father in turn arranged a better match. On one occasion negotiations went so far that I was able to meet the girl, which was a bit of an advancement. She seemed a comely, quiet sort, but things never progressed beyond that first meeting. The alliance ceased to be of import and the marriage postponed indefinitely. So far as I knew I might still be engaged to her, but had long since forgotten her name.

Of course I'd availed myself of the fleshly pleasures, cheerfully leaving abstinence to those priests who chose to give attention to that vow. I'd had mistresses here and there where my duties carried me, for I found foreign women to be very captivating. But, for good or ill, I had never been the sort to lose my heart to any one woman for any length of time. I had no desire to father children, and if I had done so, then their mothers had kept the news to themselves. The expectation of marriage had ceased to be of import to me for whole decades so Polonius had much work convincing me to even listen.

Yet for the sake of the state, I did give ear to his argument, and after much thought concluded that he was right. This would not be the first time a ruler made a bride of the previous king's wife, but I was uncomfortable that this was my brother's wife. For most, such an alliance would stink of foul incest. However, Polonius had arguments against that, supported by Holy Scripture, no less.

With a sigh, and an unaccustomed palpitation in my heart inspired by terror, not lovesickness, I gave him leave to speak to Gertrude on the matter. He must make clear the fact that this marriage was strictly for the good of the state, and that I'd never presume to make overtures to her for any other reason. I had too much respect for my brother's memory for that. She was still in the deepest mourning for him, and on several occasions we sat together in the company of her ladies and grieved together, which had provided much comfort to me. We'd known each other for over thirty years, and I thought of her as a friend, nothing more.

To Polonius I said I would consent to offer suit to my former sister-in-law *only* if she was willing, and the arrangement of the marriage bed—or beds in their separate chambers—was entirely up to her. There was no need for us to beget an heir, after all, so a consummation was not necessary.

Polonius, choosing his moment most carefully, broached the subject with Gertrude. I know not what he said to her, but with his soft persuasions and influence he added royal matchmaker to his list of duties.

What another shock it was to learn that Gertrude *desired* to be my bride—in the traditional sense. Whether she wanted me for myself as a man or as some remnant of her late husband, as her protector or a means to continue as queen, perhaps all and more, I did not inquire. Let it suffice that I spent some hours talking with her with this new aspect included in the conversation and began to see her in a whole different light. She had happily retained a great portion of her youthful beauty and charm and used it to good effect. Combined with her artless sincerity of warmth toward me, I stood no chance and suffered the supreme loss of composure that occurs when a man of middle years falls in love for the very first time.

After that, events set their own course. The nobles supported me to take the crown, which I did, and within a month of leading the procession for my poor brother's internment I was leading the wedding party in to feast. Though the crowning and especially the marriage were scandalously quick, the results were as Polonius predicted. Fortinbras held back to see what direction I would take. Certainly, the quick activity in the Danish court had served him an unexpected turn. I made sure his spies had every chance to observe how busy the shipyards and armorers were—the first orders I issued as king were to give them custom. With no other hint of my intent, Fortinbras was free to draw his own conclusions, and so he hesitated. All to our advantage.

There was some grumbling in my court about the expense of arming, particularly for a battle that might not happen, but I knew it was cheaper to build for war than to have war itself, and with the building, stave off conflict. By spending a hundred on weapons that might never come to use, I saved the land ten thousand and more in bloody conflict—an excellent bargain.

Of course, it did not hurt to write in secret to the old uncle of Fortinbras, a longtime friend of mine, and let him know what his nephew was about. Though ancient in years, he still held influence over the boy, and with a stern lecture, a bribe, and a suggestion to direct his wrath and energy against our common enemy, the Polack, disaster for us both was turned aside.

All seemed well—except for the dark shadow of my brother's most strange and unnatural demise hanging over my heart. Polonius and I devoted many hours to discussion of this man or that, trying to discover who could have been responsible. One by one we proposed and ultimately discarded them all. None in the court had anything to gain by Hamlet's death and much to lose. They knew the crown would have gone to young Hamlet, and if anything happened to him, then an election would be held to decide the next king. No one of them held so much power or the esteem of his fellows to guarantee to influence the vote to himself and there likely would have been factions and perhaps even civil war as a result.

My next progression, which I kept very much to myself, was toward Laertes, Polonius' son. Laertes was a fit young fellow and skilled to action—but in Paris at the time. He might have set some agent of his to do the actual murder, but what reason could he have to kill our liege? He was a virtuous man, though, almost monklike and full of love for others and, like the rest of us, expected young Hamlet to inherit the crown. He had nothing to gain.

Who was left? Not gentle Gertrude, who had loved her husband as land loves the rain, and I did not for an instant think she had the savageness nor the knowledge to do it.

We questioned Francisco most closely, the poor man. I daresay he thought we were preparing to accuse him of treason, but even as he stood watch at the orchard door, other guards stood their watch within his sight. Between them, their movements were accounted for and it was clear that no one had entered the orchard.

Of course, that meant nothing if the murderer had concealed himself there earlier in the day. He could easily elude the patrols of the one gardener until the afternoon, and then escape later in the confusion after the body was found.

Ultimately we concluded that some agent for Fortinbras had carried out the assassination, for he could be the only one advantaged by the crime. It must have been a sore disappointment his ploy did not work as he'd planned.

How it rankled that we could not make a fair and open accusation against him, but for the sake of Denmark's continued peace we remained silent, and publicly gave sad credence to the physician's conclusion that a serpent's sting was to blame for so strange a death. A search was made and many snakes were found, but all were the benign sort that, lacking venom, cleanse the land of rats and mice. Though innocent of regicide, they were slaughtered by an army of gardeners.

So the days and weeks passed, our griefs were gradually softened by our joys, for Gertrude was an absolute delight to me, and peaceful order replaced the disruption in our lives.

Until Hamlet arrived home.

Of course he was considerably upset, not only by his father's death, but in finding that I had—in his eyes—stolen the succession from him. He objected also to the marriage, making clear our *haste* was what infuriated him the most. Had his mother delayed and ruled as queen, then might he have made his claim. We had considered that as a possibility, but discarded it. Gertrude was no soldier, and though popular with the people, to the gathered nobles she was merely a weak woman, and they would not follow a woman's orders.

Polonius and I both tried to reason with Hamlet on the dire nature of the threat from Norway, but a disaster that never happens is easily disregarded, and he did so, rather loudly and often.

That was when we became aware of an odd change in him. As well as being versed in the rougher arts of a highborn gentleman, he had ever been a pleasant, studious sort, most charming in his manner, a trait he'd inherited from his mother. Now was he darker in his moods and raiment, surly, and given to fits of passionate rage with no cause. We seemed to be dealing with a rebellious, uncontrolled youth of fifteen, not a grown man of thirty.

He'd returned to us from Wittenberg gaunt of face, his eyes wild, and often his speech wandered in ways comparable to Polonius' convoluted, but canny method, but there was no plan in Hamlet's ramblings, unless it was to give pain to those closest to him. I was his chief target for insult, but for Gertrude's sake I endured it. She and I set some of Hamlet's old friends to watching him in an attempt to discover the source of his rash behavior, but he was as guarded with them as I was years ago while acting as ambassador to the Polish court. He could not or would not divulge the reason for those periods of turbulence that bordered on the dangerous, though he had confessed to them that he was aware of his behavior. It occurred to me that this might be some childish means to gain attention. If so, then a bout of healthy sea-voyaging might set him right again.

But before I could act upon the idea, it was with great hesitation Polonius put into words that which I feared, that young Hamlet was indeed truly losing his wits. Certainly his doting mother noticed, though she vainly hoped it to be a temporary thing brought on by his unrelenting grief for his father's death. She prayed nightly he would find a cure and be restored. She later fixed on the idea—put forth by Polonius as a straw to comfort her—that her son was mad with love for the old man's daughter, Ophelia.

"It is not for love of *my* daughter, though," he said to me in private after we'd witnessed a harrowing encounter between Hamlet and Ophelia that reduced the poor girl to tears. " 'Twas love for another's daughter that's the root of this."

"Whose?" I asked.

"A nameless trull in the brothels of Wittenberg has obviously passed the French pox to him."

Oh, dear God, no. I objected greatly to this. I did *not* want it to be.

"My lord, I have seen its like before. He shows the signs, and his mind grows more bewildered each day."

"I know the signs, too, and it takes years, even decades for the madness to establish itself. 'Tis a slow process or so I've always been told."

"Who is to say it has not? When he was yet beardless, the first cravings of manhood might have taken him to a whore tainted with the rot. It could well have happened fifteen or more years ago and *now* the pox begins to briskly manifest. That which pollutes his blood is proceeding with its foul work far faster than normal, or so it appears to us who have not seen him in over a year. His friends are perhaps unaware of it for they've grown used to its gradual rise. He has his lucid moments, but they decrease in duration, while his ravings increase. You've yourself marked his deterioration. He is sinking into madness as surely as a ship stranded on sharp rocks, battered by the waves, is taken apart piece by piece. At this

pace, within a few months he will be wholly lost
to us."

I loved my nephew, so the sight of the change in
him was most painful to me. For those with eyes to
see—myself and Polonius, among others of the
court—young Hamlet's doom was upon him like a
black cloud over his head.

Poor Gertrude. Poor Denmark. "We must do
something."

"I know of no cure, lord."

"Nor I." I gave some quick thought to the matter,
recalling what others in my position had done to deal
with such difficulties. There were few choices open,
and now I had to also freshly consider the succession
since he would likely die before me.

The contagion gnawing at his brain would con-
sume him to full madness in too short a season. Even
if in that time I arranged a marriage and he bred an
heir, the child would likely also suffer enfeeblement.
My duties in other courts had been depressingly in-
structive. I'd seen firsthand how the indiscretions of
one generation were passed to the next, resulting in
malformed or simple-minded progeny who died
young. Yet often would they come to the rule of their
land regardless of their competency, which ever and
always led to disaster.

I discarded that possibility and put off for the moment the succession issue. Now was I a stepfather as
well as an uncle and had to think how to deal with
this coming tragedy.

Had Hamlet been suffering from any other kind of
pox, plague, or cancer, there would be no question

of our providing him the best of care here in his home for as long as needed. It would have been highly painful to his mother and myself, but in that pain we might find a kind of comfort in knowing that one is trying one's best to give succor to a much-loved child.

But madness such as this would be far too terrible to endure. His outbursts, so unlike his normal self, were an agony to Gertrude and promised to become worse in time. Should her last memory of her son be of him tied to a bed raving and spitting vile words at her blameless self? I would not put her gentle soul through that hell.

"He cannot remain here," I finally said. "We will spare him the humiliation of having his family and friends watch his decline. He can go to England and live out what time remains there. We'll tell him he's to collect their tardy tribute to give purpose to the journey so it doesn't appear to be banishment."

"Might he not raise a force against you, lord?" Polonius was ever worried about upstarts disrupting the peace of the land.

"Hardly. Their king has no stomach for foreign wars. We will also send a letter for his eyes only, requiring him to keep Hamlet under watch and out of mischief. When the boy is no longer capable, he's to be placed under care in some kind monastery. A portion of the tribute money will pay for it. We trust our ambassador there. He will see to it our prince is looked after according to his station."

This news was hard received by little Ophelia, despite her distressing encounter with Hamlet, who

had shown a side of himself that none should see.
But the hearts of young girls can become fast fixed,
even when it means their own destruction. She was
a sweet child and quite unspoiled, but for this love
fantasy of hers that had once been fueled by Hamlet
himself. During one of his summer visits he'd spent
some time with her, and she had taken his casual
attentions rather too seriously. Indeed there was a
time when the girl expected to be Hamlet's bride,
and put it forth among her ladies as though it was
inevitable. The rumor was enough for my brother
and Gertrude to see her privately. Apparently Gertrude was in favor of such a joining, but a royal
prince is not free to marry as an ordinary man might.
This was most clearly explained to Ophelia. Gertrude
said the child fled the room in tears, but such is the
way of things, and in time she recovered.

When Hamlet returned, though, Ophelia's feelings
for him were stirred up again, and Polonius and even
her brother Laertes had to step in to curb her spirited
affections. Hamlet inadvertently helped with his bru-
tal rejection of her. Polonius had ordered her to return some small gifts the prince had given during
lighter days, and he took it badly, venting his temper
on her. Polonius and I had watched the sorry show
from hiding, ready to emerge to protect her should
Hamlet turn violent. Thankfully, he did not, but the
encounter was a traumatic one for us all, and I was
very relieved when Hamlet finally stormed out.

Ophelia, in that moment, must have finally realized he was mad, but still she pined for him. Certainly there could be no match between them now. I

would have no objection were he robust and back to his former gentle self, but to inflict a diseased lunatic upon that fragile girl would be cruel folly. Her father made an end of the suit, and though it was hard for his daughter, better that than a ruinous marriage.

So might we have peacefully proceeded in the plan to send him packing had I but known Hamlet was hatching a plot of his own to bring me into disrepute. Its culmination took place the night a troupe of traveling players came to Elsinore. What a dreadful outcome did they, unknowing, bring about.

Things began well, for Gertrude took Hamlet's interest in holding a play for the court as a good sign. He had been in a high humor that day, more like his old self, but to me there still seemed to be a sharpness to his manner that was not quite right. Many times I caught him throwing looks my way that might as well been daggers. It made my heart ache, but I'd grown used to the fact that he would likely never forgive me for my expedient actions to save the throne. It was also in my heart that he was well aware of his deterioration, and knew he would never live to inherit that seat. Of course, he could never admit it to himself. It was far easier to blame me for all offenses.

Members of the court took their places in the audience, and Gertrude and I came in and settled ourselves. Hamlet made a bit of a scene with Ophelia, which caused a general discomfort to those who heard. Gertrude tried to distract him over to herself, but he continued to walk on the brink of provocation with the girl. Though sweet of temper, she wasn't particularly clever, and he still possessed enough of his wits to sting her with gibes and near-insults. She understood that he was bullying her, but wasn't quick enough to hold her own against attack, retreating into red-faced silence until the play began. I thought I should try to have words with him afterward, but Gertrude shot me a glance that said she would deal with him. Clearly he still had some control over himself and harrying an innocent like Ophelia was not gentlemanly behavior. He'd been raised better than that.

The players went through their traditional prologues and miming to which I paid scant attention, focused as I was on Hamlet. If he continued to be a nuisance to Ophelia, I would step in and halt things.

Would that he had done so, but he seemed aware of my attention and behaved himself, more or less. He shifted to making comments about the presentation, which was more generally irritating but tolerable. The player king and queen stumbled through their lines as though they'd but learned them in that same hour, and the whole time Hamlet's old school friend from Wittenberg, Horatio, held his gaze on me like a hawk. I knew some devilry must be afoot, but could not imagine what it might be. The man was too far distant to make a physical attack on my person, which was what I most dreaded. My guards would cut him down quick enough, so I felt safe, but hated the idea of more tales of scandal being heaped upon my court.

There, too, was the possibility that Hamlet might, while others were distracted by the show, attack me.

He was armed with sword and dagger as was the fashion and necessity of the time. However, I had instructed my guard to be particularly alert to any threatening move on his part. After that awful business with Ophelia, I concluded that he might eventually give in to a violent impulse and direct it at me. They were well aware of Prince Hamlet's growing madness and prepared, I hoped, to deal briskly with it should he lose control.

But he had no need. I was the one who fell into a fit, maneuvered there by a cunning made vicious by his disease.

Rumor has it I stopped the play out of guilt, for the players enacted a performance of a man's murder in a garden, his assassin, who was his own nephew, marrying the shallow and betraying widow in order to inherit everything.

At first I could not comprehend what I was seeing. I thought I must be interpreting it the wrong way, but as each ill-memorized line pressed upon my ears the more my disbelief gave way to rage.

The parallels to my brother's demise were too great and too offensive to be ignored, nor could I possibly contain my fury at so brazen an insult. I'd loved my brother, and to be accused of killing him by a boy I loved as much as a son was vile beyond imagining, yet Hamlet had imagined it, and it was at his instigation that the show was carried out. Only true madness could have created and birthed such a twisted thought from his innermost mind.

I rose and roared for lights, bringing an end to the mockery. The players stood rooted in place, horror

on their painted faces. They knew they had committed a supreme offense, but were obviously ignorant
of what it might be. My gaze next fell upon Hamlet.,
On his face was a look of such vicious, lunatic exulta-
tion that I actually felt sickened at the sight. I'd not
had such a reaction since the day I'd fought at his
father's side in my first battle. The fighting itself inspired a perilous euphoria, but afterward, when one
sees the bloody bodies strewn helpless and twitching
in their death throes on the field . . . I was not imper-
vious to pity or revulsion and had staggered to one
side to spew my guts on the red-stained grass. It
took all my self-control now to keep from repeating
that youthful weakness in front of all. I gulped back
the impulse, breathed deep of the thick, smoky air
from the lamps and torches, and inwardly vowed
that he would pay dearly for this indecent cruelty.

This was not the time or place to confront him. It
must be done in private—after I'd mastered myself.
Until now his tragic disease had been a family matter; by this display he'd made it devastatingly public.

The disaster of the play alone was more than
enough woe, but on this terrible night an army of
troubles began ravening within Elsinore's walls.

After leaving the great hall in considerable disorder and disarray I took myself in haste to the chapel.
It was one place where I thought I'd be left in peace
by the constant press of courtiers, but two of them
turned up to disturb my attempt at calming devo-
tions. As there was no ignoring them, I ordered them
to prepare for their instant despatch to England with

my wayward nephew. They fled, quickly to be replaced by Polonius who informed me that Gertrude had summoned Hamlet to her closet. My old friend promised to listen in on that exchange and acquaint me of the details soon after, and took himself away.

Alone for the moment, I bent both knees and spent time in sincere prayer in an attempt to soothe myself to coherence, but it availed me not. I was not a man used to being angry, and containing it did not sit well with me, nor was I in a position to express it as before my rise in rank. There were many times when I saw my father and brother bound by the same circumstance. How it rankled them that they could not be forthright, but had to bury their feelings deep for the sake of the state. I had little to no practice at this bitter portion of royalty, and certainly those waiting without quickly backed down when at last I emerged from the chapel, still thunderous of aspect. None offered useless words of kindness or comfort, but maintained a wise silence.

I shortly called a small gathering to my council room to formally deal with the crisis. This very night Hamlet would depart for England, in fetters if need be. The timing was wretched, for it would indeed appear that I'd been stung with guilt inspired by the mummery of the play. In truth, I had put off sending him to sea, for his presence was a dear thing to Gertrude. She seemed to take her very breath from his glance, and I was loath to bring her pain. But I measured the brief sharp hurt of his leaving against the ongoing agony of months of subjection to his out-of-control rants and accusations. If he turned his wrath upon her . . . better to cut the festering limb off now before the poison spread to the rest of the body.

While I made more detailed arrangements to carry the wretch to foreign shores where his ravings would be ignored, Gertrude attempted to impart some measure of parental authority to Hamlet in her chambers. At the least she would keep him busy while I set things in motion for his removal. I judged she of all would be safe, especially while Polonius played both watchdog and witness as he'd done so many other times before under a variety of circumstances.

But young Hamlet, deranged and worked into a frenzy, did, in the violence of his madness, discover and murder loyal Polonius right in front of poor Gertrude, running him bloodily through with his sword.

Oh, God, what a foul and fell deed it was, and when I learned of it, I was torn between boundless grief and a matching fury at the senseless death of a harmless old man. In my heart I called Polonius my second father; if depth of grief could be measured by depth of love, then never would I struggle free of the darkness that enveloped my heart.

But . . . the demands and duties of office forced me to rouse, put off my feelings, and deal with the calamity. There would be no trial, sparing Gertrude that agony. There could be none, since lunatics are not responsible for their wildness. Hamlet would depart for England that night, and so he did, under the close guard of two watchful courtiers.

Then all that remained was this second anguish to live through, and I felt it even more keenly than the loss of my brother, for I might have prevented this death by arresting Hamlet immediately after the disrupted play. Again and again I berated myself for not sending a guard along with Polonius, or instructing him to have a trusted man within close call.

Alas, Gertrude withdrew from me. The ordeal of seeing gentle Polonius murdered had been too much. She'd witnessed a side of her son she never knew existed, not only his mindless ferocity, but his staring awe when he conversed with empty air as though his father stood before them. This reminder of her first husband must have plucked a deep chord of guilt in her heart. I wanted to give her comfort, and perhaps in the giving receive some crumb of it for myself, but from that night on, she held herself aloof from my solitary company, even if only to talk as one friend to another. Without her, without Polonius, I was utterly and wretchedly alone.

Time might have eventually closed even these bleeding wounds to our family, but it was not to be. Young Ophelia was unable to accept her father's death at the hands of the very man she loved to distraction. She had ever been excessive in her affections; now did she also slip into madness. Hers was not violent though, and her wandering speech soft, if disturbing. I conjectured then if Hamlet had not at some time pressed his attentions to the point of lying with her, and thus passed on his affliction. I consulted several physicians about the progress of such a disease and was again assured its onset toward madness was slow. It was her mind and spirit that were shot through with lunacy, not her body.

But I had other concerns to keep me engaged.

The news of Polonius' murder ran fast to the general rabble, causing much unrest, for the old man was popular with them. We gave him an obscure burial, which turned out to be a mistake on my part. As a lifelong servant of the court he deserved better, his bier heaped high with honors and ceremonial ostentation, with proclamations about his virtues made to the people, but at the time I thought it might better to keep things quiet and private. Instead, the scandal of his death was only magnified by this seeming suppression of his passing.

Rumors flew about like scattered birds, the worst being that I had killed him or commanded his death be carried out by a man masquerading as the virtuous Hamlet, then spiriting him away to safety. It was folly, of course, but if a lie is repeated often enough it becomes truth, and there were those in the court who would be glad to see me toppled. There would be no surprise in me to learn Hamlet, in the forefront of that gathering, turned out to be the source of that falsehood.

A garbled version of events traveled swiftly to Paris and thus to Laertes. He sped along the roads with few companions, changing mounts and pausing to sleep only when he actually fell from the saddle. By the time he reached the borders of Denmark, there were crowds waiting to greet him and declare him to be the next king. He used them to expedite his safe passage to Elsinore and to break through my own guards, storming into my chambers threatening hot revenge.

However much the mob hailed him, though, he persuaded them to stand down and wait without, and that was how I knew him to be uninterested in the crown itself. He was a hurting son wanting his father, nothing more.

Gertrude's presence also brought him up short, made him more willing to listen. She was like a second mother to him and bravely seized upon his sword arm lest he raise it to strike me. I had no fear of him, though. After so many batterings from other quarters I could deal with one angry young man, but it did take all my skill of reasoning to turn him around. Once he saw my own ravaged face, some understanding came to his that our hearts were the same in our mourning for a lost parent.

Then did Ophelia come wandering barefoot through the chamber, festooned like a bride in blossoms and weeds alike, singing ribald songs a maiden should not know. Gertrude collapsed into tears from this, and Laertes was frozen by such a shock as to be struck dumb. Ophelia recognized him not, but happily insisted on decking us with some of her garlands as if in celebration of a wedding. For each she had a story or saying that herbalists use to memorize the qualities of each plant.

That is when the awful truth came to me, painful as a knife in the vitals. I felt my legs go weak in reaction, as sick at heart as I'd ever been. I had to sit lest I drop into a womanish faint.

Gentle Ophelia—who knew the name and nature of every flower in the land, who distilled their petals into sweet perfumes and their leaves into cures for small ills—could she not just as well concoct a deadly brew of henbane and other poisonous plants and roots? She knew the story of the gentleman's revenge that I'd brought from Italy as well as any; might she also have learned the ingredients for making juice of hebenon from some forgotten volume in Elsinore's book room?

She had right of entry to the orchard when the king was not there. If she hid herself within its twisting paths well before my brother's arrival—then all she had to do was wait until he slept, then steal soft upon him and . . .

And let herself out later. Or, if there was sufficient confusion attending the discovery, add herself to the gathering and thus make her egress. I'd not noticed her presence that day; like all others, my attention was elsewhere.

But *why*?

For her thwarted love of Hamlet?

It seemed a foolish, petty motive to me, but to an inexperienced girl caught in the excessive throes of first love . . . I recalled the heat and anguish of my own youth. In those hasty days there is no restraint to the extremes of emotions, and one chafes bitterly against the reeking, unfair limits set by others.

And—most telling of all—it was less than a week before my brother's murder that he'd forbade Ophelia's marriage to his son.

With this in mind it was like a book opened to a telling page that revealed all. No man would benefit by the king's death, only this otherwise innocent young girl. In the course of time Hamlet would assume the throne and claim her as his bride, sweeping her off to be his queen as in some old tale told in the nursery. How she must have repeated it to herself in the dreaming dark of her virgin's bed. How must she have resented and despised my brother for trampling upon her perfect musings.

The fates can be kind in their way, for it was just as well that Polonius was dead, never to know this terrible truth. Would that they had granted me a similar ignorance.

Never could I speak to Gertrude about this, for she might well reproach herself for indirectly causing her first husband's death. If she'd argued just a little harder for the marriage . . . that was where her mind would take her.

Nor could I speak to Laertes. He had enough misery.

Dear God, but I wanted someone to talk to, but a king's lot must needs be lonely, his burdens heavy beyond bearing, and only death can bring him to lay them aside.

Laertes and I did come to an accord on one matter, and that was our blaming Hamlet for Polonius' murder. Yes, it is wicked to hold a lunatic responsible for his rash acts, but a man's nature can only endure so much and no more, and we had reached our limit. When I received notice that Hamlet had somehow slipped his watchers' leash and was returned to Denmark, it was too great for either of us to continue without taking action. Laertes was all for waylaying him on the road or cutting his throat as he prayed in church, but I with a cooler head and more experience had a better plan. Ironically, it was with Ophelia's unknowing help.

While visiting Polonius' chambers ostensibly to sort out state papers, I also made a sortie to the maid's own room. It was in considerable disorder as might be expected given her deranged state, but there did I find all the evidence needed to confirm that it was she who murdered my brother. Upon a long bench did she store and refine her perfumes and potions, and in certain bottles hidden behind more innocent distillations she kept the deadly results of her shadowy delvings. There was no mistaking them. Though the bottles were sardonically labeled with names like *Heart's Desire* and *Maiden's Wish* they stank foul of the grave. I took them away with me, confident she would not miss them now and in secret tested each on vermin supplied to me by the castle rat catcher.

It was quite frightening to see the effect of her dire inventions, more so to realize that she'd gone unsuspected all these months. At any time she might have taken it into her head to deliver a cruel finish to all of us had she chosen.

But I mentioned none of this to Laertes and only produced one of the poisons, along with a design to remove Hamlet's destructive presence from us altogether. All Laertes had to do was meet his father's murderer and make a public reconciliation with him. Then they would conduct an apparently friendly passage of arms as a means to settle a wager. During the course of their demonstration I would see to it Hamlet drank from my own cup of wine. Within the hour he would be dead, seemingly from overexertion, and that would be the end of the matter. It was not unknown for an otherwise fit and hearty man to fall if pressed to his limits. His mother would be sore grieved, but hold none to blame and accept it as God's will.

Some might think this a cold and malicious action on my part, but along with the burdens of state it is also a king's grim lot to order the execution of those who threaten the stability of the state. I would have been entirely within my royal duty and powers to have him arrested and beheaded the same night of the old man's murder. Only my love for Gertrude held me back from meting out justice.

Laertes then surprised me by also producing a poisonous unction. The smallest scratch would finish Hamlet off, he said. I knew he'd bought it to commit royal murder on my nephew and perhaps even myself, but held back from comment. I, the king, was about to sanction that nephew's death, changing it from murder to a lawful execution by my word alone. Besides, Hamlet was dying already, we were but speeding the process. Such was my power, and, Heaven knows, I took no pride in it.

For all that sorrow, the thought came to me of who to declare as my heir once Hamlet was gone. With the troubles that issue from bearing the weight of a heavy crown, it was not a responsibility I would willingly lay upon anyone. I had discussed several possibilities with dear Polonius, one of whom was Laertes himself. He was a good and studious man, perhaps too good of heart to be a ruler, for one is often required to do unpleasant acts for the health of the state. But his fiery resolution to avenge his father, tempered by his willingness to hear my side before taking rash action decided me to name him my heir after the duel.

He has my pity, but I can think of none better suited. I've learned to my sorrow what a terrible burden it is to be king. The state lives on, hopefully in health, but in the effort to preserve that health for others my own life has been ripped to shreds and patches. May it please God to spare me from further miseries.

Here Gertrude comes, and there is a look on her weeping face that augurs further sorrows for us. In my heart I fear some evil has befallen Ophelia and her sins have found her out. . . .

Last night I dreamed of my dead brother walking the upper platform of Elsinore as was his habit in life, but dressed in warlike raiment. This bodes ill for my beloved Denmark. Dear God, whatever transpires in the days ahead, I pray You send me wisdom enough to do right for all. In the meantime, angels and ministers of grace defend us.

Claudius Rex

Kristen Britain

GREEN RIDER

As Karigan G'ladheon, on the run from school, makes her way through the deep forest, a galloping horse plunges out of the brush, its rider impaled by two black arrows. With his dying breath, he tells her he is a Green Rider, one of the king's special messengers. Giving her his green coat with its symbolic brooch of office, he makes Karigan swear to deliver the message he was carrying. Pursued by unknown assassins, following a path only the horse seems to know, Karigan finds herself thrust into in a world of danger and complex magic.... 0-88677-858-1

FIRST RIDER'S CALL

With evil forces once again at large in the kingdom and with the messenger service depleted and weakened, can Karigan reach through the walls of time to get help from the First Rider, a woman dead for a millennium? 0-7564-0209-3

To Order Call: 1-800-788-6262

DAW 7

Tanya Huff

Smoke and Shadows

First in a New Series

Tony Foster—familiar to Tanya Huff fans from her *Blood* series—has relocated to Vancouver with Henry Fitzroy, vampire son of Henry VIII. Tony landed a job as a production assistant at CB Productions, ironically working on a syndicated TV series, "Darkest Night," about a vampire detective. Except for his crush on Lee, the show's handsome costar, Tony was pretty content...at least until everything started to fall apart on the set. It began with shadows—shadows that seemed to be where they didn't belong, shadows that had an existence of their own. And when he found a body, and a shadow cast its claim on Lee, Tony knew he had to find out what was going on, and that he needed Henry's help.

0-7564-0183-6

To Order Call: 1-800-788-6262

DAW 46

Marion Zimmer Bradley
& Deborah Ross

A Flame in Hali
A Novel of Darkover

On Darkover, it is the era of the Hundred Kingdoms—a time of nearly continuous war and bloody disputes, a time when Towers are conscripted to produce terrifying laran weapons—weapons which kill from afar, poisoning the very land itself for decades to come. In this terrifying time of greed and imperialism, two powerful men have devoted their lives to changing their world and eliminating these terrible weapons. For years King Carolin of Hastur and his close friend, Keeper Varzil Ridenow, have dreamed of a world without war. But another man, Eduin Deslucido, hides in the alleys of Thendara, tormented by a spell so powerful it haunts Eduin's every waking moment—a spell of destruction against Carolin Hastur... and all of his clan.

To Order Call: 1-800-788-6262
www.dawbooks.com

MERCEDES LACKEY

The Novels of Valdemar

ARROWS OF THE QUEEN	0-88677-378-4
ARROW'S FLIGHT	0-88677-377-6
ARROW'S FALL	0-88677-400-4
MAGIC'S PAWN	0-88677-352-0
MAGIC'S PROMISE	0-88677-401-2
MAGIC'S PRICE	0-88677-426-8
THE OATHBOUND	0-88677-414-4
OATHBREAKERS	0-88677-454-3
OATHBLOOD	0-88677-773-9
BY THE SWORD	0-88677-463-2
WINDS OF FATE	0-88677-516-7
WIND OF CHANGE	0-88677-563-9
WINDS OF FURY	0-88677-612-0
STORM WARNING	0-88677-661-9
STORM RISING	0-88677-712-7
STORM BREAKING	0-88677-755-0
BRIGHTLY BURNING	0-88677-989-8
TAKE A THIEF	0-7564-0008-2
EXILE'S HONOR	0-7564-0085-6
SWORD OF ICE: and other tales of Valdemar	
	0-88677-720-8

To Order Call: 1-800-788-6262

Mercedes Lackey
& Larry Dixon

The Novels of Valdemar

"Lackey and Dixon always offer a well-told tale"
—*Booklist*

DARIAN'S TALE

OWLFLIGHT
0-88677-804-2

OWLSIGHT
0-88677-803-4

OWLKNIGHT
0-88677-916-2

THE MAGE WARS

THE BLACK GRYPHON
0-88677-804-2

THE WHITE GRYPHON
0-88677-682-1

THE SILVER GRYPHON
0-88677-685-6

To Order Call: 1-800-788-6262

DAW 26